Charles Lan

Farthest North

Charles Lanman

Farthest North

1st Edition | ISBN: 978-3-75241-058-7

Place of Publication: Frankfurt am Main, Germany

Year of Publication: 2020

Outlook Verlag GmbH, Germany.

Reproduction of the original.

FARTHEST NORTH;

BY

CHARLES LANMAN.

1

PREFACE.

It is believed that this book, with its true but none the less stirring adventures, will be of much interest to the general public, as well as gratifying to the many warm friends of Lieutenant Lockwood. It will likewise correct any erroneous impressions which may have arisen from the publication of garbled extracts from the official journals kept by the different members of the Greely party and, by order of the War Department, laid open to the public. By this order, Lockwood's journal and those of others became public property, and hence any reference to them in advance of their official publication is allowable.

The few pages devoted to the early life can not be expected to especially interest the general public, but will gratify Lieutenant Lockwood's friends. They are here produced to give them permanency, and to show his sterling character.

No attempt is here made to give a history of the Expedition, and only so much of Lockwood's journal is produced as shows his connection therewith. The voyage to Lady Franklin Bay is given more in detail, as it presents a lively picture of an interesting people not much known, and as it exhibits the buoyant spirits with which he entered upon the work, before dissensions in camp had checked them, though without marring his faithfulness and energy. The important part he had in the enterprise, his zeal, energy, and loyalty to his chief and to the cause, all are fully set forth, and will be more clearly seen when the more elaborate history of the Expedition shall be published by Lieutenant Greely, as will shortly be done.

Although the journal has been freely used, its language and style have not been closely followed, except in those parts quoted which refer to Lockwood's sentiments and feelings. The deep pathos of these could be expressed as well in no other words.

His journal is very full and complete on the perilous boat-voyage to Cape Sabine, and in the heart-rending struggle for life in that ever-memorable hut where he and so many others laid down their lives. This has purposely been reduced to a few pages, giving the story only so far as Lieutenant Lockwood was connected with it. The same, may be said as to the home-life at the station on Lady Franklin Bay.

The portrait of Lieutenant Lockwood is from an excellent photograph taken a short time before he started for St. John's, and two of the woodcuts are from photographs by Sergeant Rice. "Arctic Sledging" was made up from a description and a sketch by Sergeant Brainard, and "Farthest North" from a sketch by Lieutenant Lockwood.

The map is a reproduction of that published by the London Geographical Society, which is an exact transcript of maps drawn by Lieutenant Lockwood and submitted by him to Lieutenant Greely with reports of sledge-journeys. This map gives the names agreed upon by Lieutenant Greely and Lieutenant Lockwood, and are those referred to in the journal and in this book. It is much to be regretted that many of these names differ from those on the official map published by authority to the world. The names first given commemorate events connected with those wonderful sledge-journeys, as will be seen in the text; and, if a few unimportant lakes and points were named after friends and relatives, this might have been conceded to one who accomplished so much, and that much so well. The map of the London Geographical Society will probably live, and the other perish, as it should.

Captain Markham, Royal Navy, soon after the return of the Greely Expedition, declared, in articles published in a leading English magazine, that Lockwood never got beyond Cape Britannia, and that he mistook Cape May for that cape, etc. It was thought that, when the history of this sledge-journey was better known, Markham would be glad to withdraw this ungenerous aspersion. This is done so far as to admit that Lockwood did reach 83° 24′ north latitude, 44° 5′ west longitude; but it is now said, in the article "Polar Regions," of the new Encyclopædia Britannica, written by the captain's brother, that all this region had previously been explored and exhaustively examined by the English expedition of 1875-'76.

This is very remarkable, in view of the fact that Lockwood Island, which was reached by Lockwood, is one hundred geographical miles east and forty miles north of Cape Britannia which Beaumont saw at the distance of twenty miles, but never reached.

In the same article are expressed sentiments in accord with those contained in this book, viz.: "If the simple and necessary precaution had been taken of stationing a depot-ship in a good harbor at the entrance of Smith's Sound, in annual communication with Greely on one side and with America on the other, there would have been no disaster. If precautions proved to be necessary by experience are taken, there is no undue risk or danger in polar enterprises. There is no question as to the value and importance of polar discovery, and as to the principles on which expeditions should be sent out. Their objects are exploration for scientific purposes and the encouragement of maritime enterprise."

I.
EARLY LIFE.

In the following pages, it is proposed to record the personal history of an American hero whose fortune it was, at the sacrifice of his life, to visit and explore the utmost limit in the Arctic regions ever attained by human skill and enterprise. Aside from the information communicated to me by his family, the materials placed in my hands consist of his private correspondence and various journals which he faithfully kept while serving his country on the Western frontiers, as well as in the inhospitable domain of the North. As the poet Fitz-Greene Halleck wrote about a kindred character—

"He lived, as mothers wish their sons to live,"

and, on the score of fidelity to duty,

"He died, as fathers wish their sons to die,"

leaving a name that will long be honored in every civilized land as that of a martyr in the cause of geographical exploration.

Many of those connected with the Naval Academy at Annapolis, Maryland, before the civil war, will remember a playful and mischievous boy, whose ready smile and cheerful ways beguiled them in their hours of relaxation. Others who were at that school after the war will remember the same boy, grown into a youth of sixteen years, rugged in aspect, devoted to manly sports, and assiduous in all his duties. It is the story of his brief but eventful life to which this volume is devoted, written for the information of his friends and all those who admire true heroism and rare abilities when allied to sufferings for the public weal.

JAMES BOOTH LOCKWOOD was the second son and third child of General Henry H. Lockwood and Anna Booth Lockwood. He was born at the Naval Academy, Annapolis, on the 9th of October, 1852, at which time and place his father—a Professor of Mathematics in the Navy—instructed the midshipmen in the military branches, as he had done for many years before. Both his parents were from the State of Delaware, and came from the best stock of that State; and, as his father taught his students "how to shoot," and prepare themselves for the conflicts of life, it was quite natural that the son should have acquired a love of noble deeds and adventure.

Like many boys, he had his narrow escapes from death, one of which occurred in April, 1860, when, having fallen into the river from the dock, he was rescued in an insensible condition, and restored to life with great difficulty. This escape must have been recalled by him with special emotion in after-years amid his struggles with the ice of Smith's Sound.

His innate love of fun had been one of his characteristics from childhood, nor was it subdued even when recovering from the accident which nearly cost him his life; for, while lying in his bed, he peered into his father's face with a quizzical smile, and remarked, "I was drowned, but not drowned dead."

When the Naval Academy was occupied by a general of the army, in 1861, and the students and professors were transferred to Newport, Rhode Island, young Lockwood accompanied his father and family, and was placed at a public school in that place. After a brief residence in Newport, his father, being a graduate of the Military Academy at West Point, was called upon to command a volunteer regiment of Delaware troops, and having been subsequently commissioned a brigadier-general of volunteers, he was placed in charge of the Eastern Shore counties of Virginia and returned to the region of hostilities, making his headquarters at Drummondtown, in Accomac County. In this quaint and quiet place, and while a mere stripling of ten years, young Lockwood displayed his love of adventure and active life by forming a company of all the colored boys in the village, erecting earthworks in a vacant lot, and, all armed with corn-stalks and broom-handles, meeting a company of white boys in mimic war—noisy, if not dangerous to life or limb. The vanity of personal strife, however, soon becoming irksome to his mind, he turned his attention to horsemanship, and explored the surrounding shores of Accomac on a Chincoteague pony belonging to his father. He also spent many quiet hours conversing about horses and their habits with the soldiers in the garrison, with whom he was a special favorite. After a while, his father was transferred to the command of troops at Harper's Ferry, and there a new field of adventure occupied the attention of the incipient hero. He was foremost in climbing the neighboring mountain-heights and scaling precipices, and always on the lookout for adventure along the waters of the Potomac. Afterward, when living with his family near the city of Baltimore, he displayed his activity and energy in other ways. When neighboring boys were wont to trespass on his father's grounds and fruit-trees, he was quite as ready to defend his home as he had been in Accomac to maintain the national struggle then rending the land. And here it was that he often accompanied his father on his rounds among the military works near Baltimore, and always attracted the attention of the troops by his skill in riding. But these experiences were not deemed satisfactory for molding the character of a boy, and then it was that his father sent him to a boarding-school at Bethlehem, in Pennsylvania, kept by a Mr. Schwartz, a good scholar and strict disciplinarian. Of course, like those of all boys, his letters teemed with complaints. He was *very homesick*—a mere child separated from all he loved. In one letter he spoke of praying to God to make him satisfied. In after-years, and when suffering all the horrors of the Arctic, his mother's prayer was that his childhood's star might again arise, and lead his sorrowing heart to that comfort found only above. His chief grievances were a Dutch dish regularly given to the boys, called *scrapul*, and the discipline of *powers* administered to those who failed in their studies. In this latter punishment, the delinquent was required to raise to the fortieth, fiftieth, or one hundredth power any number given him. However distasteful to him at the time, he seems to have changed his mind upon the subjects of food and discipline afterward; for he became, after his return home, a strong advocate of *scrapul* as a physical, and of "powers" as a mental diet. Returning, in 1866, with his father to Annapolis, he was sent to St. John's College in that place, and at that time in a flourishing condition, under the able administration of James C. Welling, now the accomplished President of Columbian College. Although his mental abilities were acknowledged as superior, he preferred action to books, and his success there was not satisfactory to his father. Others known to be his mental inferiors took a higher stand. He, however, read some Latin, and made considerable progress in mathematics. Here we come to a new illustration of his character. During his residence within the walls of the Academy, a species of tyranny existed among the sons of naval officers of his own age with whom he associated, which he could not endure. Rank in the father was supposed to give rank or prestige to the son. This theory young Lockwood was unwilling to acknowledge, and the consequence was that he soon found himself beset by those whom he opposed. But then, as always with the free and brave, right prevailed, and the aggressors were sent to the wall, while the fearless victor very soon became the peer of his associates. The situation of the Academy offering peculiar facilities for boating, fishing, swimming, etc., the professor's son became an expert in all these exercises, making pets of his sail and row boats, as he had done with the ponies of Chincoteague. Many of the Annapolis students, now high officers in the navy, have spoken of his frolicsome pranks at that time within the grounds of the Academy—for example, how he mimicked the strut of the drum-major, how he teased the watchman by hiding among the trees and bushes, personating an intruder on the grounds, and how he alarmed the servant-maids and the children by appearing suddenly before them like a phantom. He was more fond of reading than of study, and among his favorite books were those of De Foe, Mayne Reid, and others of that class. To what extent he was familiar with the histories of John Ledyard and Joseph R. Bellot can not be stated, but there is a striking similarity in their characters, and indeed it was the fate of the latter, like Lockwood, to lose his life in the Arctic regions. They form a trio of remarkable explorers, whose fame will be perennial, but it was the fate of the last one mentioned to reach the highest success. During the latter part of his residence at Annapolis, he spent many of his spare hours on his father's farm. By way of encouragement, his father assigned to him a patch of ground for his special cultivation, with fertilizers and the use of a team. To the surprise of all, his success seemed amazing, and his crops were good and profitable. With the money thus secured he purchased for himself a watch and a sporting gun. He had a special fondness for dogs, and exerted over them great influence. His favorite in this direction was a short-legged, long-bodied, common rat-terrier. In the purity of this dog's blood, he was a decided believer, which faith he maintained with many hot arguments, and exemplified by teaching the animal a great variety of tricks. Indeed, the high degree of training to which he brought the dog Jack was remarkable. He was always quiet and positive toward the animal, and Jack gave his commands a serious and implicit obedience. One of the feats performed by the dog was to carry a candlestick with a lighted candle wherever ordered to do so. Another was to this effect: the boy would place a small scrap of paper on the parlor wall at a height which Jack was hardly able to reach. Jack's attention would then be called to the paper, and the dog and master would retire up-stairs. Some time afterward, Jack, in obedience to a mere word, would proceed to the parlor, and, to the amusement of those congregated there, launch his body at the paper until he finally secured it, and then would carry it to his master. Although this dog had a special dislike for fire, he would, under orders, pull chestnuts out of the hot coals, even if it took him an hour to perform the task; and it is also related of him that on one occasion, when he slipped his muzzle on the Academy grounds, he picked it up and took it to his master. When the lad's father was ordered to the National Observatory, the family removing to Washington, the pet dog accompanied them, and the intimacy between the dog and his master was unabated. They often rambled through the streets together, and it was during one of their walks along Pennsylvania Avenue that the dog disappeared, and was never recovered by his owner, whose grief was most sincere and manifest. He published an advertisement, and, true to his regard for the departed, he spoke of it as a pure-blooded animal; which statement was probably the reason why the dog was never returned, as no stranger could have believed in the alleged pedigree of such an ungainly creature.

After young Lockwood's father and family had become settled in Washington, it was decided that he should return to Annapolis and take charge of the farm until some more suitable or congenial employment should come into view. In looking over the home letters which he wrote at that time, I find a few developments of character which are worthy of mention. For example, in February, 1872, he writes as follows:

"I find Annapolis the same as ever. It would hardly do for Rip Van Winkle to go to sleep here, for, when he awoke, he would find no change, not even by death."

After speaking in the same letter of a man going to purchase implements in Baltimore, he says: "I think it would pay one capable of judging of such things, or one endowed with 'Lockwood Common Sense,'" this allusion being to an imaginary manual which the children had attributed to their father. The quiet humor of the youthful farmer is manifested in another letter after this fashion: "I have been suffering all the week from the effects of a poison most probably communicated from some vine. It manifests itself pretty much as Job's troubles showed themselves, and no position of body except standing affords relief. I haven't yet got down into the ashes. If tartar emetic produced these eruptions, they might be attributed in some way to the evil agency of Mrs. W——."

The person here alluded to was the one who became notorious for the alleged poisoning of General W. S. Ketcham, in Baltimore. Young Lockwood had met her at a boarding-house in Annapolis after her release from prison, and was agreeably impressed by her conversation and manners. On a subsequent occasion, when visiting his family in Washington, and some severe remark had been made against the lady in question, he demanded that the company present should not abuse an absent friend in his presence. Being of a sensitive nature in regard to the weather, as is proved by several of his Annapolis letters, and by such passages as the one now to be quoted, it seems surprising that he should ever have decided to visit the icy regions of the North.

"This gloomy weather," he says, "is by no means calculated to elate one's spirits, but, on the contrary, makes everything appear in its most dreary and desolate light, especially on a farm like this, and, though the spring will bring more work and attention, yet I shall hail its appearance with joy. I must confess that I can not prevent a feeling of loneliness from coming over me, particularly in the daytime, for at night my lamp and open wood-fire make things more cheerful, or rather less dreary."

As these letters were written from a farm, and by a mere boy, they are chiefly devoted to asking for advice as to how he should manage affairs, and to reporting the condition of the crops; but, in their way, they prove that there was much solid manhood in the lad, and that he looked upon life as something substantial, and not as a kind of dreamland.

On one occasion, when visiting his home, he noticed that one of his sisters was manifesting what he thought an unreasonable excitement about the advent of cockroaches in the kitchen, whereupon he drew the figure of a vessel under full sail, beneath which he wrote the following: "The brig Anna Baby, bound to the north pole for a load of cockroaches."

On another occasion, after consulting the family copy of Webster's Dictionary, he wrote upon one of the fly-leaves, opposite the indorsements of Henry Clay, Daniel Webster, and other distinguished men, these words: "I regard this dictionary as very good, especially when you can not get any other."

These incidents, though unimportant, help us to appreciate the character of the critical and independent youth.

The following example of the boy's ingenuity is also worth mentioning:

In 1870 a brother-in-law gave him a small, cheap clock, about four and a half inches in diameter, which he at once adapted to the purpose of waking himself in the morning. After joining the slats of his bed together with battens, he sawed them through in the middle and hinged the parts. That half of the arrangement which was at the head of the bed was supported only by a single prop. A minute collar of lead was supported by one of the hands of the clock. At the proper time the lead slipped from the hand automatically, and, in falling, set in motion a system of levers which were connected with the prop by a string. Thus, with unfailing regularity, the prop was jerked from its place, and the young occupant of the bed was pitched headlong to the floor among his pillows and bolster. When he tired of this apparatus, it became his custom at night to hitch a string around his foot, the end of the string being passed out of the window and allowed to trail down to the kitchen-door. At a definite time in the morning, previously ordered, the colored cook pulled the string until she received intimation of a successful result.

In the hope of finding more congenial employment, young Lockwood now fixed his mind on engineer work in connection with railroads. He joined a corps on the Texas and Pacific Railroad line, and went to the northeastern corner of the State of Texas, where, for four months, he drove pegs and cut down bushes in the virgin wilderness, which employment was only terminated by the failure of the company to go on with its enterprise. What with the rough people with whom he was compelled to associate, the hard fare at the rude taverns, and a severe attack of sickness, he had a very disagreeable experience, which was enhanced by the non-payment of wages by the company, and by the temporary loss of the spare money furnished by his father, which was taken from him by the rascality of a pretended friend, an employé of the railroad company. By careful financial engineering, he managed to leave the wilderness of Texas, went to Shreveport, and thence to New Orleans, where he took a steamer for Cincinnati, and on this trip he met with one small bit of good fortune. Owing to his limited means he contracted with the captain of the steamer that he should be carried to Cincinnati, O., for a specific sum, all his meals to be included in the passage-money. It so happened, however, that the steamer was detained by floating ice for three weeks, but this caused no detriment to the traveler's pocket, as time was not "nominated in the bond." About eleven years after that experience, the same traveler was fighting his way through the ice of the Arctic seas and enduring the horrors of Cape Sabine, finding it difficult to secure necessary rations at any price or of any quality.

On reaching home, he began the study of bookkeeping with a view to the civil service. With others, he was examined for a position in the Treasury Department. He passed the examination with credit, and received a mark much above the number required for passing, but, when the office-mark was thrown in, as was then the custom, his average was reduced, and those who had personal influence and understood the "tricks of the trade" became the successful applicants.

II.
ARMY-LIFE IN ARIZONA.

After finding that farming and railroad engineering were not exactly the employments he had fancied them to be, young Lockwood resumed his studies under the direction of his father. Not long afterward, however, he was seized with the idea of entering the army, and, at the very outset of this venture for a useful life, he was met with a blending of good and bad fortune. Securing the influence of many friends, he made a successful appeal to the President and the War Department. He received orders for an examination before the proper tribunal, and, out of thirty-eight young men who were examined in Washington, he passed No. 1. He also had a higher mark than any of those examined in other places at the same time; hence he was entitled to the highest commission as second lieutenant, and at one time it was resolved to give it to him; but, as the examinations were conducted in different places and before different boards, it was decided to settle the rank of the applicants by lot, and Lockwood's number was forty, instead of one to which he was justly entitled. He was, however, promised a crack regiment, and hence became second lieutenant in the Twenty-third Infantry, then commanded by two officers who had gained distinction in the late war— Colonel Jefferson C. Davis and Lieutenant-Colonel George Crook. He soon after joined the recruiting station at New York for instruction.

The few letters that Lieutenant Lockwood wrote home from New York contained very graphic pictures of what he there observed. His reception at the recruiting-station was most cordial, one of the first things done there by the recruiting-officers, to his surprise, being to bring forth a demijohn of whisky; but from this hospitality he begged to be excused, only one or two other young men following his example.

After a service of several weeks at the recruiting-station in New York, he conducted recruits to the Territory of Arizona by the way of Panama. The party left New York in November, 1873, and, on reaching San Francisco, went by steamer to Fort Yuma, near the mouth of the Colorado River, and thence marched over the rugged and dusty plains of Arizona to McDowell Post, a distance of more than one hundred and fifty miles in the interior.

From the few letters that he wrote respecting his trip from New York to San Francisco, we gather the following items:

"Aspinwall is a dirty, sandy town, of no architectural pretensions. I cannot better describe it than by asking you to imagine Lockwoodville [1] with a lot of palm- and cocoanut-trees growing in the vacant lots, plenty of the sand and filth aforesaid, all the darkies of Annapolis sauntering around, plenty of children and many dogs, pigs, etc. However, I must do Aspinwall justice—it has a neat little church, a marble monument erected to some of its chief benefactors, and, what I should call, a remarkably fine statue of Columbus, in bronze. It has an enormous trade passing through it, from one ocean to the other, and is really a place of great importance to the mercantile world."

"We reached Panama between four and five in the afternoon, after a very interesting ride across the country, and were immediately embarked for the Constitution—which lay two miles from shore—so that I had no opportunity of seeing Panama, except from the water. The ship left during the evening, and ever since has been 'plowing the angry main' toward San Francisco, excepting when stopping at some of the towns along the coast. We have seen several of these, and they are all of one type, that of Aspinwall, though on a much smaller scale. Some that I saw had not half a dozen wooden houses, but consisted merely of reed-huts covered with straw. One of these—Mazatlan— claims to have twenty thousand inhabitants, but does not appear to have more than one tenth of that number. All the tropical fruits were abundant at these places, and could be purchased for a trifle. The Constitution is a side-wheeler of four thousand tons, and has little motion, and, while sea-sickers are abundant, I am not one of them. I have gained ten pounds, and now weigh one hundred and sixty-one."

Lockwood's stay in San Francisco was too brief to afford him much opportunity for observation, but here is what he said of the Chinese: "I visited Chinatown this evening, and saw the Celestials in all their glory. I saw many strange and amusing sights in their stores and shops and along their streets, as they are very slow in adopting civilized customs. I send along with this some Chinese pictures which I purchased. I am very much pleased with San Francisco, and shall leave it with many regrets. A walk through the Chinese quarter is like a visit to some Chinese city on the other side of the Pacific."

The few events of his trip along the coast to Yuma were to this effect: Soon after leaving the Golden Gate, he experienced a storm that was far from pacific in its character, far worse than any he had witnessed since leaving New York; he visited Magdalena Bay, which impressed him as a barren, miserable place, chiefly noted for its want of houses, and yet of some importance as the shipping port of a dye-wood found in that region; he also stopped at Carmen Island, where large quantities of salt were found in the dry bed of a lake, and at Cape St. Lucas, but brought away no favorable impressions from any of these remote places. With Yuma City he was better pleased, describing its houses as small, one-story affairs, built of adobe, more

Mexican than American in character, and its streets as far more dusty than those of Washington City; and the mountains surrounding the city as very imposing. The Colorado reminded him of the Red River—the channel winding and running between great mud-flats and islands, all constantly changing, and abounding in many kinds of water-fowl. He was interested in the Indian inhabitants, whom he pitied for their poverty and degradation; occasionally seeing a number of squaws reclining like quadrupeds on the mud-flats or in front of their tiny oval huts.

The sojourn of Lieutenant Lockwood in Arizona lasted into the summer of 1874, and from the letters which he wrote home from Post McDowell may be gathered some interesting particulars, illustrating his habits of close observation in regard to men and events.

His journey from Fort Yuma to Camp McDowell was full of interest and was greatly enjoyed. He had for companions two brother officers and three ladies; traveled by ambulance, making marches of only about fifteen miles; camped out every night, Lockwood himself sleeping on the ground outside. As the country was very desolate and barren, they traveled generally along the valley of the Gila, but their last march was over desert land forty-five miles wide. They saw many relics along the route, mounds, ruins, and immense ditches for irrigation. One immense pile of rocks, called the Painted Rocks, was entirely covered with pictures of lizards, Indians, beasts, and birds—supposed to represent a great battle in which the Apaches conquered the Maricopas. There were also along the road graves of men murdered by the Indians. One grave, near Gila Bend, was of a man named Lumley, a station-keeper, murdered by two Mexicans—his successor exhibited a knife, used by one of the murderers, which had been found, and he pointed out the spot where Judge Lynch had disposed of the only criminal that happened to be captured. While the travelers did not spend any money at hotels, they were obliged to pay from twenty to thirty dollars for being ferried across the Gila and Salt Rivers at different points.

In one of his letters, written to his sister after the rainy season, and soon after his arrival at Camp McDowell, young Lockwood says: "I wish you could see the pretty flowers around here; they are principally yellow and red, and each kind grows by itself. They grow so close together that the ground is covered as with a carpet. To the west of this post there is a wide plain covered with these flowers. There is also a species of cactus called the Suwarrow, which grows fifteen or twenty feet high—a sort of tree without branches, but covered with thorns; the outside of this tree is of a green color and nearly as soft as young asparagus, but inside it has a frame of wood. These are all over the plain, in fact all over Arizona. I often walk out here after dinner with a large dog that belongs to one of the officers, and start up the rabbits—great big Jack-rabbits, as they are called—as large as a small dog. They can run very fast, faster than any dog except a hound. Among other curiosities about here are rattlesnakes and lizards—the lizards as common as flies; also crows as big as hens and almost as tame. The post is entirely surrounded by mountains." By way of contrast to this pleasing prospect, in another letter he gives the particulars of the murder of two men by the Indians within twelve miles of the garrison, their bodies having been fearfully mutilated. "I am still in the land of the finite and material," he writes, "and the Apaches have not yet disturbed the arrangement of my back hair; in short, I am alive and kicking."

On the 14th of May, Lockwood writes that "there has been nothing new at the post except the arrival of Lieutenant Schuyler, Fifth Cavalry. He has been out on a scout for several months past, dropping in at various posts now and then. He reports that he came upon the Apaches southeast of here, killed twelve and took fourteen prisoners. He is accompanied by Dr. Corbasier and a party of thirty-one soldiers and eighty-one Indian scouts. These scouts are composed of Apache-Mojave, Tonto-Apaches, and other tribes, closely allied to the Apaches proper. It seems strange that they are thus willing to join the enemy in exterminating their brethren; but such is their nature. They are hardly superior to the beasts, except in shape, and even there the line of demarkation is not very distinct. The Pimos, to the number of one hundred or more, were here about a week ago, on their way to punish the Apaches for stealing some stock from them. When they returned, they reported the killing of quite a number of their foes—some sixteen or more—and taking many prisoners. Schuyler's party confirm the report; they came across the camp of the Apaches, and the doctor said he counted a large number of slain. The Pimos surprised the Apaches when asleep and almost exterminated them. They were armed with war-clubs, and of course mangled their bodies horribly. When found their heads were all beaten in, and their bodies stuck full of arrows and partially burned. The doctor says it was the most sickening sight he ever beheld. The Apache bands, off their reservations, are fast becoming exterminated, over a thousand having been killed during the last winter. General Crook will not allow them to return to their reservations unless they bring the heads of several of the ringleaders in the late outbreak."

In another place, after alluding to the extravagant accounts published about Arizona, he says: "One would suppose, from reading the pamphlet I send you, that Arizona is a fine agricultural country—which is absurd; and that it contains many flourishing cities and towns, whereas even the river-bottoms require irrigation, and the 'cities' are merely the nuclei of towns."

On one occasion, after alluding to his enjoyment of the newspapers sent him from home, and to the early transfer of his regiment, he says: "It would probably have been removed this spring but for the financial panic and other commercial disasters. I suppose if the rest of the year goes by prosperously, and nothing occurs to prolong the gingerly, penny-wise, pound-foolish policy of Congress called economy (?), that the Twenty-third will probably be removed next spring or fall." And again, he continues: "Grant appears to have obtained great credit by his veto of the Inflation Bill. How Congress could pass a bill which seems to be unacceptable and repugnant to the whole people, I can not understand."

Alluding a second time to the *pleasing* characteristics of frontier life, he tells his father that "a party of Indian scouts arrived here yesterday from Schuyler's command. They brought the news that the lieutenant had *jumped* the Indians at Four Peaks—a high mountain, forty miles off—killed eighteen and captured six. The party brought in a wounded scout, shot through the head, who is now in the hospital. He was the only one wounded in the fight, or rather slaughter, for these Indians rarely fight a party of any size. I suppose these Arizona tribes are the most degraded, cowardly, and despicable savages in the country. Schuyler, as I understand, generally sweeps a breadth of country fifty miles across, by means of flanking-parties on the right and left, and has been quite successful."

In speaking of his duties at the post, he says: "I am officer-of-the-day every other day; I mount the guard every morning, attend all roll-calls, accompany the captain in his inspection of quarters every morning, and afterward recite tactics. I also am present with him at company-drill every evening, command the company at Sunday morning inspection, sit on boards of survey and perform other irregular duties."

After announcing the arrival of the paymaster at the post, and alluding to expenses, he says: "Servants in this country are paid enormously. The post-trader pays his Chinese cook thirty dollars per month, and has paid as high as one hundred dollars. Officers in Arizona are compelled from necessity to employ soldiers in this capacity, though contrary to the regulations."

In one of his letters, Lieutenant Lockwood gives his opinion about some of his father's landed property, and then goes on after this fashion: "The old farm has additional charms for me now, after living in Arizona, and I have come to think that there are many worse places. Does distance lend enchantment to the view? or what is it? I often long after some of the delicious peaches and other fruit that the much-abused farm produces in such abundance. However, if you can dispose of the farm as you suggest, it will, no doubt, be for the best, as the Lockwood family have become so *high-toned* that I am afraid they will never *stoop* (?) to live on a farm and become *grangers*."

In one of his letters written about this date, he makes the following remark respecting his education at Annapolis: "I don't think I care about being present at the meeting of the alumni of my *Alma Mater*, or, what she would be more pleased with, contributing anything in the way of money. Enough has been thrown away in teaching me what has never been of any use. However, the *old woman* has my good wishes."

In another letter, after speaking of an entertainment he had attended, he said: "I don't know that I should have enjoyed it, but for the presence of a very pretty Spanish girl with whom I fell in love; she danced charmingly, but as she could not speak a word of English, nor I a word of Spanish, our conversation was somewhat limited."

On the 4th of July when arrangements were commenced for removing the Twenty-third Regiment to Yuma, the lieutenant thus touches upon the national anniversary: "I have celebrated the day by being very busy writing up the proceedings of a board of survey, and have a like job on my hands for to-morrow; indeed, I shall be fully employed now till we leave. Some of the men, however, have been otherwise employed, viz., in parading before the guard-house with logs of wood on their backs, as the reward of a drunken frolic. Our march to Fort Yuma will doubtless be very disagreeable, and for two weeks we shall have dust and heat together with the fatigue of travel; but, on the other hand, the daily march will not be more than fifteen miles, and as we shall be well provided, I can't say that I look forward to it with much dread. The wife of our captain is even now interesting herself in the culinary arrangements, so I presume the *vitals* will be good." From the time of his uttering this amusing pun until the following September, the letters of young Lockwood give us no incidents of special interest, and we now follow him into the State of Nebraska, his regiment having been assigned to the favorite post of Omaha.

III.
ARMY-LIFE IN NEBRASKA.

Having entered upon duty at the barracks of Omaha, he seems to have made himself especially useful there, while enjoying some of the comforts of civilization, including good society. On the 25th of September, he wrote that he had been busy for a week as the recorder of a court-martial. "We settled nine cases, and, while we now stand adjourned *sine die*, I suppose the court will soon be reconvened to try half a dozen more men against whom charges have been preferred. There have been, since my arrival here, as many as sixty men in the guard-house, and courts-martial are the order of the day. I have to attend drills, etc., every day, and hence my leisure and opportunities for visiting the town have been limited. However, I did go last night to a concert in town given for the benefit of the grasshopper sufferers, several of these sufferers from the country being present. You can not realize what a nuisance these insects are in this country. I have not yet seen them in any numbers, or the effects of their ravages, but I am told they sometimes actually stop the railway-trains. The incredible number of bed-bugs in this country is another curious fact. I sleep so soundly that they do not disturb me. They infest every house at the post, and they are also numerous in the city, the fences between here and there being painted in many places, 'Go to Smith's for the great bed-bug buster.'" He became a favorite in the refined society of Omaha, at that time on the confines of civilization, but appearing to him like a bit of New York city cut off and set down in the wilderness, where, only a few years before, the buffalo ranged in his native freedom. During his residence at Omaha, young Lockwood was on the most friendly terms with all his fellow-officers, with one exception. After giving his father a very manly account of that trouble, he writes a paragraph about himself in these words: "With regard to myself, I find this army-life about what I expected. It has its pleasures and its crosses. I should prefer the cavalry to the infantry, and am sorry I did not apply for that arm of the service. I should like to remain in the army two or three years longer, I think, and yet, with a good opening, might do better in civil life. Promotion is very slow, and the accumulation of anything is not easy. These, of course, are rude impressions and but half formed, but, as you ask for impressions, I feel bound to give them just as they are. I have not been in the army long enough to rise, nor have I had the opportunity to gain any particular reputation, but suppose mine is as good as the average—that is, I think I have displayed as much aptitude for my profession as is generally exhibited by men of average ability, for of such I regard myself—perhaps below the average. I hope this peroration will answer your inquiries, and prove satisfactory in that respect. Excuse the necessary egotism. I will thankfully receive any advice or corrections which the reading of this, or your acquaintance with my characteristics, may suggest. I feel as though I had written a lot of foolishness; if you think so, please excuse."

To the writer of this personal history, it seems as if such sentiments as the above could come only from a young man endowed with the highest instincts of ambition, honor, and true manhood, and can not but be considered, with others of like character, as a suitable passport into the land of Odin and the glories of Valhalla.

During his stay at Omaha, Lieutenant Lockwood was detailed by General Ord, the commanding officer, to visit those counties of Nebraska where grasshoppers had destroyed the crops, for the purpose of determining to whom contributions which had been sent to the general should be given. In this journey of several hundred miles, made in the coldest weather, he visited the several county towns, met the citizens, and afterward laid before the general such testimony as to the destitute, that the bounty was distributed to the satisfaction of all. While on this duty, he traveled ninety miles in twenty-four hours. The county people with whom he conducted business, he designated as "Grasshoppers." He greatly enjoyed the prairie scenery through which he passed, especially the valley of the Blue.

On the approach of Christmas at Omaha, our young friend had an attack of chills and fever, which sent him to his bed. After deploring that he could not perform his duties on the pending court-martial, he gives us this holiday information: "Yesterday was Christmas, and I am glad that the day comes but once a year. With a large party I was occupied until late in the afternoon making the rounds of the many houses here at the post. In the evening, I ate a fine dinner at General Ord's, and on top of that, danced in the parlor until eleven or twelve o'clock, and, as a consequence, am coming on as officer of the guard to-day with a most gorgeous headache. So much for Christmas. I have received two or three presents, but have made none myself, from want of funds. I just now heard a tremendous crash, and, on going out, found a fine lunch, sent by Mrs. Ord, scattered on the ground, and in the midst of the *débris* of broken glass and china, the unfortunate bearer, who had slipped and fallen on the ice in front of the door. I was not particularly sorry on my own account, as I could not have eaten the good things 'anyhow.' Upon the whole, Christmas has passed away as it usually does, pleasantly, though at the expense of many unfortunate turkeys. I am sorry I could not send home any presents, my pecuniary affairs being in a straitened condition. I should like very much to be at home about this time. I often wish I could hear Lidie and Anna sing, although I suppose I would find the girls, including Julia and

Mary, much changed."

Remembering young Lockwood's remarks about whisky-drinking in New York, the following statement is worth quoting: "Most of the ladies at the post received visitors on New-Year's-day, either singly or in groups. One marked feature of the day was the general absence of liquor, its place being supplied by coffee, chocolate, and other refreshments of a more solid and less stimulating character. I noticed the same thing in town, or rather that at those places where I saw liquor, the ladies were less urgent than is usually the case in pressing it upon the gentlemen. However, there is less drinking at this post than at any other I have seen, as large as it is. Although, with few exceptions, all drink here, it is done quietly at home and without excess."

As our young friend had narrowly escaped with his life from drowning at Annapolis, so did he from the pranks of an unruly horse at the Omaha Barracks. He was about mounting the horse for a ride, when the animal started on the run before he could get into the saddle, when he was thrown forward upon his head. The trouble was owing to a defect in the bridle. In accounting for his escape, he remarked that his thick head was what saved his life. True to his native pluck, he tackled the same horse a number of times afterward, until the animal—a special favorite—was subdued.

In the month of June, 1875, it would seem as if something like homesickness was weighing down his spirits, for he then began to write about employment in civil life. Not that he disliked the army, but he longed for some business that would enable him to make a little money. He thought he could supply a sufficient amount of energy to prosecute a commercial venture. He felt that there was a great difference between the roads that lead to wealth and to military glory. If his father should chance to see an opening that might give him a fortune in a few days at the expense of a few hundred dollars or some hard work, he wanted to be promptly notified. He broached these business ideas at that time merely for the sake of having a subject for discussion when permitted to visit his home.

The life at the Omaha garrison, during the summer of 1875, was comfortable but monotonous. The faithfulness with which the young officer corresponded with his parents is eminently characteristic of a dutiful son. When not writing about his surroundings and daily duties, or sketching the character of his associates, he ventured to discuss business matters with his father, frequently volunteering a bit of advice. He often alluded to the Annapolis farm and to people and events connected with Georgetown, now a part of Washington City, where he expected the family to remain permanently. On every subject discussed, he manifested a clear head, and enlivened his more serious talk with an occasional joke, for which he seemed to have a fondness. In expressing his opinions on men and things, it seemed impossible for him to hesitate or equivocate; he always went directly to the point, and, though charitable, he could not refrain from looking out for the demands of justice, as, for example, when alluding to the death of a man who had been untrue to himself and friends, he said "to die was about the best thing he could do." As to his jokes, they were not confined to his private letters, as will be shown by one of them practiced upon the post trader during a dull period in the garrison. The trader in question, a young fellow, had removed the balls from the pistol of one of his clerks, with the intention of playing a ghostly trick upon him that night. He told Lockwood and another friend of his intention, and they determined to turn the tables upon the trader. They notified the clerk, and at midnight the amateur ghost rose from his bed, enveloped himself in a white sheet, and stole softly into the room of the *unsuspecting* clerk. Just then an improvised noise was made outside the door, when the clerk seemingly awoke with an exclamation of terror at seeing the ghost. The report of the pistol was duly followed by the return of the ball held in hand, *à la ghost*, but immediately after, the poor ghost found himself completely drenched with a bucket of water, which had been coolly set aside for that purpose. At this unexpected turn of affairs, the trader fled in the greatest consternation, leaving his "trade-mark" behind, and, as he passed out of the door, received a second pail of water from one of his ghostly companions. The result was that it took a long time for him to dry his saturated skin, and a much longer for his title of Mr. Ghost to be lost by the garrison boys. Not long after the above incident, this personage found that there was not "the ghost of a chance" of his continuing in business, as he became insolvent and had to retire. It would appear that while many of these military merchants on the frontiers have a chance to make fortunes, those who are located near a city like Omaha find it difficult to make both ends meet in their business affairs.

On reading the proceedings of Congress during the winter of 1875, he writes to his father as follows: "Congress seems to be looking around for some scape-goat on which to pile the odium of the millions legislated away, and, as usual, pitches on the army. It seems to be the opinion here, however, that no reduction will take place this winter. If Congressmen consulted occasionally others than the staff-officers living in Washington with regard to military affairs, they might find out the true whereabout of the tremendous rat-hole which swallows up annually the sum of thirty-four millions of dollars. It does not go to support the army proper, but to support that enormous, overgrown, expensive adjunct of the army, the staff, which, created merely for the administration of the *army*, now masters that which it was intended to subserve, and has become superior to it in rank and influence, and in everything that rank and influence can bring. But Congress seems to be blind to the fact that expenditures are credited to the army, under the army appropriation bill, which have no legitimate connection with it, and which would still be required if no army existed. Why is it that the army is the perpetual foot-ball of these demagogues? Is it thus, at every session, to be bantered about by those who do not understand the requirements of the country in this respect? Is not the causing of this periodical uncertainty respecting his fate the most pernicious thing that Congress can do to an officer? O consistency, thou art a jewel! How is it that the navy and other branches of the public service are not subject to this constant tinkering? But I am not in Congress, and had better subside." The assertions here made can not be controverted, and, coming from a young man who had but recently passed his majority, prove him to be the possessor of very substantial abilities. He also expressed decided opinions in regard to various noted officials charged with improper conduct in Washington at the time alluded to, all of which have been sustained by subsequent developments.

Remembering what he said about the drinking customs of Omaha, on New-Year's-day, 1875, it is pleasant to have him record the fact, on the 2d of January, 1876, that "the most noticeable feature during the previous day, in society, was the entire absence, at most houses, of any intoxicating liquors, and that he did not see a case of drunkenness during the entire day—a thing very rare even in the cities of the East." On a subsequent occasion, he mentions the fact that, when one of his sergeants had been drinking to excess, he put him in arrest, but released him the next day, after warning him of the consequences of a repetition of the offense, and "preaching him a sermon on the evils of intoxication, moral, mental, and physical." On one occasion, when his father had asked how he spent his leisure time in the barracks, he replied that he read, so as to combine pleasure with profit, played on his flute, and studied the art of short-hand, which had long been a hobby with him, and was to be in the future an important accomplishment. In an effort to read Draper's "Intellectual Development of Europe," he could only manage about one half of the work, and to counteract its dullness resorted to a novel, "The Wandering Jew." As he was frequently called upon to act as recorder of the military court, he found his knowledge of stenography very useful and very much of a relaxation, and, on receiving a letter from one of his sisters which was good but not very plainly written, he said that he had been able to make it out by means of his skill in shorthand writing. As to his studies, he had formed a regular plan for prosecuting them, but was constantly interrupted by extra official duties. Among other things, he devoted himself to the German language, and subsequently to French, and attained considerable proficiency. An idea of his habits of industry may be gathered from what he wrote to his father, when the General was placed on the retired list of the navy: "So you are retired this month. You ought to open an office, or do something to occupy your mind. Every one needs something in the way of business or duty. You will soon get tired of reading continuously." On the approach of spring, and with the expectation of obtaining a leave of absence during the coming summer, he resumed a discussion with his father about leaving the army for civil employment. He had entered it well posted in regard to its disadvantages, and chiefly for the sake of having something to do. He had now become more deeply impressed than before that promotion was so slow, that his prospects of increased rank and pay offered no inducements to any young man of energy and industry, qualities which he certainly possessed. He was not then ready for decisive action, but he was determined to support himself, and would, therefore, be on the lookout for advantageous prospects in some other line of employment. In one of his letters, after commenting upon the school which two of his sisters were attending, he gives us this bit of experience: "I am a school-teacher myself; my pupils, the non-commissioned officers of the company. They waste the midnight oil, however, only in *boning* the tactics. I go down and dilate and expatiate very profoundly on the reasons and logic of this and that. This is a pleasant school to have; the authority and influence of the officer have their full weight in the ordinary school-room as elsewhere in the army." In May, 1876, after giving an account of a proposed demonstration, under General Crook, against the Indians on the Yellowstone, he thus relieves his mind: "Would that I belonged to the cavalry! I like motion, action, and variety. To be sure, I would rather be here (in Omaha) than where the other companies are, but still would rather be in the field than here." In June, 1876, the monotony of his life was relieved by an order to take some convicts to the State prison near Fort Leavenworth, which he described as the largest post in the country, containing the post proper, the department headquarters, and the military prison. The State prison is about six miles from the town. "Here," he writes, "are sent all the enlisted men who are dishonorably discharged, convicted of theft, or other not purely military offenses. The inclosure is an immense yard, surrounded by a high stone wall —the building, which is on one side, having an appearance somewhat like the Smithsonian Institution. In the inclosure are various other buildings, each one used as a workshop for some trade, almost all the common trades being represented. The prisoners, numbering about five hundred, are together in the daytime, but not at night, and are not allowed to talk with each other. It was from this prison that the best features of the new military prison were obtained, the board of officers on the management of the prison at Fort Leavenworth having decided it to be the best one to imitate."

In the autumn of 1876, when he was granted a leave of absence to visit his parents, they found him in personal appearance wonderfully improved and developed, the boy of 1873 having become a handsome and accomplished gentleman. He was not slow, as may be supposed, in making his way to Philadelphia to visit the Centennial Exposition, which he greatly enjoyed.

IV.
ARMY-LIFE IN KANSAS.

During Lieutenant Lockwood's absence on leave, his regiment was transferred to Fort Leavenworth, and there we find him early in 1877, and for about two years thereafter. Of course, the garrison life of an officer, in times of peace, is somewhat monotonous; but the letters which the lieutenant wrote from this station contain some passages which are interesting and illustrate his character, as will be seen in the following pages. Here it should be stated that, during his sojourn at Fort Leavenworth, he made many pleasant acquaintances, which ripened into friendship; among them being the widow of an officer, with whom he boarded for some time, and whose friendship he particularly valued.

At a time when there was quite a rage at the garrison for private theatricals, one of the superior officers took the liberty, without previous consultation, of putting Lockwood on the list of performers, whereupon he declined the honor, as he thought Nature never intended him for a star. In speaking of a little difficulty between two of his friends, he manifests his love of fun by stating that one of them had denied the allegation and defied the alligator. When commenting upon some disagreeable March weather, he said, "I don't think the ground-hog has seen his shadow, and hence the latter part of the month ought to be pleasant." After a remark on the proficiency he was making in the study of French, he quietly continues, "There are many here who speak it '*à l'Américaine*,' as if they thought that 'the chief end of man.'"

As if never satisfied with his acquirements, he writes in one of his letters as follows: "My latest hobby is telegraphing. The signal officer of the department has loaned me a small battery and an instrument. We have put up the wires and are progressing well. Telegraphy, like phonography, is easy to transmit after some little practice; but it is difficult to recognize the sounds as they come over the wire, and it requires as much practice as it does to recognize the phonographic characters. I have the instrument on the table before me, and can not fail to gain some proficiency at any rate."

In July, 1877, when the strikers and rioters were making trouble in St. Louis, Mo., Lieutenant Lockwood's company and five others were ordered to that city on duty. After their arrival, they waited in daily expectation of mowing down the mob, but there was little fighting, as the police and militia were found to be amply sufficient to subdue all disturbance. He was greatly pleased with the city and military quarters of St. Louis, and felt that he would like to remain there on permanent duty. The feature which pleased him more than any other at St. Louis was a private garden of about fifty acres, exquisitely planned, and containing the rarest and most beautiful flowers and trees. The floral display, there, he thought superior to that at the Centennial Exposition. The owner, a bachelor named Shaw, nearly eighty years of age, and a man of enormous wealth, paid out yearly in expenses twenty-five thousand dollars. At the garden residence of this millionaire, young Lockwood and a friend were hospitably entertained—a wonderful contrast to the accommodations at a beer-saloon, near the arsenal gate, where the army officers were obliged to take their meals while in the city. Altogether the trip was pleasant, but too expensive for men with limited means. On their return to Fort Leavenworth from the Eden-like garden of St. Louis, they were informed of Indian troubles in Montana, and startled by a rumor that they must soon be off upon a hunt for Indians—illustrating the vicissitudes of army-life.

It was about this time that a specimen of American royalty visited Fort Leavenworth with his daughter, to whom young Lockwood had an opportunity of being polite. This was a great cattle-man from Texas, who was said to have fenced in a grazing-farm of a million of acres, and who numbered his cattle by tens of thousands. His name was King, and his title in all the West was the "Cattle King of Texas." The father and daughter were much interested in an inspection of the fort, where they were hospitably entertained. From that time onward for several months, the dullness of garrison-life was only relieved by parties, dinners, and theatrical amusements in the city, by the presence of an encampment of Indians near the post, and by attendance at a grand reception and ball given at Kansas City by the Governor of the State. The letters written by young Lockwood during all this period are elaborate and full of interest to his parents, but not enlivened with any incidents of public interest. The garrison courts seem to have demanded very much of his attention, because of his skill in taking down testimony by short-hand, and he was frequently compelled to devote many of his sleeping hours to the duty of writing out his notes.

While going from the fort into town one day, he witnessed what he called an awful spectacle—three little boys in a state of intoxication. This recalled the fate of one of his former companions in the East, who had become a drunkard, and in a letter to his father he recorded the following: "Liquor is certainly a terrible curse; one constantly sees illustrations of this in the army. You rather startled me in a recent letter by telling me you had taken the pledge. Had you departed from your abstemious habits in this respect? was my first thought, but I was at once relieved by seeing that your allusion was to something else. A rule that I have had for a long time and seldom depart from, is not to drink before sunset and never to do so in a saloon. It is rather superfluous in me to have any such rules, as it is very seldom that I have a desire to touch spirituous drinks, and then I partake only for the sake of not appearing to be rude in social matters."

On one occasion, after describing a splendid dinner which he had attended, he branches off upon his own experiences in that line, stating that he had been caterer for the "Bachelors' Club" during the current month, and playing housekeeper for the first time in his life. He was striving to feed the mess well and to reduce expenses, the individual assessments amounting to twenty-four dollars.

"We have a good deal of fun," he says, "at the mess; among other ways, by a resolution of the officers that I shall keep a record of the puns, jokes, profane expressions, etc. Any one indulging in these is put back or set forward on a regular motion and vote by the members, and any one getting a record of fifteen has to send to the store for a supply of cigars. One of the mess, having the bad habit of saying, 'O Lord!' and 'Damn it!' when excited, gets a great many bad marks, and is made unhappy. The standard of wit being very high, one seldom 'goes ahead.'"

In May, 1878, when it was doubtful what Congress would do about reducing the army, and Lieutenant Lockwood thought that he might decide to leave the service, he discussed with his father the question of future employment. He thought favorably of a position in some telegraph company, thereby proving that, in all his studies and leisurely occupations, he was practical, and no visionary. Another idea that he had was that he might play Cincinnatus, and again go upon the farm. He also thought of a position in connection with the Signal Service as one that would suit him should he, from any cause, be compelled to leave the army; and this suggestion, taken in connection with his subsequent career, is notable. He went so far, indeed, as to ask his father about the practicability of securing such a position in that corps, and desired especially to know all about the necessary qualifications.

On one occasion, after alluding to the possibility of his being transferred for duty to some other place, he says that it might be a good thing for him, as he could not remain at Leavenworth always, and yet he dreaded to be sent to some "far-distant and isolated post." When he wrote those words, how little did he imagine that he would eventually close his earthly career in a land of supreme desolation within the Arctic Circle!

Subsequently—July, 1878—he resumed with special earnestness the consideration of being detailed for duty in the Signal Service, and, with his father's approbation, made the proper application. He thought the proposed transfer would be of benefit to him in many ways, and if he failed to make it so, he would very quickly be ordered back to his regiment.

In September he was ordered to St. Louis for the purpose of conducting some recruits westward, and for a short time it was uncertain whether he would have to go to Texas or the Territory of Wyoming, whereby were shown the uncertainties which attend life in the army. He took the recruits to Fort Laramie, and, on his way, was in danger of being embroiled with the Cheyenne Indians under Sitting Bull, but returned in safety, by way of his old camp at Omaha, to his company at Fort Leavenworth. During another trip, which he soon after took with his company, he saw in western Kansas many Russian immigrants. They were poor, and had settled at great distances along the streams to be near water, not always easily found in these regions. They knew nothing of the recent outbreak of the Indians, and, indeed, many of them had never seen an Indian. The lieutenant also stumbled upon a colony of Swedes, and at one place saw three women, whose husbands had been killed by the Indians, and who were weeping bitterly in their distress. While his company was on the march he generally kept at the head of the column, thereby receiving the title of Pedestrian of the Command. Much of the country over which they traveled was monotonous in the extreme—wide stretches of prairie reaching to the far horizon. Antelopes and Jack-rabbits were frequently seen, and sometimes were fired at without success. But, to his mind, the most wonderful features about the country were the countless tracks and bones of the buffalo, while not a living animal was seen. One of his guides informed him that in former times he had killed three hundred in a single day, so that it was no wonder that they were now extinct.

In a letter to one of his sisters, in October, he speaks of his return from this chase after Cheyenne Indians, and then goes on to mention some amusing incidents that had occurred at the post, and gives her this bit of artistic advice: "I hope you will profit by your talent for painting, *not bury it in the ground, like the foolish steward*. Painting is a great and very popular accomplishment; there is none perhaps more so." No matter what happened in or about the garrison, he seemed always ready with his common-sense opinions referring to passing events. For example, after alluding to the burning of a stable, with thirteen mules, when some of them that had been released ran into the fire from fright, he thus proceeds: "I was talking 'over the wire' with one of the men on our telegraph line, and what he said is no doubt true, and shows the short-sightedness of the Government. He said that he and many of the other soldiers had damaged or lost their clothes, and that if soldiers were reimbursed for their losses on such occasions, they would work with much more *vim* and energy, and that he heard one man say that he would not lose his new pantaloons for all the mules in the stable. Of course, in the case of a private house on fire, I believe the enlisted men would risk everything; but in cases of this kind, where Government property only is concerned, this feeling has its existence. There is, too, some reason for this feeling; for, no matter how hard a soldier or officer may work at a fire to save public property, the Government will not reward him even by the restitution of his clothes. Nothing short of an act of Congress would be authority for such an issue."

That the heart of this young man was as pure as his mind was bright, may be seen by reading the following remarks concerning the death of a little niece: "I learn with deep regret the death of poor little Agnes, and sympathize heartily with Lidie and her husband in their affliction, the depth of which none but a parent can know. It should be a consolation, however, that the disease carried the little one away in all the innocence of childhood, before her mother's love had been intensified with years, and her own intelligence had taught her to love and cling to life. The sad news reached me on the day of the funeral of the little daughter of a brother lieutenant. The little baby seemed very amiable in life, and after death lost none of her sweetness. I sat up with the remains during the night before the funeral." Alas! when this noble-hearted young man gave up his own life, his only night-watchers were the stars and the icy mountains of the far-distant North!

In December, 1878, the Twenty-third Regiment received orders for service in the Indian Territory, and a few weeks afterward entered upon its line of march. In the mean time, the lieutenant made himself useful in performing the duties of an engineer for the sanitary benefit of the Leavenworth garrison. After some appropriate studying, he soon got the knack of running the levels and measuring angles with the theodolite. He found these new duties interesting, preferring the field-work to the making of the necessary profiles and other drawings, involving measurements to the $1/1000$ of an inch—rather a confining employment.

V.
ARMY-LIFE IN INDIAN TERRITORY AND COLORADO.

From the spring of 1879 until the winter of 1881, Lieutenant Lockwood spent a part of his time in the Indian Territory, but chiefly in the State of Colorado. The first duty of his company was to establish a cantonment on the Canadian River. On their way thither, they made a halt at Fort Supply, where the country was sparsely settled, and where the rolling prairies seemed desolate and interminable. Those of his regiment who had been ordered to Supply, he found in miserable quarters—log-huts covered inside with canvas—old, cold, and forlorn in appearance inside and out, and yet the canvas walls thus used and useless were furnished at a cost of hundreds of dollars. After leaving that place for the Canadian River, he was made the engineer officer, and, with a view of making a map of the route and surrounding country, devoted his time to the science of topography, being rewarded by the hearty approbation of the officer in command.

He had counted upon having some good hunting on this route for turkeys and other game, but was disappointed, owing to the fact, as was supposed, that several hundred Indians had passed through the country some weeks before and had gobbled up everything, including a host of *gobblers*. On reaching their destination, the company went into camp under a bluff on the Canadian River, where they were to remain until buildings could be erected in the immediate vicinity. At the conclusion of his first letter written home from this camp, he says, "I am lying at full length on a buffalo-robe with my paper on 'Daniel Deronda,' and the position is not comfortable."

In June, Lieutenant Lockwood was sent with a small party to Post Reno, where troubles were apprehended with the Indians. It was not necessary to do any fighting there, however, for the reason that the chief inhabitants of the region were rattlesnakes, tarantulas, and prairie-dogs, and the Indians in the vicinity did not seem to be in a blood-thirsty mood. Returning to the cantonment on the Canadian River, he was depressed by the discomforts of the place—no society and many extra duties—but he, nevertheless, found time and inclination to study the Spanish language, as if determined not to leave a stone unturned in his efforts to make himself useful, or ready for any emergency. After confessing his fondness for social intercourse, he writes: "At times I get the *ennui* and *blues* very much. Still I try to preserve a philosophic mind, and when the dark side of the picture presents itself, I take a different stand-point, and thus force myself to see, by contrast, the bright side. I find, and ever have found, that the more occupied I am, the better contented I feel."

In April, 1880, he went upon a kind of exploring expedition, riding in ten days a distance of nearly three hundred miles, and on returning was glad enough to have a little rest in his camp. But, before he could fall into any idle habits, he was ordered westward, with his command, on still more arduous duties. In a letter from a camp near Saguache, on the borders of Colorado, he sent home the following account of what he had seen and experienced: "We left Fort Garland on the 17th of May, and have since been traveling across 'San Luis Park,' the 'Valley of the Gods.' This is a vast level plain in southern Colorado, surrounded on all sides by high, snow-capped mountains, which always seem within a few hours' travel, and yet are miles and miles away. When one considers that Blanco Peak is over fourteen thousand feet above the sea-level, one does not wonder that it is very plainly seen from where I am now writing. This Paradise of the Gods is some two hundred miles long by over sixty across, and is a veritable desert. I have met nothing like it outside of Arizona. The vegetation consists of greasewood and sage-brush— sometimes not even this; the irrigation-ditches that one meets near the few streams seem hardly able to produce a feeble, stunted grass. For miles and miles, all is pulverized dust, which, blown by the winds in blinding clouds, covers everything like the ashes of a volcano. Night before last one of these *pleasant* zephyrs blew down several of the tents, and filled the air so thickly with dust, that several of the command, who had their hats blown off, were unable to find or recover them. They say it sometimes rains here, but I very much doubt it. The few ranches we have encountered are on streams descending from the mountains, which sink in the plain after running a short distance; and bordering them are the squalid adobe houses, the only habitations in the country.

"Improbable as it may seem, the owners say that they raise potatoes, etc. Surely these mountains should be of gold and silver to compensate for the sterility of the soil." The prospect did not make Lockwood hilarious, and he frankly said that he was tired of army-life, and that eating almost nothing but bacon, and going without any comforts caused him to sigh for a return to the old Annapolis farm. He had not the ambition to enjoy the glory of army-life in such a wilderness. It might, indeed, give one a competency, but it was a gold-mine in Arizona that had recently given a fortune of fifty thousand dollars to one of the officers of his regiment. After a short stay at Garland and Alamosa, and catching a glimpse of the Del Norte, the command reached the Cochetapa Pass, near Los Pinos and the summit of the Rocky Mountains; and now the lieutenant began to experience a kind of mountain-fever, which he called a weird condition of the system. He was troubled with the shortness of breath usual at great altitudes. The six hundred mules drawing the train of one hundred wagons had great difficulty in passing through what he called the terrible cañons. Early in June, 1880, he reached the Uncompahgre River, where the command encamped. Hardly had he obtained any relaxation before an order came from Fort Leavenworth, detailing a general court and making him the judge advocate, thereby proving that there was not much rest for an officer of recognized ability. While anxious to make money, he did not, while among the mountains, follow the example of certain fellow-officers, who devoted some attention to mining speculations, their mode of operating being as follows: "For example, they secure the services of a competent man, provide him with food, etc., and send him out to prospect. Those in the Nineteenth have received a very flattering letter from their man, who has struck a very rich vein, *according to his account.* But this and all similar ventures are mere chance. Money, to the amount of twenty-five or fifty dollars, seems little to invest in enterprises that may pay thousands; but these investments count up and are not pleasant to consider when all ends in failure. One of the officers has invested not less than thirty-three hundred dollars in this mine-hunting business. He goes it alone, and has all the enthusiasm of an old miner." Not caring to waste his money in speculations of this sort, he improved his leisure in exploring the scenery of the region, especially some cañons where the walls were several thousand feet high, and also a stream called Cow Creek, where he had some superb fishing and caught the largest trout he had ever seen, while his companions killed a number of deer. Among the scenes in which he was especially interested was a hot spring which measured thirty feet across, a waterfall two hundred feet high, and a small mining hamlet nestled in a pocket of the mountains, and where, funny to relate, he and his companions were suspected to be tramps or horse-thieves. Returning to his regular cantonment on the Uncompahgre, he was informed of a pending trouble with the Ute Indians, when, according to his habit, he expressed this decided opinion: "If the sentimentalists on Indian questions in the East could be brought out here and made to feel and suffer the outrages which these savages inflict on isolated settlers, there would not be so many to support the Interior Department in its abominable prejudice in all questions of Whites *vs.* Indians."

In one of his letters, written from a cantonment in Colorado, he mentions with pain the temporary fall of one of his brother officers, who, while playing a game of poker, was charged with dishonesty, thereby pocketing a hundred dollars. The poor fellow had been placed in arrest and was to have a trial. In speaking of his manner of killing time in his Colorado camp, he alludes to the fact of having two setter dogs, which he was training for use and his own amusement, and further says that when not playing a game of billiards at the store near the camp, he spent his time in reading, the books then occupying his attention being, Tyler's "Baconian Philosophy," which he greatly admired; Swinton's "History of the Rebellion," which he criticised with some severity; and Green's "Russian Campaign in Turkey," which interested him greatly.

VI.
PREPARING FOR THE ARCTIC REGIONS.

From this point, the story of Lieutenant Lockwood's life will be chiefly given from the records which he kept during his sojourn in the Arctic regions. For reasons which the general reader will appreciate, all merely technical and official remarks have been omitted, and only those retained which are calculated to illustrate the personal character of the man and officer, it being understood that his journals, illustrating his merits and labors, will be fully set forth in the official history, to be hereafter published, of the expedition with which he was so honorably identified.

In 1880 it was proposed by an International Polar Commission, for the purpose of elucidating in behalf of science the phenomena of the weather and of the magnetic needle, that meteorological stations should be established by various countries in different parts of the polar regions. The Congress of the United States made an appropriation for establishing a scientific colony at the two places designated for the occupation of the Americans—viz., Point Barrow, in Alaska, and Lady Franklin Bay, in Grinnell Land. These stations were to be occupied for from one to three years. At the time the expedition was being organized in Washington for the latter place, Lieutenant Lockwood was on a visit to his parents in that city. Taking a special interest in the operations of the Signal-Service Bureau, which had the business in charge, he forthwith volunteered for the proposed expedition, and his services were accepted by the Secretary of War. When the party for the Lady Franklin Bay station was fully organized, it consisted of First-Lieutenant Adolphus W. Greely, U. S. A., commander; Lieutenants F. F. Kislingbury and James B. Lockwood, U. S. A., as assistants; and Dr. O. Pavy, as surgeon and naturalist; with a force of twenty-two sergeants, corporals, and privates, all connected with the army, and whose names are given as follows: Edward Israel, Winfield S. Jewell, George W. Rice, David O. Ralston, Hampden S. Gardiner, sergeants in the Signal Corps; William H. Cross, sergeant in the general service; David L. Brainard and David Linn, sergeants of cavalry; Nicholas Saler, corporal of infantry; Joseph Ellison, corporal of infantry; Charles B. Henry, Maurice Connell, Jacob Bender, Francis Long, William Whistler, Henry Biederbick, Julius R. Fredericks, William A. Ellis, and Roderick R. Schneider, privates in various branches of the army; and, finally, two Esquimaux, Jans Edwards and Frederick Christiansen, of Greenland.

In view of the possibility that Lady Franklin Bay might become a permanent station, all the preliminary arrangements were made as complete as possible.

A steamer called the Proteus was secured for conveying the expedition to Lady Franklin Bay, and she was ordered to await the arrival of the explorers at the port of St. John's, in Newfoundland. Lieutenant Lockwood sailed in a steamer from Baltimore with the party and reached St. John's late in June.

Here it may not be out of place to submit a few remarks on the utility of these Arctic explorations, which are sometimes criticised by people who, without due consideration, jump to hasty conclusions. In former times their main object was to find open passages between the northern regions of Europe, Asia, and America, and to settle the problem of the north pole; and statistics show that when these expeditions have confined their operations within reasonable limits, the mortality attending them has been remarkably small— less than in ordinary commercial voyages. Sir John Franklin went far beyond these limits, and left no monuments by which he could be traced. De Long put his ship into the polar ice with the design of moving with the polar drift. The Greely Expedition was expected to be confined, and was confined, to the well-known waters of Smith's Sound. It could, therefore, be reached at any time, and, if necessary, it could fall back upon a point accessible at all times. All that was required to secure its safe return was *a well-chosen base, and an absolute certainty that this base would be maintained.* Unfortunately, neither requirement was fulfilled, and hence nineteen men lost their lives. Sledge-journeys from established bases, though fraught with great labor and discomfort, have never been attended with serious loss of life. It is now about one thousand years since the first Arctic voyage was made, and their aggregate usefulness can hardly be questioned when we remember that they have developed fisheries that have built up the commerce and navies of nations, and that the direct return into the exchange of England has been far more than the cost to her of all her Arctic explorations. The Polar Commission, already alluded to, inaugurated a new policy in regard to Arctic explorations, and one whose utility can not be questioned. It had its origin, in 1875, in the mind of a German discoverer named Carl Weyprecht; and in the opinion of many of the leading minds of the world, the meteorological observations inaugurated by him have done much, and will do much more, to rectify errors in the polar problem and bring to light information about the ice zones, which will give the observers a prominent position in scientific history. According to Professor Joseph Henry, the problems connected with physical geography and science, which are yet unsolved, are the determination of the figure and of the magnetism of the earth, complete knowledge of the tides of the ocean, the winds of the globe, and the influence of extreme cold on animal and vegetable life. Surely the men who voluntarily toil and suffer in their efforts to obtain the needed light on all these subjects, are quite as worthily employed as those who struggle for riches or political fame. In the Professor's opinion, all the branches of science above mentioned are indirectly connected with the well-being of man, and tend not only to enlarge his sphere of mental activity, but to promote the application of science to the arts of life. A French writer, after applauding the plans of the Polar Commission, concludes his remarks as follows: "The larger number of the civilized nations are striving by scientific means to wrest the mysterious secrets of the deep from the hidden recesses of the North." In 1884 the number of nations that had entered heartily into the project was thirteen; fifteen polar stations, and over forty auxiliary stations, had already been established. That the reader may fully understand the operations and exploits which are to be chronicled in the subsequent pages of this volume, it may be well to submit the subjoined extract from the official report of General W. B. Hazen, Chief of the United States Signal Service, for the year 1881: "Owing to the very mobile nature of the atmosphere, the changes taking place on one portion of the globe, especially in the Arctic zone, quickly affect regions very distant therefrom. The study of the weather in Europe and America can not be successfully prosecuted without a daily map of the whole northern hemisphere, and the great blank space of the Arctic region upon our simultaneous international chart has long been a subject of regret to meteorologists. The general object is to accomplish, by observations made in concert at numerous stations, such additions to our knowledge as can not be acquired by isolated or desultory traveling parties. No special attempt will be made at geographical exploration, and neither expedition is in any sense expected to reach the north pole. The single object is to elucidate the phenomena of the weather and of the magnetic needle as they occur in America and Europe, by means of observations taken in the region where the most remarkable disturbances seem to have their origin."

While the foregoing were to be considered as the primary considerations, it was expressly stated in the official instructions, that sledging parties, generally, should work in the interests of exploration and discovery, and should be conducted with all possible care and fidelity. Careful attention was also to be given to the collection of specimens of the animal, mineral, and vegetable kingdoms. It will be seen that all that was accomplished by Lieutenant Lockwood was instigated by the mandate connected with the use of the sledge.

It thus appears that the Greely expedition was not only intended to accomplish a good work, but that in all human probability the same might have been accomplished without serious loss of life. That there was a deplorable loss of life, we can only lament, leaving for others to point out the causes of the disaster which befell the expedition.

VII.
FROM NEWFOUNDLAND TO LADY FRANKLIN BAY.

All things being ready, the Greely Expedition left St. John's, Newfoundland, for Lady Franklin Bay, on Thursday, July 7, 1881, in the steamer Proteus, Captain Pike. She was a barkentine, measuring two hundred and fifty feet in length, and having a burden of six hundred tons. Built in Scotland for the whaling and sealing service, she had already made several successful voyages within the Arctic Circle and on the Labrador coast. The departure of the ship elicited no demonstration from the people on the dock, excepting a few cheers from some warm-hearted fishermen. Whether the good people of Newfoundland were disgusted because they could not sell any more supplies at extravagant prices, or were displeased with the Yankee explorers for presuming to compete with Englishmen in the icy North, are questions not to be easily solved.

During his stay in St. John's, Lieutenant Lockwood wrote a letter to his mother, in which he gave the following account of the city:

"St. John's is a queer and forlorn old place; everything is antiquated, slow, and behind the times in every respect. The few hotels are more like third-class boarding-houses; a livery-stable is not to be found in this city of thirty thousand. This condition of affairs is said to be due to the religion of the place, which is Roman Catholic. It is charged that ignorance and poverty are what this church most thrives on, and it is certainly a thriving church here. The other day the shops were all closed, and the place assumed the appearance of Sunday—it was a holy day for their patron saints, Peter and Paul. Only two classes here—the poor and the rich—and everything accords with the former class. Crooked streets and mean, forlorn, dirty houses everywhere. The only respectable public buildings are the Catholic churches and the convents."

With the wind favorable, the sea calm, the sky clear, and all in good spirits, away went the vessel on her voyage to the North. A steam-launch, called the Lady Greely, rested securely on the main deck. It was arranged that the sergeants of the expedition should sleep in the cabin, eating at the second table, and the rest of the men live forward; and, though somewhat crowded, it was hoped they would all be comfortable. During the first twenty-four hours, two hundred miles were made. Lieutenant Greely and most of the men were sea-sick. At sunset on the second day out, the first iceberg was seen, and attracted the special attention of the land-lubbers. On the 9th, gales from the northwest set in, and the sick men became worse—the thermometer marking forty degrees, the air being damp and uncomfortable. The wind moderated in the evening, but left the sea very rough, so that the steam-launch had to be secured in her cradle by braces. Although then in the track of the St. Lawrence trade, not a single vessel was seen, suggesting the idea that business was not flourishing. As to Lieutenant Lockwood, he was in good spirits, and amused himself by reading Kennan's interesting book on Siberian life. On the following day the sea went down, and the sick men came up from their berths and were able to resume their places at the table, Lockwood and Kislingbury being the only ones who had escaped sea-sickness. When the former had finished Kennan's book, he took up Barrow's "Voyage within the Arctic Circle," reading it in the presence of several icebergs, which appeared as if they intended to welcome the band of Yankee adventurers to their inhospitable domain.

On the morning of the 11th, notwithstanding the promise of fine summer weather, the sky became overcast, and at noon the captain, assisted by the volunteers, including Lockwood, Israel, and Gardiner, could hardly succeed in getting observations, and though they reckoned the latitude at 58°, it was not reliable. Rain, attended with high winds or gales, succeeded, the sufferers from sea-sickness finding refuge in their berths. Ellis, one of the sergeants, suffered more than the others, having refused all food since leaving port. They could give him no aid save a little wine and beef-tea. The cold, cheerless weather depressed the spirits of all, but they hoped to get used to it. The days were sensibly growing longer, beginning at 1.45 A. M. and closing at 10 P. M. They now remarked the absence of icebergs and ice-floes, and wondered whether this meant that the previous winter in the north had been so mild that but little ice had formed, or that the spring had been so backward that but little had become detached and drifted southward. They had learned at St. John's that the late winter had been the mildest ever known there. At the close of the 11th, no land was in sight, and they had made seven hundred miles. The steward informed Lockwood that the men were growling about their food, which was the same as that received in the cabin. He thought this a bad sign for Arctic explorers, but tried to make matters more satisfactory.

The next day was disagreeable, a cold rain falling; and though a strong head-wind was blowing, the sea was smooth, betokening land or ice, it was supposed. Accordingly, at 9 P.M., they were aroused by the cry of "ice ahead," and, sure enough, there was seen, extending over 90° of the horizon, the white line indicating an ice-floe. Coming up to the ice, they found it to consist of detached pieces flowing southward. Some of these assumed the most fantastic shapes—dogs, seals, and other animals, and even houses and castles, readily presenting themselves to the imagination. One piece looked like an old ruin. The pillars, dome, and vaulted roof, all were there; indeed, the effect was perfect. Again, other pieces presented varieties of color most beautiful and remarkable. Generally, the lower parts being dark blue, were surmounted by a stratum of pure white, resembling snow, but really the purest ice. They were two hours in getting through this floe. Although daylight was continuous, they could not, because of fogs, distinguish the hours of sunrise or sunset.

On the following day the weather was still cloudy, and another ice-floe detained them two hours. They also saw many isolated pieces and large icebergs in the distance. This ice, it was said, came from the east coast of Greenland with a current which, flowing around Cape Farewell, passes up the west coast half way to Disco. It still proved interesting to the voyagers by reason of its fantastic shapes and diversified colors—white, blue, and green. It rose a few feet above the water-line, and the submerged portion of the floe colored the water a most beautiful green. Seals were then seen for the first time, basking in the sun on the ice. Judging from the increased seas, they expected no more ice-floes in front. The temperature also indicated this, for it was sensibly warmer. Lockwood, who seemed never to be idle, now finished Barrow and took up Captain Nares's "British Expedition of 1875-'76," reading, writing, and Bowditch occupying much of his time. The crow's nest was hoisted to the main-top on that day. This was a large barrel or hogshead with peep-holes on the side and a trap beneath. This afforded shelter for a man posted there who looked out for the ice and the best way of getting through it.

On the 16th, fogs detained them and interfered with noon observations, but, lifting at three o'clock, they sighted the Greenland coast on the starboard bow, distant fifteen miles. The coast-line appeared exceedingly rugged and broken, and the interior, mountainous with deep ravines running very abruptly down to the sea. The mountain-tops were covered with snow, but generally the sides were bare of snow except the ravines, which seemed to be filled up entirely. This range of mountains reminded Lockwood of the Uncompahgre chain in Colorado as seen from Los Pinos Valley. They saw the usual number of gulls and a species of duck called the sea-pigeon, also several whales blowing and spouting in the distance, surrounded by flocks of small birds which seemed to feed on their offal. Kislingbury and the steward tried rifles on these whales, but without success. One whale being near by, with apparent design to cross the track of the vessel, was met by the rifle-ball, but with no other effect than to cause him to throw up his tail and dive below the surface. The thermometer rose to 50° on that day, rendering the deck, where all were assembled to view the prospect, quite comfortable. They then first witnessed the sunset since leaving St. John's, because of the fogs and clouds that had constantly attended the voyage. The sun's disk seemed greatly flattened just as it disappeared at 10.20, and presented much the appearance of a huge mushroom seen edgewise. Enough of twilight remained at midnight to render the horizon visible.

On the 16th, they steamed cautiously through the fog, making but fourteen knots between noon and 6 P. M. Then the high, bold bluffs forming the southern coast of Disco Island loomed up in the distance directly ahead. These bluffs are almost vertical and probably five hundred feet high, and are desolate and barren in the extreme. Their continuity is interrupted only by deep ravines, or cañons, which break through at various angles to the sea. They there found themselves in the midst of a hundred icebergs of every conceivable form and size, and in color of the purest white, resembling in the distance huge mountains of chalk. One of the sights that attracted special notice consisted of two bergs connected by an immense arch high enough overhead for the ship to sail beneath, reminding Lockwood of the Natural Bridge of Virginia. On near approach it looked like marble and was quite as smooth. Some time afterward, and when two miles away, a signal-gun was fired for a pilot. This was followed by a rumbling noise, which caused the voyagers to look back, when they were surprised to see this immense arch tumble over and fall into the sea, throwing the spray a hundred feet into the air and producing a commotion of the sea sensible two miles away, and soon after followed by a noise like distant thunder. Most truly sublime were both spectacle and catastrophe! Icebergs are regarded as very dangerous both by the Esquimaux and by experienced Arctic travelers, and are given a wide berth.

Moving on at a low speed, the steamer was finally boarded by a white man attended by an Esquimaux, the former introducing himself as Mr. Gleichen, the Governor of Godhaven, Lively, or Disco, as the capital is variously called. The vessel was soon twisted through the narrow opening behind which the town lies, and the voyagers found themselves in the snuggest and smallest harbor, for its depth of water, that any of the party had ever seen. On one side were the high cliffs, barren and rugged, and on the other the few habitations which constituted the place, the only dwellings presenting an appearance of anything more than squalid huts being those of the governor and of the inspector, a Mr. Smith. Besides the dwellings, there were several warehouses and a church, all of wood. The huts of the natives were to some extent of wood, but strengthened and made warm by thick walls of sod reaching to the eaves.

Greely, Kislingbury, and Lockwood immediately went ashore to visit the inspector, whose house stood near the water and presented a neat appearance. Within they found quite an air of comfort and refinement. A piano, a small billiard-table, a well-filled book-case, carpets, pictures, and many other evidences of civilization and even elegance were there. They found the wife of the inspector very pleasant and speaking English fluently, while her daughter and a governess, though speaking English with difficulty, were well dressed and ladylike. After taking wine with these hospitable ladies, the lieutenants left their commander to continue the conversation and wandered forth to view the town. Passing without mishap several cross-looking Esquimaux dogs, they found themselves in what seemed a carpenter's shop, on the large, bare floor of which a dance was in progress. After playing spectators for some time they indulged in a waltz with the prettiest girls in the room, and were surprised and pleased to find how well they got along together. Their round dances were found to be like many figures of the "German" as danced in the United States. Kislingbury gave the natives an exhibition of the Indian dance, and thus became a favorite with them.

The dress of the men consisted of a pair of sealskin pantaloons and a woolen or checked shirt. That of the women was very peculiar—indeed, unique. One of the girls, whose dress may be taken to illustrate all, wore a pair of seal-skin pantalets bound at the hips by a red scarf and terminating just above the knees, where they met the white canvas tops of a pair of boots, or rather leggings. These reached to the calf, and there met the tops of red seal-skin bootlets, into which they were inserted. These leggings were starched and prettily fringed at the top, and their color indicated the state as to matrimony of the wearer, white being reserved for maidens, and colors for those that were married. This distinction was afterward found to be general. The pantalets were plain, except some red leather pieces sewed on in front by way of ornament. The upper garment consisted of a pretty, fancy-colored cassock, or jacket, extending barely to the hips, replaced in cold weather by the same of seal-skin with a hood. The upper part of the jacket was concealed by a necklace, or rather by several necklaces, sewed together flat, which formed a collar covering the bosom and shoulders. The head was covered by a kind of chaplet formed of fancy-colored cloth, and the hair was done up in a queue, which extended upward and backward from the top of the head, and was tied with colored ribbon. The wrists and neck were encircled with boas of dark-colored furs, which contrasted well with the bright-colored skin. The arms were bare to the short sleeves of the jacket, and on the fingers were a number of rings. So much for the Disco belles!

The dancing officers did not reach their ship until after midnight, and soon after the sun rose, flooding all nature with his glorious light, and seemingly affecting natives and strangers alike, for both were seen standing around to admire and enjoy the benediction of nature.

Inspector Smith visited the steamer, dressed in a military coat with brass buttons, and military cap with wide gold-lace band, but wearing seal-skin trousers. The strangers soon found themselves surrounded by a fleet of Esquimaux boats, called *kyacks*, resembling in form a cigar cut in half lengthwise and turned up at both ends. The framework of wood was covered with seal-skin with the hair removed. In the center was a hole into which the occupant inserted the lower part of his body to the hips, drawing up at the same time a cylindrical piece of seal-skin which was attached to the rim of the hole. When the top of this is gathered up and secured over his chest, the man and boat are practically one, and both are water-proof under all circumstances. The upper surface of the kyack is but an inch or two above the water when smooth, and when rough, of course it is frequently submerged entirely. In this craft the kyacker braves the billows of the open sea, and, provided with lance and harpoon to slay his game, and bladder and rope to mark its flight when struck and buoy up its body when killed, he attacks the seal, walrus, or even the narwhal. In South Greenland, where there is more open water, the kyackers become very expert, and, by means of their short, two-bladed paddles, can easily right themselves when upset, or even perform a complete revolution without changing position or posture.

On Sunday, the 17th, Lieutenant Lockwood called on the governor, and then went into many of the houses of the place; he found the natives polite and hospitable, living in clean, well-built huts, whose interior presented nothing peculiar except that about one third of the floor was raised a few feet, constituting a platform, which was used as the sleeping-couch of the whole family by night, and by day as a place of deposit for articles in daily use. The walls were adorned with rough prints or illustrations from European and American papers. In one house was seen a translation of the Psalms into Esquimaux. Their words are run together, as in the German language. Lockwood made some purchases, giving in return an old pair of pantaloons, old clothes being a circulating medium, and preferred to money. He was surprised to find that these people had a paper currency, the units being the ocre and the crown, one hundred ocres making one crown, while the crown is worth about an English shilling. In dealing with one another, the ocre seems to go a good way, but not so when a stranger is dealt with; and to do much shopping with this currency, one must carry a load of paper equal to what was required of Confederate currency in wartimes to buy a barrel of flour. The coins were of copper, valued each at five ocres.

On the following day, Lieutenants Greely, Kislingbury, and Lockwood, all dined at four o'clock with the inspector's family, by invitation of his wife, in the absence of her husband on official duty; the courses being soup, fish, eider-duck, and canned green peas, with a dessert of jelly; wines and brandy being served with the courses. The cooking and serving were excellent, the waitress an Esquimaux damsel in pantalets. Afterward, with others, they called on the governor, and with him went down to witness a dance. Lockwood learned that the population of the two divisions of North and South Greenland together was about nine thousand souls.

On the 19th, at the request of Lieutenant Greely, Lockwood made an exploration of the mountain-cliffs south of the town. After a long tramp over the soggy moss, and up steep cliffs, much annoyed by innumerable mosquitoes, he returned to dinner, with very little information worthy of mention. After superintending some stowage, he again called to see Mrs. Smith, the inspector's wife, and enjoyed her excellent piano-music, to say nothing of the wine and cigars she offered. Then he went to the dance, but not until after the men had left. These Greenland dances, as already intimated, resemble the Virginia reel, differing only in the alternate chasing of the partners through the two rows till caught.

Having completed their stowage and coaling, and having taken on board fourteen dogs with their food, they would have left Disco but for the fogs. Dr. Pavy, who had been left there by Howgate, joined the party on the 20th, as surgeon, as Mr. Clay was expected to do at Ritenbank. They had some music on the chapel organ in the evening, which was well rendered.

The penning of the dogs was a scene of excitement and amusement. Their snarling and biting and fighting had no end until one of the number present was acknowledged, for his prowess and valor, the victor by all the others.

Then the battle ceased, but only until there was a new arrival, when the battle was renewed and the *parvenu* put *hors de combat*, or declared king. In due time the steamer left Disco, and arrived at Ritenbank between 10 and 12 A. M. The harbor was found to be quite roomy and the entrance wide and deep; icebergs float into it, and thus render Ritenbank less desirable as a harbor than Disco. While there, with Mr. Clay (who now joined the expedition) and some of the men, Lockwood visited the neighboring bird mountains or looneries, rowing up a fiord some three miles distant. The approach to these was manifested by the commotion among the innumerable eider-ducks and other wild fowl flying overhead, swimming in the water around, or occupying the narrow ledges of the vertical cliffs on either side, some of which were five hundred feet high and covered with birds. The shot used being too small, would kill only at short range, and it was difficult to obtain the game; consequently they got only seventy fowls of various kinds. On their return they visited an Innuit burying-ground, which, from its antiquity, must contain many of the natives, whose blood is much purer than that of the present stock; for it is said the present Esquimaux blood is now very much mixed. The graves were oblong piles of lichen-covered stones, containing the moldering skeletons, which were generally in a sitting posture. But little regard is paid to the dead in Greenland. Influenza, and consumption induced thereby, are rapidly carrying off the natives, and this is increased by uncleanly habits, improper food, and bad ventilation, the latter aggravated by the introduction of small stoves into their close houses. The present longevity, it is said, averages thirty-three years.

The prevailing fogs greatly decreased the pleasure the explorers would have had in viewing the grand scenery in the passage to Upernavik, which they reached on the 23d of July, or in about fifteen days from Newfoundland. They had in sight numbers of icebergs, some of immense size. The whole western coast of Greenland is skirted with islands, separated from each other and the mainland by deep fiords. If it were not for the fogs, a pleasant summer excursion could be made through these fiords to the everlasting barrier of glaciers, which render the interior a veritable land of desolation.

Very soon after the expedition had arrived at Upernavik, it was found necessary for some one to go to a place called Proven, to obtain Esquimaux guides and a supply of Arctic clothing, and to Lieutenant Lockwood was assigned this duty. He and his helpers boarded the steam-launch, and, with Governor Elburg as guide, proceeded on their way through an inner passage leading to the place of destination. Their course lay along rocky and precipitous cliffs, many of them covered with auks and other wild fowl. The cliffs attained an elevation of two and three thousand feet, and were so smooth and regular as to have the appearance of having been made by man.

Without any shore whatever, large ships could lie alongside in safety. On their arrival at Proven, they saw the whole population in their picturesque costumes lining the shore, to view what they had never seen before—a craft moving without oars or sails.

Near the shore were located four large warehouses where seal-oil was deposited before shipment, and where also were kept by the Danish Government supplies of provisions for issue to the natives in case of emergency. The huts of the natives were found still more primitive than those at Disco, for here the entrance was through a long, low gallery, requiring one to grope in darkness almost on hands and knees. Lockwood softened the heart of the occupant of one by presents of tobacco, and induced him to play on his fiddle simple airs which he had picked up from whaling-crews. This brought in all the damsels of the town, and soon waltzes and other dances prevailed. The lieutenant did not consider it beneath his dignity to "show a heel." He unfortunately answered affirmatively to the question, "Are you big captain?" and was also imprudent in giving an old lady a half-dozen ocres. He was at once pounced upon by every one as lawful prey, and, what through begging, extortion, and other means, the "big captain" was soon rid of all his change, and might have been reduced to a state of nudity but for the timely arrival of the governor, who took him home to dine and to lodge. The soup, though sweet to the taste, was good; floating in it were lemon-peel and raisins. Next came reindeer-steaks cooked in wine and most delicious. Potatoes were the only vegetable. Cooking and serving excellent. Brandy, beer, and wine in profusion. The meal terminated by a general hand-shaking, according to custom, and the governor kissed his wife. The lodging was equally agreeable, affording the luxury of a clean feather bed. In the morning, and while yet in bed, a young Esquimaux damsel in pantalets brought the American a cup of strong coffee with a few crackers. That day he took on board the launch two Esquimaux, Frederick Christiansen and Jans Edwards, lashing their kyacks behind, also the seal-skin, dog-skin, and other clothing they had come for, and at midnight left amid the hearty cheers of the natives and the tears and lamentations of the friends of Jans and Frederick who had come to see them off.

After an uneventful passage, and stopping only to add one hundred and twenty-seven birds to their larder, the launch reached the ship at 10 A. M. on the 25th. Lieutenant Kislingbury and a crew in the whale-boat afterward went to Sanderson's Hope Island and secured several hundred more, so that there was no scarcity of fresh food. In the mean time some new dogs were secured, so that the total number now on hand was thirty-two.

The ship left Upernavik on the 29th, and, keeping the inner passage, made her way toward the north.

While crossing Melville Bay on the 30th, there was no ice in sight except bergs, and the sun shone brightly. That state of things was a great surprise to the explorers, as here it was that McClintock was frozen in for a whole year, and Nares congratulated himself in having passed the bay without detention. Indeed, Melville Bay has always been regarded as the *bête noire* of Arctic travel. An Arctic bear found on a broken pack of floating ice was killed by Lieutenant Kislingbury, and, when hoisted on board, was found to weigh a thousand pounds and to measure seven feet two inches in length. They were probably fifty miles from land at the time.

On the last day of July, the Proteus party sighted land, which they supposed to be Cape Dudley Diggs, north of Melville's Bay. Much old floating ice was seen, but so rotten as to offer no obstruction. Several seals and many little auks were killed and secured.

About this time Lockwood and others observed tokens of disrespect and insubordination on the part of some of the men, which were traced to a certain corporal as ringleader. Lockwood watched him with care, and urged the propriety of sending him home by the first opportunity, which was afterward done.

On one occasion, toward evening, the voyagers witnessed the overturning of an iceberg three hundred feet long and one hundred and fifty feet high. After capsizing, it continued to revolve on several axes for some time. Its change of base was preceded by the fall of several detached pieces, thus shifting its center of gravity.

The next day, August 1st, was clear and cool, and without fog. Passed Dudley Diggs at noon and then steered for Gary Islands, sighting them three hours later. The officers looked hard for the crimson cliffs near Dudley Diggs noticed by Sir John Ross, but observed only some slight discoloration of the snow. The glacier near this cape seemed to be two or three miles long; at the sea-shore, of inconsiderable height, but in the background, attaining an imposing elevation. The ship's compasses, as usual in this latitude, were all crazy, occasioning some bewilderment to the captain. The bear and seal meats were duly served on shipboard, and pronounced palatable by all, though to some the bear-meat was slightly fishy. Two boats with all the officers and others landed on the most easterly of the Cary Islands, and proceeded at once to find and inspect the *cache* of provisions—thirty-six hundred rations—left there by Sir George Nares for his own safety. They were apparently in good condition, notwithstanding many of the barrels resting on their ends afforded opportunity for rain and snow-water to enter. Some biscuits were found moldy. Replaced the Nares record by a copy, and also left a full record of the

Proteus. There was found there an excellent whale-boat, turned bottom upward, with oars and sails complete. This Lockwood urged Lieutenant Greely to take along, but he preferred getting the one at Foulke Point. The former regarded the supply of boats as too small, and circumstances might arise which would cause them to regret not using this one. They had only the steam-launch, a twenty-four-feet whale-boat, and a small, fourteen-feet row-boat—the whale-boat being the only one to be depended on in case of accident. The boat at Point Foulke was thought to be inferior. They picked up driftwood, an oar, and some burned pieces of a ship's stem or stern. They also saw some red snow, and shot several eider-ducks. The Cary Islands were found to be barren masses of rocks without vegetation.

The steamer came to anchor at Littleton Island at 9 A. M. on the 2d of August, just as the steering-gear gave way. A party went to "Life-boat Cove" and brought back a number of articles left by the Polaris Expedition of 1873. They saw neither Esquimaux nor reindeer, but shot a walrus. Lieutenant Greely made an effort to find the cairn left there by Nares, and the letters left for Nares by the Pandora. He found the letters but not the cairn, though there was a dismantled cairn afterward seen by others. Lockwood with a party of men put ashore several tons of coal, which, as it had to be carried up some thirty feet above the sea-level, he found no easy job. While thus engaged, this party had an adventure with some walruses, not unattended with danger. Having excited a drove of them by a simultaneous fire, the animals came toward the boat, and at one time held its inmates in peril. Lockwood alone was prepared to meet the foremost, and by good luck slew one of them, when all the rest disappeared. The walrus can be killed only through the brain, and when wounded, the animal is exceedingly ferocious. Numberless boats have been destroyed by them. Lamont thinks the walrus superior to the bear for food. Those they saw were evidently a female and her young, and their safety was in having killed the mother. Littleton Island affords a good illustration of these shores. The sides rise precipitously, sometimes in steps composed of immense cubes of trap-rock, sometimes in steep slopes formed from the crumbling of the same. The top of the island is seven hundred feet high, according to Nares, and generally quite level. Of soil, there is none. The summit afforded a fine view of the sound, though somewhat obstructed by fog. No floating ice; and the western coast with its snowy mountains quite distinct.

Having crossed the strait during the night of the 2d of August, in the early morning they ran along the western coast, which was very distinct and picturesque, the bluffs and headlands being reflected by the smooth sea. Striking the western coast near Cape Sabine, at 8 A. M. they reached Cape Hawkes, a headland over a thousand feet high and very picturesque. While

Lieutenants Greely and Kislingbury visited the cairn there, Dr. Pavy and Lieutenant Lockwood went to find the record on Washington Irving Island, both left by Nares. They then continued their way with slight interruptions from fogs until abreast of Franklin Island, when they were obliged to lay-to because of fog. They had not been delayed a moment by ice, and were surprised to see so little of it. Their success emboldened them to hope that they might reach Lady Franklin Bay without obstruction. Indeed, they even thought of inducing Captain Pike to run on until he reached the north pole itself, or at least till he attained a higher latitude than did Nares. One of the dogs having died, they became impressed with the thought that the poor curs suffered much from being cooped up and from the damp weather. The party continued on their way up Kennedy Channel with everything favorable, having the finest weather yet seen; air soft and balmy, sky clear, and water smooth.

On reaching the vicinity of Franklin Island and Carl Ritter Bay, they left there a small deposit of hard bread, pemmican, and rum, and continued on their way rejoicing; and so onward until nearly 10 P. M., when, just above Cape Lieber, they encountered an impenetrable pack extending all the way across the channel, and as far ahead as they could see. The ship made a savage dash at it, but in vain, and thus, but eight miles from Lady Franklin Bay, and with Cape Baird in full view, they were brought to a standstill. The mountains along the coast were covered with snow, but the valleys and low places were bare. The prominent objects of the landscape were all distinctly seen from their position—Capes Lieber and Baird on the left, Franklin, Hans, and Hanna Islands in the rear and left, and, in the far distance, Polaris Promontory and Petermann's Fiord, with the glacier beyond. A party that went on shore saw traces of the musk-ox, but no animals were seen.

Several of the officers and men attempted the ascent of the promontory of Cape Lieber, a precipitous cliff three thousand feet high, which seemed but a stone's throw away, but to reach which required a long, cold row, and then a fatiguing and painful climb. Lockwood and two only of the party succeeded. The difficulty was in the giving way of the crumbling slate-rock, which formed an incline of 45°. Those that reached the summit were rewarded by a grand view, extending to the limit of vision. On their return, after clambering over some rocks cropping out of the slippery snow and ice, they chose a short cut and came down at a run, or rather slide, followed by a miniature avalanche of *débris*. On the 6th of August, it was found that the icy barrier, which evidently came from the Polar Sea, was moving south, carrying the steamer along. Some game was seen in both air and water, but none taken. Parties attempted to reach the shore on the ice, but were recalled by signal, as moving ice was seen from the ship, and also open water near the shore.

From this point they slowly drifted south, with high winds from the north which opened up lanes of water which they did not think safe to enter. The total drift amounted to ten miles. With the lowering of temperature, it was suggested that it would be well to move across the channel, along the pack, and, if needful, land on the Greenland shore, possibly where Hall had wintered.

On the 11th of August, the ice barrier gave way under a change of wind and weather, leaving the passage open. Under full steam and sail, and with beautiful weather, they soon regained all the distance they had lost by drift, passed Cape Lieber, and came abreast of Cape Baird. Thence forcing their way through the broken ice of the bay, and reaching Bellot Island, which marks the beginning of Discovery Harbor, they cut their way to a secure spot for the ship to rest in. And thus ended the voyage to Lady Franklin Bay or Sound. As this harbor, or a spot in its vicinity called Fort Conger, was the one where the Signal-Service station was to be established, the steamer Proteus here ended her voyage, soon to return to Newfoundland. Discovery Harbor, which was to be their home, is an indentation of the bay covered by Bellot Island on the south. This indentation extends east and west some ten miles, and is probably two or three miles from north to south. Inclosing the harbor on three sides is a line of rugged bluffs and hills (or rather mountains, for they are two thousand feet high), those on the east side sloping back gradually, but elsewhere precipitous and rugged in the extreme. Thus, with Bellot's Island fifteen hundred feet high on the south, was formed a harbor, landlocked and most admirably sheltered.

VIII.
HOUSE-BUILDING AND LOCAL EXPLORATIONS.

Immediately after the explorers had anchored their ship in Discovery Harbor, they saw a drove of musk-oxen leisurely ascending the neighboring hills, which they climbed with the facility of goats. This was indeed a cheerful prospect for men in so isolated a region and without fresh meat, and many of them started forthwith in pursuit of the game, working their way to the shore on the ice, but were compelled to return after a vain attempt to follow the animals over the hills.

Hitherto there had been no opportunity to make any special discoveries, but now a comparatively new field, to which the explorers were to devote all their energies, came into view. Discovery, however, was to be always subordinated to the duties of meteorological observations. As this narrative proceeds, it will be seen that Lieutenant Lockwood was not only eminently active at all times, but most successful as an explorer.

It being desirable to establish the station as near as possible to the coal-mine on Watercourse Bay, Lockwood was dispatched with Messrs. Clay and Ryan, to report as to the practicability of carrying out this, the original intention. According to the map prepared by Nares, this bay lies seven miles distant on the strait, and is separated from Discovery Harbor by the mountain-ridge on the east, which terminates southward in Distant Cape. They attempted the passage across these hills, following a ravine leading in the proper direction, and had gone only a short distance when they saw seven musk-oxen quietly grazing. Making a *détour*, they thought to take them unawares, but soon saw them move away to some distance up a steep incline. Expending vainly a few shots at long range, they followed the animals up the hill, over a steep ledge of rocks, and into a valley on the other side. Here the men halted, concealed from view, and arranged plans for their capture. The animals were covered by precipitous rocks on one side. Clay, Ryan, and Lockwood approached them simultaneously on the other three sides, and thus had them surrounded and at their mercy. Some depressions and other irregularities of the ground enabled the hunters, by crouching low down, to approach the game unawares. Clay firing first, the whole herd rushed toward Lockwood's side, closing up as it came, and, seeing him, made a charge. Dropping on one knee, he threw his cartridges down and blazed away with great rapidity. Many shots telling, the animals halted before him only a few rods off, and at once attempted a flank movement; but now Clay and Ryan closing up, the herd was check-mated. In five minutes from the first shot every animal of the herd—five grown and two calves—lay dead before the hunters. The hunters were sorry they had killed the calves, but in the excitement it could hardly have been otherwise. They then returned to the ship to report their success, and to have the carcasses brought in. This addition to their larder was the occasion of great joy, not only as giving a present supply of fresh meat, but in its promise for the future; not only as a luxury, but as the only certain means of warding off the scurvy, so much and so justly dreaded by Arctic explorers.

After supper of that day, Lockwood, ever ready for adventure, again started for Watercourse Bay, accompanied by Clay, Ralston, and the mate of the Proteus. Following the small stream, which came into the harbor at this point, for three miles, by an easy and regular ascent between lofty mountains on either side with a slope of about forty-five degrees, and over ground and patches of snow thrown up like potato-hills, they reached its head, and there, fortunately, found another stream running in the other direction. Following this, they were brought to Watercourse Creek, which runs into Watercourse Bay. Being uncertain whether the coal-mine, said to be on this creek, was above or below this point, they followed the creek up-stream three miles, when, not finding it, they retraced their steps to the point where they entered the creek, and, finding it impossible to follow the bed, climbed the bank. Here they saw two more musk-oxen, which they slew by strategy as before, and, opening the carcasses with penknives, left them to be carried in. Coming near the mouth of the creek, Lockwood saw indications of coal, and soon after reached the exposed seam of one hundred yards' extent by twenty-five feet depth, distant about three fourths of a mile from the sea. This coal is said to equal the best of Welsh production. Near here, they saw another musk-ox, whose life they spared for the time, as they had so much meat in store. Lockwood found, and so reported, that, though Watercourse Bay had the merit of a near coalmine, and was nearer the grounds of future explorations, it was not possible to use it at once for the unloading ship without great risk and labor because of moving ice. Discovery Harbor, though full of ice from sixteen inches to ten feet thick, was perfectly landlocked and unobstructed. Ralston preceded the party home, killing one musk-ox *en route*. The Arctic summer was now at its height, lichen, moss, saxifrage, and various other little red, yellow, and blue flowers, bright red moss, and tufts of green grass at intervals, breaking the monotony of the somber rocks and earth. But the enjoyment of these beauties of nature could not then be indulged in, as all hands had to take part in unloading the ship, a labor which was soon accomplished.

The next business in order with the explorers was to build a house, and they selected a site facing the water, fifty feet from, and fifteen feet above it. While this work was progressing, the men lived in tents.

On the 19th of August, all hands were sent ashore, and the Proteus started on her return, but, passing too near Bellot Island for safety, was caught in the ice and delayed. Lockwood made an effort to follow in her wake with the steam-launch, but failed, because of the rapid closing in of the great masses of broken ice and the wedging of small ice-masses into the screw and well. The launch battled manfully with her foe, the ice. Frequently he ran her under a full head of steam against a massive floe, which would be shivered for a few inches, the recoil causing the launch to roll and pitch like a little giant. In young ice she would sometimes split a sheet for ten or fifteen yards at one impact.

Finding nothing to do while the house-building was progressing, Lieutenants Lockwood and Kislingbury occupied themselves with tramping after ptarmigans and other game over the mountains whose steep sides formed the eastern entrance of the harbor, and the northern boundary. Viewed from the house, their sides seemed gradual and their summits not over twenty minutes' walk. In fact, however, the sides were successions of slopes separated by precipices, growing greater with the ascent. What below seemed the top was only one of many that must be passed before the real summit or divide could be attained. They reached the summit marked by the English cairn, and from there viewed the scene below. How small the ship appeared! and yet it seemed as though they could throw a stone upon her. They reached home with wolfish appetites, but with no game. The ptarmigans, which they chiefly sought, are provided, at this season, with a coat so nearly resembling the shade of the rocks and grounds as to be almost indistinguishable. By a happy provision of nature, in winter the feathers of this bird become white with only a little black about the tail.

The lieutenants then extended their excursions over the mountains on the north side of the harbor, availing themselves of a ravine, called the "Black Cañon," which leads to a pretty waterfall. Climbing out of this cañon with difficulty over loose slate and other *débris*, they found themselves on the high backgrounds of the North Mountains. Thence moving west over loose rock and snow, and through pools of water, they finally came in sight of Musk-ox Bay, the western extremity of Discovery Harbor. They then retraced their steps, reaching home without having seen a living object bigger than an humble-bee.

On the 23d, the house was occupied, though not finished. Looking after their supplies, they found that the foxes had made free with the carcasses of the musk-oxen left near Watercourse Bay. Lockwood now proceeded to superintend the laying out of the observatory, digging for foundation pier of transit, etc. He found the ground frozen after reaching thirty inches, which may be taken as the depth where perpetual frost begins. The ship being still detained, but with a prospect of soon getting off, Lockwood wrote more letters home in which he expressed an opinion about the Proteus. Her chances of departing south were doubtful. Detention there for the winter would be embarrassing all around, as neither the ship nor her crew were prepared to stay, nor the explorers able to help them through the winter.

Just before her final departure, some difficulty arose between Lieutenants Greely and Kislingbury, which ended in the latter making a request to be relieved from duty with the expedition, which request was granted. One of the annoyances complained of was the rule that officers should rise in the morning with the men, and although Lockwood advised Kislingbury not to make any further trouble, he decided to pack up, board the Proteus, and return home. In this, however, he was not successful, as the steamer got away before he could reach her, and the order for his relief was somewhat modified. After explaining his action in this matter, Lieutenant Greely remarked that, if anything should happen to him, he desired that Lieutenant Lockwood should have command of the expedition. Lockwood expressed himself as very sorry for what his fellow-officer had done, and could not understand his course of action.

As soon as the building was entirely finished, on the 27th of August, the explorers found themselves very comfortable. The dull, cheerless weather and monotonous life were beginning to depress the spirits of Lockwood, but he felt that, when settled down to regular habits, he would not find the life in the north more irksome than that he had experienced on the Western plains of the United States. It may be mentioned that the final opening of the house, or government station, was commemorated by the issuing of an order from Lieutenant Greely, that the exploring expedition along the northern coast of Greenland, which had been marked out for Lieutenant Kislingbury as senior officer, was to be placed in command of Lieutenant Lockwood. He now felt that the opportunity for doing something creditable, for his own as well as his country's reputation, was at hand, and his feelings of depression gave way to those of enthusiasm.

On Sunday, the 28th of August, all work was suspended, and some appropriate notice was taken of the day. Lieutenant Greely read a chapter in the Bible, having previously stated that any one would be excused from attending the service who had conscientious scruples. The supply of drinking-water having come up as an important question, demanded attention. The water was obtained from the ice-hummocks in the harbor. Pieces of suitable size were brought to the house on sledges and then melted in a large metallic box near the stove, through which and the stove ran a steam-pipe. Thus a liberal supply was kept up.

Wishing to establish a depot on the channel for future explorations, Lockwood left with Sergeants Brainard and Cross to explore St. Patrick's Bay, lying northeast of the station and on the straits. The ground being covered with snow, the Government boots were soon soaked though, and the feet of the party became wet and cold. Following a ravine, they soon reached a lake near the summit of the hills in the rear, where they saw a musk-ox grazing on the bank. The animal fled on seeing them, but stopped farther on. Approaching him under cover, Lockwood got a standing shot and brought him down. Skinning him and dividing the carcass into quarters, they left the meat for others to carry in and went on their tramp, which took them midway between the "hog-back," an elevated plateau on the north, and the rugged broken chain of mountains which lie between Discovery Harbor and Robeson Channel. About noon they reached St. Patrick's Bay, but at a point so different from that laid down in their maps, that Lockwood felt some doubt as to its identity, to settle which, they proceeded to explore a wide river-bed, followed by a deep cañon, which led into the bay near its head. With this view, and to see the country to better advantage, they kept north along the steep rocky sides of the "hog-back," over rocks, great and small, compact and loose, and generally covered with snow. After two hours of laborious travel, they found themselves high above the riverbed and in a position giving them a good view north and east. The main stream seemed to come from the north, with a branch from the west, the whole through lands of the most rugged description. Beyond the river to the east, the hills were more sloping, yet rising to an immense altitude between the river and the channel beyond. It seemed not difficult to descend into the bed of the river, walk up its frozen course, and, taking advantage of some break in the cliffs a few miles up, gain by a gradual ascent the high hills beyond, thus obtaining a view of Robeson Channel. The descent, over rocks, stones, and snow, involving great fatigue, took two hours. This brought them to a level terrace extending from cliffs to cliffs, through the center of which ran a deep cut or channel containing the insignificant stream, the sole occupant of this immense cañon. They gained the frozen stream with difficulty, cut through the ice and got a drink, and then regained the level terrace above, and began their steep climb up the mountain beyond, through a friendly ravine. One hour's work brought them to an elevation which, at a distance, had seemed to be the main summit, only to find that farther on there were still higher points. Finally, at 6 P.M., they reached an elevation where the slope seemed to be eastward, and from which a magnificent view was obtained of the channel from Cape Lieber to Repulse Harbor, while directly east of them lay Newman's Bay and Polaris Promontory. After erecting a cairn, they started back, cold and hungry, satisfied that they had seen the true

St. Patrick's Bay.

Regaining the river-valley, they had a most fatiguing climb to attain the pass through which they had come, and where they had killed the musk-ox. Just east of the lake, they encountered Dr. Pavy and Rice, and soon after Ralston and Lynn, going to Lincoln Bay *via* St. Patrick's Bay. Our party reached home at midnight, with frost-bitten feet and empty stomachs, Lockwood finding his stockings full of ice and one toe badly frost-bitten.

He was laid up for a week with frosted feet, and had apprehension of losing some of his toes. Although suffering greatly, he was made especially unhappy by the thought of being disabled so early in the campaign. Discussing the subject of scurvy with Lieutenant Greely, they agreed in regarding the explorers much better provided against it, than was the British expedition, in that their dietary list was more complete. The English issued fresh beef but once a week; the Greely Expedition three times or oftener. This expedition had also the great advantage of a dry, warm, well-ventilated house.

Lockwood's report as to St. Patrick's Bay settling that as the place for their first depot, Sergeant Brainard with others proceeded to establish the same there by means of the whale-boat, moving around Cape Distant. Lockwood was much annoyed that his disability prevented his being one of those to carry out this important feature toward their future explorations. He took advantage of his non-active condition to figure out a design for an "ice-sledge," which he thought would be an improvement on the Hudson Bay sledge they had in use. Lieutenant Greely approving the plan, he proceeded at once to build one by way of experiment. The duty assigned to Brainard was duly accomplished, and Depot A was established at St. Patrick's Bay.

Having received a gentle reminder from Lieutenant Greely for oversleeping himself, Lockwood said he could not complain, the offense not being his first of the kind. The singular clearness of the atmosphere had enabled him to make satisfactory sketches of Cape Lieber and other prominent objects in the distance, and also of the house.

Among the events which made the early days of September somewhat lively were the following: Gardiner reported a waif, in the shape of a boat twelve feet long and an eight-men sledge, on the shore near Cape Murchison. Lieutenant Greely with others, and Lieutenant Kislingbury as a guest, went upon a two-days' trip to the Bellows in search of game and to view the land. They were successful in securing ten musk-oxen, a dozen or more eider-ducks, and some other game. Sergeant Lynn, returning from Cape Beechy, reported a wagon and lamp on the shore, left by the English.

Dr. Pavy returned from Lincoln Bay, but Rice, taken on the return with severe inflammatory rheumatism, was left four miles north of St. Patrick's Bay. A party was at once sent for his relief, which brought him in, in a bad way. Great difficulty was found in lifting him up the steep cliffs between the station and St. Patrick's Bay.

Lockwood, having recovered from his injuries, went upon an expedition to the Bellows with Gardiner and the Esquimaux Frederick, using an eight-dog sledge and carrying rations for four days, consisting of roasted musk-ox, baked beans, butter and sauce, hard bread, and chocolate. They visited Bleak Cape, the entrance of the Bellows. The Bellows they found to be a long, level valley, walled in by lofty hills and cliffs, in some places two or three thousand feet high. It bears the impress of having been, at some far-distant period, the channel of a glacier, its level surface being thickly strewn with stones, while there are masses attached like shelves to the sides of the cliffs and slopes. For twenty miles, the valley preserves a width of nearly three miles; beyond this, it narrows and changes direction toward the west. A small creek runs through its entire length, which generally they followed. The route was difficult, owing to the large number of stones imperfectly covered with snow, and hence all riding ceased after they entered the valley; for the dogs could scarcely pull the sledge and its load, and often required aid. Here they met a piece of drift-wood, indicating that the tide once flowed up the valley, for no tree or wood had ever been seen away from tide-water. One of the dogs becoming sick was turned adrift, trusting to her following the party or returning home. Reaching "Devil's Head," they went into camp by turning up the sledge and hanging rubber blankets around to shield them from the cold wind, and then ate a supper of warmed-up beans and hot chocolate, and tumbled into the sleeping-bags, all of which they found most enjoyable.

After a breakfast of chocolate, hard bread, and some frozen cheese, they were delighted to see the sick dog rejoin them. The sledge-runners were rapidly wearing out, and they concluded to walk to the end of the valley, leaving the Esquimaux with the sledge and team while they pushed on as best they could.

Lockwood and Gardiner reached the head of the valley at four, and, proceeding up the incline to the west where it narrowed to a ravine, went on till they came to a narrow gorge—its terminus. Having seen all there was to see, and Gardiner complaining of a game leg, they retraced their steps, reached the sledge at 10 P. M., and at once, supperless, turned into their sleeping-bags. Near the terminus of the valley they met two musk-oxen, but, having only their knives with them, did not venture on an assault, though the animals stood still and quietly gazed at the intruders.

Returning, they followed the creek, finding some advantage from the ice which had formed during the night. Lockwood saw and took back with him a few pieces of wood-coal, or very soft coal, evidently of recent formation, which had doubtless washed down, but whence he knew not. Reaching Bleak Cape, they decided to make a *détour* west to a cañon near the "Knife-edge," where the musk-oxen were killed by Lieutenant Greely and party a few days before; but no musk-ox, dead or alive, was to be seen. Gardiner being still lame, Lockwood abandoned some other objects he had in view in making this trip, and, striking out directly across the bay and riding on the sledge, they reached the station without incident.

Dr. Pavy made an unsuccessful attempt to reach an estuary at the head of Lady Franklin Bay, from which Lieutenant Greely thought a passage might be forced westward to a supposed fiord or sea connected with the waters leading through Behring Strait into the Pacific Ocean. Unfortunately, finding Lady Franklin Bay open beyond Stony Point, the doctor returned without settling this interesting question, which, as will be seen, Lieutenant Lockwood afterward solved.

Sixteen, or more, large Arctic wolves were seen in one day on the ice, a few hundred yards from the house. These were the first seen by them; the English saw none here, nor do Kane, Hayes, or Hall mention them. These wolves are large, strong, fierce-looking beasts, perfectly white in color, and anything but desirable customers to meet.

Lieutenant Greely, and Sergeants Brainard, Bender, and Connell, left on an exploration above and beyond "North Valley," a deep cañon cutting through the "hog's back" north of the station. They left without sledges, carrying six days' rations, sleeping-bags, etc. Following the "North Valley" upward, and leaving it near its head, they soon found themselves in a water-course running toward St. Patrick's Bay. Turning westward, and going some distance, they came in sight of what they regarded as the United States Range; but, a heavy snow-storm coming on, they cut short the trip after traveling twenty-five miles, and returned. It was deemed unfortunate that the untoward weather prevented their getting a good view from that range. The absence of glaciers and large water-courses, the low altitude of the range, and many other features in that region, all seemed to indicate a large sea not far to the westward.

The building of Lockwood's sledge turned out a failure, for the want of proper appliances.

On the 17th of September, the party celebrated Whistler's birthday by a dinner of his own selection—oyster soup, roast musk-ox, potatoes, corn, pear-butter, cake, etc., and a glass of grog in the evening. Two-story bunks were built for the men, giving more room. The Signal-Service men—the observers —had a little corner partitioned off, where they were to sleep and work. Another corner was fitted as a wash-room, where warm water might be had, and where there was a bath-tub, which all were expected to use every week. Other arrangements had been provided productive of comfort and health. Lockwood's time was now chiefly occupied in drawing maps, making finished drawings from sketches, reading, and sledge-work.

Dr. Pavy, with a party, went to take provisions to the depots, but failed to get round Cape Murchison. Not satisfying Lieutenant Greely, the latter himself undertook the task, and, after considerable difficulty, in which the sledge broke down, succeeded. On the 21st the sun presented a remarkable appearance, having rainbows to the right and left, which nearly joined above; also radiating vertical and horizontal beams of light.

Lieutenant Kislingbury, after many futile efforts with arsenic, succeeded in poisoning many wolves with strychnine. Five of them bit the dust at one time, and by this means the party was able to get rid of these dangerous neighbors. This animal, as stated, is perfectly white, and is not unlike the Esquimaux dog, but larger and more formidable.

On the 24th of September, Lockwood started on a trip to Cape Beechy with Ellis, Fredericks, Ralston, Biederbick, and one large sledge, to provision Depot "A," distant twenty miles. They started with two hundred and fifty pounds on the sledge, intending to take on other food left near Cape Distant. Their passage around this cape was accomplished only after cutting away masses of ice. Beyond this, and with their load increased to three hundred and fifty pounds, they struck masses of rocks over which the sledge and load had to be lifted. There they left the photograph apparatus for Rice, and took lunch. Afterward they passed Watercourse Bay, and the English wagon lying on the shore, and halted for the night at 6 P. M. at Cape Murchison, without any remonstrance on the part of the tired-out men, notwithstanding some of them, about noon, had proposed going on to Cape Beechy without a stop. Indeed, Lockwood observed anxious faces among them when he hesitated about stopping. Floe-bergs of every form and shape—square, oblong, round, and pyramidal—from ten to forty feet high, were scattered along the shore. Without the barrier afforded by these, the floating floe, moving with the noise of railroad-trains, would cut away the foot-ice and render travel impossible. Using the tent at Depot "A," and the bedding, etc., there, they got supper over the spirit-lamp and crawled into their sleeping-bags. The cold, cramped position, and dropping of congealed moisture from the tent, robbed them of sleep; hence they rose at 5.20, little refreshed. Beautiful "sun-dogs" were noticed with the rising of the sun across the strait. Toward noon similar appearances, peculiar to the Arctic sun, were still more remarkable—rainbows on either side, and joined above the sun, while vertical and horizontal beams of white light pierced the sun. They passed St. Patrick's

Bay, and, after a hard and cold day's work, reached Depot "B," south of Mount Bufort and a little farther south of Cape Beechy, at 3 P.M., the 25th. On the following day, dragging an empty sledge, they returned to the *cache* at St. Patrick's Bay, loaded up with three hundred and fifty pounds, and returned to Depot "B," tired, cold, and wet with perspiration, this last being, perhaps, the greatest obstacle to Arctic travel. The great exertion soon induces perspiration, which being checked when labor ceases, you are at once sensible of cold water and ice at the same time. It was rare to have anything entirely dry after the first day of work. The sole resource was to use the heat of the body in the sleeping-bags at night. Mittens and socks were the most important to keep dry, and the most difficult. Their lamps being imperfect, they found a difficulty in preparing their chocolate. The alcohol took fire below and filled the tent with fumes quite as unpleasant as the cold. Having left their tin plates behind, they had to eat from one dish. Eating was simply cramming, that their benumbed fingers might give up the cold spoons and return to the warm pockets. Yet with all these discomforts they ate heartily, and with appetites unknown elsewhere than in the Arctic regions; and, notwithstanding dirt, cold, and alcoholic fumes, they had their jokes and songs while lying in their sleeping-bags, trying to keep warm and get to sleep. But their ills did not end there, for whenever the canvas was shaken, frost-like snow—condensed vapor —fell upon them, which melted with the lighting of the lamp in the morning. Truly, this was a rough road to glory and fame!

Two of the men, in consequence of the crowded tent, had to sleep outside with the thermometer at -15°, and left without breakfast, to return to the station. The party soon followed them, and, after stopping at St. Patrick's Bay to take on a log of driftwood observed there, which gave them an additional pull of five miles, reached the station long after dark. Having taken something to eat and drink, they got into their warm and dry beds, which never felt more comfortable.

The next man to command a party was Dr. Pavy, who had in view a long-projected trip to Cape Joseph Henry, with the object of carrying out the wishes of the Navy Department, that a search should be made there for the Jeannette, and a signal placed indicating that help was near at hand; another object was to establish a depot for spring operations. His force consisted of the Esquimaux Jans, Whistler, and two dog-teams. His "constant weight" was two hundred pounds, and he took rations for twenty days. He counted upon other rations at Lincoln Bay left by the English, and those nearer home left by Greely's men at Depot "B," near Cape Beechy. He hoped with these to establish a depot near the place where the Alert had her winter quarters, and thus be ready in the spring to surpass Markham. Lockwood was inclined to think the doctor a little too anxious to retain personal comfort while exploring, to accomplish much. He had been convinced that sledge-journeys of any considerable extent in those high latitudes could be made only by the sacrifice of every personal comfort.

On the 2d of October, there was a remarkable and beautiful sunset. The lower part of the picture was formed by the clear white ice of the harbor westward. Then came the distant mountains, whose snow-capped summits reached into a sky of beautiful green; above, a line of gold, and then blue and gold alternating, and finally the deep-blue vault studded with masses of red—on the whole a most gorgeous spectacle.

Finding this inactive life monotonous, Lockwood started on an exploration of the streams which enter St. Patrick's Bay from the north. Lynn, Bender, Saler, Henry, and himself constituted the party, and they proposed going by way of the gap through the mountains rather than around Distant Cape. They had not gone far before they regretted having taken this short cut, for they found the way exceedingly laborious from want of snow—so much so, that they were six hours in reaching the steep, rocky bluffs which overlook St. Patrick's Bay and the valley at the north of it, and they were two more before reaching the level of the bay. Indeed, this was only attained by carrying their load piece by piece down the cliffs and letting the sledge down by ropes. Here they put up their tent and went into camp. Unfortunately, they had neglected to bring candles, and hence had to eat their meal in darkness. Lockwood and Saler occupied one sleeping-bag, while the others were in another. They passed the night cold and sleepless. There being a birthday dinner at the station, they had intended to walk back to it, a distance of seven miles, but, on account of the condition of the way, abandoned the idea.

Getting off at an early hour after a cold breakfast, and reaching the bed of the water-course, they made their way over its stony bed, so lightly covered with snow as to rapidly grind away the sledge-runners, up the cañon, as grand as the stream was insignificant. Finding their progress so much impeded, they left the sledge behind and made their way without it. The cold being intense, to keep up circulation they walked rapidly, but suffered greatly in their feet and hands. Having volunteered for this expedition, they were ashamed to give it up, though often disposed to do so. Thus, for three tiresome hours, they kept on their way, either following the bed of the stream, or along the mesa-like formations, which projected like shelves from the mountain-sides. Finally, the valley and mesas alike disappearing, the stream entered a narrow gorge. Gaining an eminence, the further course of the stream was indicated to them, and its probable terminus in table-lands of great elevation seen in the distance. Returning by the bed of the stream until the valley had attained a width of half a mile, they entered from the west a very picturesque cañon thirty feet wide with walls one hundred feet high. Its walls were worn smooth, as though by the action of ice, and there were small, basin-shaped holes apparently made by bowlders caught by glaciers. They also met with blocks of quartz much larger than could possibly be moved by the force of any body of water now passing through the cañon. Notwithstanding their exhausted condition, and the worn state of their foot-gear from the numerous stones and rough ice they had passed over, they concluded not to spend the night where they had left the sledge, but to go on to Depot "A," near Cape Murchison. Adding their outfit to that of the depot, they had a night of less discomfort than usual. On passing Cape Distant, they noticed a broad channel of open water in the strait, preventing any passage at that time.

On reaching the station, they found that the temperature had been -16°, and it was probably 4° lower where they had been. Lieutenant Greely was putting in order a variety of reading-matter for the men. Sergeant Brainard was absent at the Bellows, with Rice and Bender, after musk-ox meat. They returned later, badly frosted, but brought the meat to within easy sledging distance.

The 7th of October, being Mrs. Greely's birthday, was celebrated with a dinner made regal by the following-named dishes: gumbo-soup, biscuits, old sherry, Columbia River salmon with sauce sauterne, boiled ham, asparagus, sago, corn, lima-beans, cold bread, chocolate cake, strawberry and pineapple ice-cream, dates, figs, grapes, prunes, candied fruits, coffee, and Benedictine.

In Payer's "History of the Austrian Expedition to Franz-Josef Land," Lockwood found much of interest in connection with the requirements for a sledge-journey—details of clothing and other matters best suited to fit one to stand the cold. The book he considered of great value to any novice in Arctic sledging. He supposed that they themselves were much better off than any expedition that had wintered within the Arctic Circle. The most serious difficulties—dampness, want of ventilation, and darkness—were reduced with them to a minimum, while of fresh meat, anti-scorbutics, and fuel they had an abundance; and if their assortment of clothing—particularly foot-gear —had been better, they would have had nothing to desire.

Besides the large stock of coal left by the Proteus, they had the coal-mine within ten miles. The men seemed comfortable and contented. They had a bathroom and bath-tub, with hot and cold water ready at hand, and books and periodicals in abundance. Their heating arrangements were generally perfect and quite effectual. The light from the sun amounted to little, and artificial light within-doors was required all day; but with a full moon, bright sky, and everything covered with snow, they had a flood of light almost an equivalent. They had musk-ox meat almost every day, and a large store on hand. They also had a large supply of the best pork, lime-juice, cider, sour-krout, pickles, onions and cucumbers mixed, and other anti-scorbutics. The men were comfortable, seemed happy and cheerful, and found many sources of amusement—among others, from an anti-swearing society. Delinquents were fined five cents each, the proceeds to pay for a grand dinner on returning to the United States. Several members incurred such enormous fines as to become bankrupt, and were expelled. These outcasts lay around and beguiled the unwary, thus affording amusement to all except the victim. Rice and Israel had a way of carrying on ridiculous discussions. One evening they had an apparently angry dialogue, in which Rice personated a tipsy lodger complaining of the fare and demanding his bill, and Israel, an insulted landlord. Both seemed entirely in earnest, and kept their countenances amid roars of laughter and gibes from the men.

IX.
PRELIMINARY SLEDGE EXPEDITIONS AND LIFE AT THE STATION.

Among the amusements which helped to kill time at the station of Discovery Harbor, officially called Fort Conger, was that of celebrating certain birthdays, and this chapter begins with what was done when Lieutenant Lockwood attained his twenty-ninth year. He confessed that he did not wish a "happy return of the day" in the Arctic regions, and yet he would be contented if they should all be as pleasant as the one just experienced, in spite of the cold winds, ice, snow, darkness, and anticipations of exposure and fatigue when his spring travels should begin. He spent most of the day in sewing canvas leggings to his moccasins and altering his trousers, while Lieutenant Greely entertained him with recollections of his army experience during the rebellion, fighting his battles over again. His birthday dinner was something quite formidable, consisting of:

Pea soup à la Proteus,

Scalloped oysters à la Eastern Shore,

Deviled crabs à la Chesapeake,

Musk-ox à la Franklin Bay,

Potatoes à l'Irlandaise,

Macaroni à l'Italienne,

Rice and curry à la Pacific Mail,

Blanc-mange, fruits, nuts, cake, ice-cream, and black coffee.

Lieutenant Greely kindly added, from private stores, some very good California port wine. Lockwood's reflections, however, carried him to his distant home, and he longed to know that all there were well—that his dear parents and sisters were happy as when he was with them! Perhaps, even at that hour, their thoughts and words were of him. On this day, as frequently on his sledging journeys, he pictured to himself the family circle in the far-off home. The cold, fatigue, and monotony attending him and his companions were rendered endurable by thus breaking away from the present.

On the morning of the 10th of October, Lockwood started on a trip with Jewell across Lady Franklin Bay for Cape Baird. Had no difficulty for a mile or two beyond Dutch Island, but mist and fog then obscuring their way and blotting out the landscape, they kept on their course by compass. Soon they encountered heavy snow-drifts and many floe-bergs and fields of rubble-ice, all unfavorable for sledging. Fortunately, they had only themselves to transport. Though the weather was cold, they soon found themselves oppressively warm from the labor attending the journey. Profiting by past experience, Lockwood had this time come out warmly dressed—viz., with two flannel shirts, a woolen jersey, an under-shirt of light buckskin, heavy woolen drawers, a seal-skin over-all, and two pairs of socks under light buckskin moccasins. He then became convinced, that it was quite as great a mistake to wear too much as too little clothing. Even when they could ride on the sledge, which was not often, there were numerous bad places where they had to run with the dogs and lift the sledge over obstacles. Trying to avoid the moving ice, they struck too far westward, so that when they approached land they found themselves some two miles within the cape for which they had started. Stopping only to take a bite of crackers and meat, they started to retrace their steps, but not before daylight had left them, and they had only the moon to show them the way. After some time they thought to reduce the distance by taking what they supposed was a short cut, but soon found themselves scrambling over hummocky ice of the most formidable character. They regained their track, but not till overcome by thirst and fatigue. Resting at short intervals, they finally came in sight of Dutch Island, and soon afterward were gladdened by the sound of distant shouts. Dr. Pavy and Sergeants Brainard and Connell had come out to meet them, and not empty-handed, for they bore a bag of hot coffee, and never did coffee taste more delicious. Though the mercury was nearly nine degrees below zero, when they reached the house everything they had on was as wet as if they had fallen overboard.

The result of that reconnaissance was that they decided to establish a "depot" near Cape Baird, which labor was duly carried out by Lockwood, Ellis, Saler, and Bender. The weather being open, they started directly for Cape Baird, but, finding that route impracticable, inclined westward and got into their old track. After much delay and great labor, they reached a point on the farther side, where they found it necessary to encamp for the night. The tent was pitched, chocolate boiled, and beans thawed out, after which they crawled into their sleeping-bags, trying to forget, if possible, that the thermometer stood at -24° without. Resuming their journey, but now with the discomfort of wind added to intense cold, they made their way ashore, established the depot of provisions, and with lightened sledges and hearts retraced their steps. Noses were frozen during the day, and only restored by friction, which made them raw and uncomfortable. Very soon after starting back, twilight disappeared, and they had only the moon to light them on their way. Passing the resting-place of the previous night, they concluded to make the journey to the house without stopping. They stumbled on in the dark, a used-up party, Lockwood having a sprained tendon Achilles, and also a lame back. The air becoming calm, they were enabled to stop sometimes and rest, which they could not have safely done in their perspiring condition had the wind been blowing. When near Dutch Island, Dr. Pavy and Lieutenant Kislingbury met them with hot coffee, which so much refreshed them that the rest of the journey seemed easy, although it was probable that Lockwood's raw red nose, frosted toes, lame back, and tender heel, would be reminders of this trip for a long time.

On the 16th of October the sun disappeared, to rise no more until February. With the mercury ranging from -28° to -40°, Lockwood amused himself by scraping off the accumulated condensation of moisture from the room on the window-panes near his corner, the ice being one inch thick.

About this time Lockwood took up a course of Arctic literature, with which they were liberally supplied. This was chiefly in view of his sledge-journey in the coming spring. Feeling the need of exercise, he left the station on the 23d for Depot "B," Cape Beechy, with Brainard, Connell, and the Esquimaux Frederick, and a sledge with eight dogs. At Depot "A" they took on a small stove and a bag of coal from the mines, and thereby the tent at Depot "B" became more comfortable than anything they had experienced away from the station; notwithstanding, they had a comfortless night, as the crowded condition of the tent compelled some of them to lie so near the stove as to endanger their safety. Lockwood woke up to find a large hole burned in his blanket. Afterward, the fire going out, they suffered more than when they had had no fire at all. They erected a snow-house for a depot here, forming the sides of tough blocks of compact snow, and covering it with the boat-sail supported by oars, and, by imitating the natives in some particulars, had a house impervious to cold.

While there, Lockwood, with Brainard, ascended Mount Bufort, near at hand, and had an uninterrupted view of the straits as far down as Cape Lieber, and of the opposite coast, between which and them hung water-clouds, indicating open water. This fact was also indicated by the roar, like a moving railroad-train, made by the crushing of the ice in the current. Having passed another night in their warm snow-house, they made their way next day to the station in less than five hours, and found all hands there engaged in erecting an ice wall around the house as high as the eaves, and filling in with snow. This proved most effectual in keeping the house warm.

Lieutenant Greely had an uncomfortable experience while assisting to make a tide-gauge. He fell in and got a ducking—not his first experience in that direction. Wolves were daily seen near the house, and were so bold and fearless that the men deemed it prudent never to leave the building without fire-arms; for, as the animals were of the same color as the snow, they could not be easily distinguished.

On the 29th, a singular aurora made its appearance, consisting of a ribbon of white light a degree wide, stretching through the zenith from north to south; then another arch, 10° westward, whose base touched the first; and still another, also passing through the zenith, and cutting the others at right angles.

On the 30th, Lockwood commenced preparations for a preliminary journey to Hall's winter quarters, whenever the straits could be crossed and the weather and light were suitable. Among other things, the saddler, Fredericks, made a tent to hold eight men, using to that end two common "A" tents.

About this time, while cogitating on his room and room-mates, Lockwood said: "Surely this is a happy quartet occupying this room! We often sit silent during the whole day, and even a meal fails to elicit anything more than a chance remark or two. A charming prospect for four months of darkness, such gloom within, and penned up as we are in one room! I have doubts of getting over the straits, but I must be off as soon as possible, for I find a relief in getting away."

Lieutenant Greely had felt himself compelled to show his dissatisfaction with Dr. Pavy's explorations, or rather attempted explorations. He and the doctor had also adverse views as to how explorations should be made. The doctor wanted to take along many creature comforts, while Greely thought, with Lockwood, that nothing could be accomplished without sacrificing all beyond bare necessities.

Having everything complete, Lockwood started on the 1st of November to try the passage of the straits, with Brainard, Lynn, Saler, Biederbick, Ellis, Fredericks, and Connell, dragging an eight-man sledge, weighing, with load, one thousand pounds. They left sledge and load beyond Cape Distant, and returned to lodge at the house, where all hands fortified themselves with a first-class dinner, preparatory to the labors of the next day.

They got off early, but, owing to the limited light and other difficulties, found themselves some distance from the snow-house near Cape Beechy when darkness overtook them. Having all in readiness on the 4th, they again got off, leaving Ellis at the snow-house with an injured foot. This was unfortunate, as he was a strong, willing fellow, with lots of pluck. The prospects of crossing the straits at this time were not encouraging, both from the short duration of light and from the open waters. Still, they determined to make the effort. This they first did with the whale-boat, which they had picked up on their route.

They mounted it on the sledge, but soon found they could not drag so heavy a body, and returned to the snow-house. Rice, whom they found there, was then sent with a dog-sledge to bring up a small boat from Cape Murchison. Dr. Pavy, Lieutenant Kislingbury, and Jans coming along *en route* for another attempt northward, were surprised to see how comfortable they were in the snow-house.

After extensive repairs to the small boat, they again got off at noon, seven men and Lockwood himself dragging the sledge, on which were the boat and one hundred and fourteen pounds of rations. On reaching open water, three only were to proceed in the boat, the others to fall back on the snow-house. They got along pretty well until they came to the hummocks, through which, with extreme labor, and frequently using an axe, they made their way, till they heard, in the distance toward Polaris Promontory, the roar of the grinding ice, indicating open water. Moving on ahead of the party over very rough ice, and crossing some wet, slushy ice fifteen or twenty yards wide, Lockwood found himself on a level floe. He had gone only a short distance over this toward a dark streak beyond, which he took for open water, when he found that the floe upon which he stood was in motion. Retreating over the bed of slushy ice, he found this to be really only a thick mass of broken pieces intermediate between the moving floe and the firm ice. He could readily thrust his ice-hook down through it to the water beneath, and did so. Reaching the sledge-party, and viewing the difficulties of the situation, he decided, all agreeing, on the impracticability of crossing at this season. They accordingly displayed signal-torches from the top of an iceberg, as agreed upon, that Lieutenant Greely might know that they had found the crossing dangerous and had abandoned the effort. They returned in darkness, and with considerable difficulty, guided somewhat by a signal-torch displayed by Ellis at the snow-house. They remained all day at the snow-house, which the men found so comfortable that they preferred it to the restraints of the station. At noon Lockwood and Brainard went upon a tramp, and found the condition of the open water to be such as to demonstrate the wisdom of their return the evening before. The men made some additions to the snow-house, which were regarded as a great success. The return to the station on the 7th was attended with more difficulty and labor than had been expected, arising from a strong south wind having worn away the foot-ice, and the small amount of light; hence, they soon had wet feet, which in that region always means frost-bitten feet. So much were some of the men used up by this journey of twenty miles, which had before been made in one day, that they had to be conveyed on the sledge, and did not reach the station till the third day. At Dutch Island they met Whistler, who, missing Biederbick at the ropes and seeing a human form on the sledge, came to the conclusion that Biederbick was dead, and repeatedly exclaimed, "Poor

Biederbick! poor Biederbick!"

During a period of dullness at the station, Rice and Henry projected a newspaper, to be called the "Arctic Moon," and Lockwood, to whom, also, the idea had occurred, agreed to join them as one of the editors. They wanted something to dispel the monotony which was depressing all hands, as all were tired of reading, of cards and other games, while two of Lockwood's room-mates were gloomy and taciturn. To counteract this, he resumed his reading, especially history and travels—anything but novels. Kane's work interested him especially, and he considered him a remarkable man, courageous, energetic, and determined. Their own manner of life just then reminded Lockwood of a rainy day in the country intensified. "Yet," says he, "why not be contented? Books and leisure afford an opportunity for reading and studying which we may never have again. We have a warm, comfortable house, plenty of food, and other things which many are without. Life in this world is just what one chooses to make it. Man can make of it a heaven or a hell." He felt anxious as to the effect of one hundred and thirty sunless days upon himself and men, as this might tell on their sledging in the coming spring. Nares's people broke down under it, and, when sledging, were decimated by the scurvy. They themselves were fortunate so far in not having had a single man sick enough to keep his bed.

True to his intellectual instincts, Lockwood formed a class in geography and grammar, consisting of Ellison, Bender, Connell, and Whistler, while Lieutenant Greely taught them arithmetic. On the 22d of November appeared, with a flourish of trumpets, the first number of the "Arctic Moon." Of course the editors thought it a great success. It had for the frontispiece a sketch of the house, drawn by Lockwood, while Rice made fair copies of the paper by the hectograph process—enough for all, and many to spare.

These trifles served to shorten, apparently, the many hours of gloom and darkness, which were wearing away the spirits of all. The men were now far less hilarious than they had been, and, with the game of chess to assist, silence reigned supreme.

Thanksgiving-day, with its games, sports, and dinner, gave them a pleasant variety. First, came the snow-shoe race of one hundred yards, Brainard, victor. Next, the foot-race, with many contestants, but Ellis coming out ahead. Then the dog-team race to Dutch Island and return, under the Esquimaux Jans and Frederick, the latter, victor. And, finally, a shooting-match, necessarily at short range, and with torches, Henry, victor. These and other out-door exercises were followed by the grand feature of the day, the Thanksgiving dinner, and not a poor one either, even for a lower latitude than eighty-two degrees. In the evening Lieutenant Greely gave out prizes to the victors and second best, Rice acting as master of ceremonies, rigged out in swallow-tail coat, black pantaloons, white vest, and "boiled" shirt. The mercury froze on that day, and Lieutenant Greely brought in a teacupful, which looked like lead as it comes from the mold. The moon also made its appearance, and all fully appreciated the blessing of this luminary.

"What a change," exclaimed Lockwood, "when she comes forth in all her beauty and loveliness, flooding the landscape with her refulgent beams and cheering the drooping spirits of benighted mortals! Even the poor dogs feel her influence!" On the 1st of December, they had an almost total eclipse of the moon, more remarkable there than an eclipse of the sun elsewhere. During the phenomenon, the exposed part of the disk was of a dull-red color. Lockwood took the altitude of the moon while crossing the meridian, using a saucer of molasses as an artificial horizon. She flooded the whole region with a light, electric in appearance, and causing deep shadows. In the evening they were treated to a display of mock moons, with a circular band of bright light connecting them, and several bands or ribbons of light at various angles, but all passing through the moon.

The Esquimaux, Jans and Frederick, having of late been much depressed, efforts were made by kindly attentions on the part of Lieutenant Greely and others to dispel their gloom and assure them of the friendly feeling entertained toward them by all. These good offices, however, all failed. Dr. Pavy said this state of mind was not infrequent among the natives of lower Greenland, and often resulted in the wandering off of the subjects of it, and, if not followed, by their perishing in the cold. One morning Jans was missing, and at once his tracks were followed by Dr. Pavy, Brainard, Rice, and Whistler, with the dog-sledge. Late in the afternoon they returned with poor Jans, who was found nine miles away, following at a rapid pace the ice-foot around Cape Murchison. He returned unwillingly, and gave no reason for his strange conduct. Rice and Whistler were both rendered *hors de combat* by the journey, the former by a fall from an ice-hummock, the latter by congestion of the brain owing to having shaved before going out. Both Dr. Kane and Dr. Rink (in his book on Greenland) refer to hallucinations similar to that of Jans, and the frequent fatal consequences.

On the 14th of December appeared the second number of the "Arctic Moon," which was thought to be an improvement on number one, and was well received. Lieutenant Greely gave a lecture on the "Polar Question."

On the same day also, Esquimaux Frederick came to Lieutenant Greely and asked permission to leave the station, and, when asked why, said some one was going to shoot him—a strange hallucination!

On the 20th Lockwood writes: "The sun now begins his journey to the north;

the backbone of the winter is broken! Walking out at noon to-day, I was just able to see the hands of my watch by holding it close to my eye. The profound silence of this region is quite as striking, and almost as disagreeable, as the darkness. Standing still, one can almost hear his heart beat. The sense of solitude is sublime." Speaking of Arctic literature, he says that "Hayes' book, though beautifully written, is far below that of Kane as to information and reliability. No one who has been up Smith's Sound can fail to notice this."

On the 24th of December, after eating a birthday dinner, the Christmas presents from an unknown friend to every one of the party, were distributed. The rooms were appropriately decorated, and everything was done to render the occasion cheerful and pleasant. Those articles not specifically assigned by the donor were disposed of by lottery.

Lockwood indulged in the following reflections: "How suggestive of home and of the dear ones there! How often do my thoughts wander away to them! Has Providence been equally kind to them as to me? The day with me suggests alternately the past and the future. Will next Christmas find me here, with everything around as auspicious as now, and shall I then be able to look back with satisfaction and self-complacency on my labors along the Greenland coast? Or will the future bring a record of dreams unsatisfied, of efforts unproductive, of labor in vain? My mind is far away with that group at home assembled together and doubtless regretting that the absent one is not of their number. Could I but see them for an hour, or know that all is well with them, I should rejoice, indeed!"

The "Lime-Juice Club" gave an entertainment on the same evening, at which Snyder affected Jans to tears by his personation of an Esquimaux lady, and Connell brought down the house as a martinet captain, by exclaiming, when a soldier who had shot himself was brought in: "Very sad affair, very sad, indeed! Charge him with two cartridges expended, Sergeant."

Lieutenant Greely also gave the party as a lecture, "Reminiscences of the Battle of Fredericksburg," which was interesting and two hours long, though entirely *ex tempore*; and Lockwood was announced to lecture on "Arctic Sledging."

On the 31st, rations of rum were issued to help the men welcome in the new year. They were also to fire a salute with rifles. Fiddles were in full blast, with singing and other marks of hilarity.

Lockwood's lecture on "Arctic Sledging" was given January 3, 1882, and was well received. Being confirmed in his opinion that he was no public speaker, he intended to leave lecturing for others thereafter. On the 9th he took his usual walk, notwithstanding the thermometer was at 60° below zero, and felt the cold chiefly on his nose. It seemed curious to him, that when the thermometer was lowest, the air was stillest. Were it otherwise, he supposed existence in the Arctic would be an impossibility.

But severe as was the weather, it did not deter him from the study of science, as will be seen by the following record, made on the 9th of January: "I have been looking up the subject of nautical astronomy for some time past, and to-day and this evening, taking sextant, mercury, etc., and establishing an observatory on top of an old barrel in front of the house, commenced observations on the transit of Markab, Capella, and other stars, but have not been very successful. Everything conspires against one in this climate. It reminds me of my observations last spring. However, I hope by dint of practice to do better. The winter is passing away slowly but surely. The time is coming when I shall look at these stars from grassy fields, on a summer night, in the temperate zone, I hope. The stars up here are very bright, and a great many of them circle around the pole and never set. It is a beautiful sight. Arcturus, Aldebaran, and others, besides being very bright, show different colors, red, violet, and green. Jupiter looks immense."

Still absorbed with his astronomical studies, he gives us the following on the 13th of the same month: "The moon appeared after noon. How welcome she is! How a poet would rave over the moon could he once experience a polar winter!—not simply an Arctic winter, for anywhere north of the Arctic Circle is the Arctic, and the dark days which most expeditions have seen are trifling compared with ours. I think it would be a good idea to exile a first-class poet into these regions for the purpose, but give him to understand he was never to return. How he would sing!"

On the 12th, they had a phenomenon they had never heard of—the precipitation of vapor with a perfectly clear sky. It resembled a heavy mist or light rain.

On the 16th occurred the first hurricane of the season. It began in the morning with heavy south wind and sudden fall of barometer. At noon the wind whipped round to the northeast and blew with indescribable fury, filling the air with snow-drifts, and blotting out the view of everything even a few feet distant. The anemometer registered sixty-five miles, and then broke down. The noise of the storm, as heard from the house, was as though on shipboard. It must have given way but for the ice walls around it.

On the 20th, Lieutenant Greely issued a circular letter, calling attention to the order that all should be up for breakfast. Kislingbury and Dr. Pavy took exceptions to this, and the latter declined to lecture in his turn.

The next evening occurred a beautiful and unique auroral display, the chief features of which were many broad bands of pure white passing through the zenith and reaching to the east and to the west horizon, which blended, twisted, and curled in upon each other in a very remarkable manner. The spectacle was viewed with wonder and amazement.

On the 26th, the twilight at noonday was quite bright. The moon also lent her aid; but low spirits and a sense of oppression and homesickness prevailed, all induced, doubtless, by want of exercise, and loneliness.

"Another twenty-four hours," wrote Lockwood, on the 6th of February, "of this interminable night nearly gone! Thank God! Sometimes it seems as if this life must hold on forever, but *tempus fugit* up here as well as elsewhere. The days and weeks seem weeks and months in passing, and yet, in the retrospect, time seems to have passed quickly, because there is so little in the past to mark its progress, I suppose."

Lockwood could not realize the extreme cold, and seldom wore his gloves when going out for a few minutes. Though he put on a thick dog-skin coat and seal-skin over-all when taking his daily walk, he really did not regard so much clothing necessary. Exposure to such low temperatures, however, for several hours, and particularly at night, was to be dreaded. Many authorities —among others Lieutenant Greely—spoke of a peculiar sensation in the throat on first encountering a very low temperature, as when going out of doors from a warm room, but such was not Lockwood's experience. Provided it was calm, he could stand any degree of cold he had yet met with. Owing to the peculiar and admirable construction of their house, the men were able to keep up 50° of heat within, however cold without.

On the 13th of February, Lockwood with two men went to see what damage had resulted from the late storm to the observatory on the summit of Bellot Island. Contrary to their expectations, they found the snow not only deep, but with a crust just firm enough *not* to bear. Consequently, they sent the dog-sledge back, and proceeded on foot, frequently sinking down knee-deep. Though the thermometer stood at -65°, they got into a profuse perspiration, which was not lessened by the steep and slippery ascent of two thousand feet. From this point the station-house seemed only a black spot, and was hardly recognizable as a house. Having made their inspection and fired their rifles several times as agreed upon with Lieutenant Greely, who was experimenting on sound, they returned. The result of these experiments was, that at -65° sound travels nine hundred and fifty feet per second. This was the coldest day they had yet experienced, and still they did not suffer with the cold.

The return to a warm house was an indescribable comfort, and Lockwood thought that if this could always be done, Arctic journeying would then be nothing. It was unprecedentedly cold even for that latitude. Pure brandy and also glycerine were frozen hard. The poor dogs suffered, yet many of them preferred to remain curled up on the snow-banks outside, to occupying the tent and holes prepared for them.

On the 19th, Lockwood made a dog-sledge trip with Brainard and the Esquimaux Frederick to Depot "B," to look for a good place to cross the straits. Found that the snow had drifted so as to form a continuous inclined plane from the bluffs far outside the snow-house and tent, thus almost concealing them. They recognized the spot only by seeing the stovepipe jutting above the snow. Knowing how the mouth of the tunnel lay from this point, they dug through the hard, compact snow, cleared out the tunnel, and soon found themselves within the snow-house. The little stove was swallowed up in a cone of snow reaching from roof to floor. This had drifted through a small aperture where the pipe pierced the roof. The fire going out after they turned in, the room became extremely damp and chilly. However, they made up for the discomforts of the night by a rousing fire in the morning, over which they got up a grand breakfast of musk-ox steak, beans, coffee, and hard-tack. They next sent the team with Frederick down to St. Patrick's Bay for a bag of coal, while Lockwood and Brainard walked over the straits toward Polaris Promontory. Going out some four or five miles over ice of varied nature, some exceedingly broken and hummocky and some quite level, they returned, satisfied that the time for crossing over was not yet. Frederick had, in the mean time, returned, mended up the hole in the roof, made a good fire, and prepared a warm meal.

They again started out to test the important passage, taking a route farther north. There the rubble-ice reached only two hundred yards from the shore, beyond which, as far as they walked and could see, smooth ice extended. They returned, satisfied that this was the place to attempt the passage when the time should arrive for their contemplated exploration farther north.

They made the trip over the foot-ice to the station (twenty miles) in four hours, thus proving the fine condition of the sledge and dogs for traveling, and the eagerness of the dogs to rejoin their companions and pups. All the way, they had before them to the southward a rich glow on the horizon like the sunrise of a fine morning at home. They found the men celebrating the 22d of February by match-games of various kinds, and, after listening to an appropriate speech on the Father of his Country, enjoyed a good dinner.

X.
"THE ARCTIC MOON."

As already mentioned in this narrative, among the events which occurred at the Greely Scientific Colony, or Fort Conger, was the establishment of a newspaper, the first ever issued so near the north pole, the nearest approach to it previously having been "The Ice-Blink," issued by Kane's Expedition in 1854. It was projected by G. W. Rice and C. B. Henry, but Lieutenant Lockwood was the editor-in-chief. The sheet was fifteen by nineteen inches in size, first prepared in manuscript and then multiplied by photograph, published on the 2d of November, 1881, and semi-monthly as to time. As the musk-oxen, the walruses, and the bears and wolves of Grinnell Land took no interest in the enterprise, the patrons of the paper were confined to the colony of explorers. In his opening address, the editor proudly claimed that his corps of contributors embraced the finest minds in the country; that his reporters would always be "on the spot"; that the journal was certain to be superior to any other in the country; and that the subscription list numbered not less than twenty-five thousand—the last assertion being a servile imitation of what often appears in the papers of New York and other American cities. And now, by way of giving the reader an idea of the style and character of this unique journal, it is proposed to reproduce in this chapter, as specimens, a collection of its editorials, contributions, items of news, and advertisements. In an article on "Christmas," the editor gives us the following pathetic reflections:

"Our Christmas-time has come and gone, and, although our geographical position is not a favorable one for the complete observation of this joyous anniversary, it was attended with many of the happy features that make its memory a pleasant landmark of the dying year. No boughs of 'evergreen were berried bright' (our crop of evergreens failed this season), but had they existed, the conditions for making them 'white with rime' were very favorable.

"Christmas always attracts a crowd of joyous faces, and, although we missed the pleasure of 'childhood's grace and fair maiden's blushes' under the mystic mistletoe, the stalwart, bearded men who grasped hands under our smoke-begrimed roof felt indeed the inspiration of the gladsome time when the voice of man's good-will to man speaks forth in everything. Could the possessors of the kind hearts and hands that contributed so much to the pleasure of the party have looked in upon the happy, smiling faces, living again a day of their youth in the anticipation and surprise attending the bestowal and opening of the mysterious packages containing the presents, they would have felt more than rewarded for their kind thoughtfulness. Lips unused to the task framed grateful acknowledgments of the kind act. The interest in our happiness taken by the wife of the commanding officer was repeatedly shown, and when, as we sat down to our inviting Christmas dinner, we contemplated a crowning proof of her kind good-will, repressed enthusiasm could no longer be restrained, and three rousing cheers for Mrs. Greely were given with an effect which proved beyond cavil the vigor of our lungs, and rendered unnecessary the weekly examination of the doctor.

"Of course, the festive season brought with it regrets that would not be repressed, and longings that could not be satisfied, when processions of absent loved ones and severed friends followed the funerals of other Christmas-days through thoughts that would wander over snow, and ice, and land, and sea, to the happy firesides where we knew they were gathered. But every one looked on the bright side of things, and extracted as much comfort and pleasure as possible under the circumstances; we even knew one sordid individual who congratulated himself on the immunity of his exchequer from the heavy drafts generally entailed by the purchase of Christmas presents. We have not space to enter into a detailed account of all the happy features of the holiday. Altogether, our Christmas was a great success."

By way of showing that there was nothing very frigid in the hearts of the explorers, another editorial is submitted, on the New Year:

"Christmas is gone, with all its pleasant associations, and we find ourselves on the threshold of a new year. What thoughts the day recalls to a reflective mind! the exodus of the old, the advent of the new year; the past and the future, history and prophecy, the ceaseless alternation of life and death, the eternity of nature.

"The day is suggestive in another way. Where were we a year ago? what doing? what looking forward to? Where shall we be a year from now? what will be our surroundings, and what shall we look back upon? How distant seemed this day a year ago! how short now seems the time that has since elapsed!

"The new year of 1882 finds us a community of twenty-five men, living through the cold and darkness of an Arctic winter, in a small house near the north pole, thousands of miles beyond any civilized habitation. A year ago saw us scattered—some in the cities, some on the plains of the far West, some occupied in quiet routine, some in the ceaseless changes and activity of the field. Will the next year find us here with our surroundings as satisfactory and auspicious? We trust so, and this day is eminently a day for making good resolutions. We are free agents, and the future depends, in great part, on ourselves. Let us, then, determine that, so far as lies within our power, we shall have no cause to look back with regret on the year just ushered in. The phrase is hackneyed, but none the less true:

'Of all sad words of tongue or pen,

The saddest are these—it might have been.'"

And now we come to a contribution addressed to the editor of the "Arctic Moon," as follows:

"As Grinnell Land is a recognized Territory of the United States, and has a territorial form of government, a delegate from this Territory is to be elected who is to take his seat at the opening of the Forty-seventh Congress. The undersigned offers himself as a candidate for the office, on the following platform: I am in favor of reaching the north pole by balloon, a liberal appropriation for the purchase of lime-juice, compulsory education, unlimited emigration, a homestead and sixty acres of land, one musk-ox and two Esquimaux dogs to each actual settler. I am also a strong advocate of woman's rights, but there is no good in rights without the woman. I am prepared to 'chaw' the points on the above platform; I think it is 'plump,' and will stand without being propped up.

(Signed)   "CONNELL."

And now, under the general heading of "*Moon-Beams*," we come to the following paragraphs, which are not only spicy, but characteristic of the time and place with which they are identified:

"The British expedition found the ice in this harbor, January 1, 1876, twenty-eight and three-quarter inches thick. Measurements made this day showed thirty-four inches. Our average temperature for December was nearly eight degrees lower than theirs for the same month.

"The darkest day being a thing of the past, we shall soon find ourselves sliding down hill quite rapidly. We have made complete arrangements to have the sun interviewed on his return to this country the latter part of February.

"The walrus seem to have emigrated, so that the Dutch Island people now take their daily exercise in *peas*.

"'I wonder what is in the mess-boxes?' is the oft-repeated query. Have patience, brethren, time will show.

"Old Probabilities will be surprised to learn, that his enterprising colony at this point is indulging in outdoor sports with the thermometer at 40° below zero.

"To-day, at Dutch Island, Lieutenant Kislingbury was able to see the time of day holding his watch about one foot from his face.

"Sergeant Cross has made another addition to his already numerous trades— that of bottling samples of air for the examination and scrutiny of those not favored with a sniff of Arctic breezes.

"Sergeant Brainard is excellent authority for the statement that the gate-money taken at the racing contest will be devoted to the advancement of geographical knowledge within the Arctic Circle. Such being the case, the number of aborigines present will be a crucial test of the desire on the part of the Grinnellites to bring their country into more general knowledge.

"Wanted—A good family horse. Will buy it cheap, or will take for his keeping, or keep for his taking. To be used on good country roads and for family driving. Must be very gentle. No objections to a Government mule. Address Jacob Doboy.

"Wanted—A poet for the 'Arctic Moon.' Must be strictly temperate and a good speech-maker. No tailors need apply. Address this office.

"Wanted—A humoristic writer for the 'Arctic Moon.' The present incumbent has suddenly become ill from too close application.

"Information wanted of the Greely Arctic Expedition. It strayed away from home last July, and was last heard from at Upernavik, Greenland.

"We beg leave to announce to the public that we have made extensive improvements in our establishment, whereby we can furnish at the shortest notice bread, twists, rolls, cakes, pies, tarts, and, in fact, anything in the baker's line. Wedding cakes made a specialty. Are thankful for past patronage, and respectfully ask its continuance in future.

> "FREDERICK SHOOTMAN,
> "SAN FRANCISCO LONGMAN,
> "Merchant Bakers."

XI.
EXPEDITION TO LOCKWOOD ISLAND.

On the 29th of February, Lieutenant Lockwood went upon an experimental trip to Thank God Harbor preparatory to his proposed grand expedition along the coast of Northern Greenland. His companions were Brainard, Jewell, Long, and the Esquimaux, Frederick and Jans, with two dog-teams. As the dogs, constantly yelping and howling, competed for the mastery, they traveled rapidly, and, after many twistings and turnings, reached their destination, where they found the observatory still standing. They took a necessary inventory, and, after a survey of the dismal plain, visited the grave of C. F. Hall, where Lieutenant Lockwood recorded the following touching notice in his journal: "The head-board erected by his comrades, as also the metallic one left by the English, still stands. How mournful to me the scene, made more so by the howling of the winds and the thick atmosphere! It was doubtless best that he died where he did. I have come to regard him as a visionary and an enthusiast, who was indebted more to fortune than to those practical abilities which Kane possessed. Yet he gave his life to the cause, and that must always go far toward redeeming the short-comings of any man. The concluding lines of the inscription on the English tablet, I think good: 'To Captain Hall, who sacrificed his life in the advancement of science, November 8, 1871. This tablet has been erected by the British Polar Expedition of 1875, which followed in his footsteps and profited by his experience.'"

The American inscription on the wooden headboard was as follows:

IN MEMORY OF
CHARLES FRANCIS HALL,
LATE COMMANDER U. S. STEAMER POLARIS,
NORTH POLE EXPEDITION.
Died November 8, 1871.

"I am the resurrection and the life; he that believeth in me, though he were dead, yet shall he live."

After various struggles with the snow, fog, and cold weather, ending in frosted feet and faces, and after inspecting a boat left by Buddington, they returned by way of the snow-house at Cape Beechy, and, all very much exhausted, reached the station, receiving a hearty welcome. Greely had been very anxious about the party, owing to a storm of great violence, and had sent Dr. Pavy with men to their relief. The trip thus made covered not less than one hundred and forty miles. Lockwood now decided that on the 1st of April he would start upon his proposed expedition. This trip occupied his mind continually. He hoped he might be successful, yet there were many chances of failure. Who could divine the future? He felt that he ought to be able to reach Cape Britannia, but that was not enough; he desired to do more.

As the time for taking his departure approached, Lockwood was greatly troubled with rheumatism, but still was very busy in maturing his plans. Lieutenant Greely wrote him a flattering letter, putting the whole plan of operations in his hands and placing at his disposal the entire *personnel* and material of the expedition. This would include almost all who could take the field. The men were becoming enthusiastic and were showing an admirable spirit, although they knew from experience that they were to engage in no child's play. Almost all of those selected had shown pluck hitherto. Without this element no one could endure the hardships that they might have to undergo. Should any of those selected break down early, there were excellent substitutes among those left behind. Lockwood was pleased with an exhibition of pluck by Ellis, who walked all the way from Depot "A" with a frozen foot, refusing the offer of Jewell to bring him on the dog-sledge. Jewell, on returning from Lincoln Bay, had orders to convey stores to the "Gap," where the boat previously sent over the strait lay. Hence, before starting, supplies would be placed at Depot "B," at the "Gap," and at a point intermediate on the frozen strait.

Having all things complete, Sergeant Brainard was to proceed at once with the supporting parties to Cape Sumner. He was to leave Depot "B" with a weight to drag of one hundred and thirty pounds per man. Lockwood was to follow with dog-sledge loaded with five hundred pounds of pemmican. Thus they would concentrate at Cape Sumner with the six hundred rations in hand, together with seven hundred pounds of dog pemmican. The stores embraced pemmican, bacon, corned beef, roast musk-ox, raw musk-ox, English beef, hard bread, canned beans, potatoes, sugar, tea, chocolate, and coffee, besides which they carried alcohol for cooking and lime-juice as an anti-scorbutic. Their sledge ration had been made up by consultation with Lieutenant Greely, though, of course, it might be departed from if circumstances required. The diet list was purposely a varied one. No rum or spirits were taken except as a medicine. The main supporting party consisted of Sergeant Lynn, Corporal Ellison, and privates Biederbick, Whistler, and Henry.

Lieutenant Lockwood, Sergeant Jewell, and the Esquimaux Frederick formed the advance party, while Sergeants Brainard and Ralston, Corporal Saler, and privates Connell, Fredericks, and one other man constituted the second supporting party.

Sledging over the Arctic Floe.

On the 2d of April, the main and second supporting parties moved off in good style, amid the waving of flags, firing of pistols, cheers, and other demonstrations. Both Lieutenants Greely and Lockwood took occasion to address the men a few words of encouragement and advice. Lockwood confined his remarks to the necessity of co-operation and subordination as the chief essentials to success. He would follow with Jewell and the dog-sledge, and, if he knew himself, would not return unsuccessful. He got off at 8 P. M., with Jewell, Frederick, and the dog-sledge Antoinette. The team of eight consisted of "Ritenbank, the king," a large white dog, at whose growl all the rest trembled; "Major," a friend of Ritenbank, and a very useful, good-natured old fellow, hard-working and quiet, without any special characteristics; "Howler," a large, lean, mean, ill-natured brute, whom they took on board at Disco, and who lorded it over the rest till Ritenbank came on board at the place of the same name, when Howler was dethroned; since which he had been morose and misanthropic, and never associated with the other dogs. He set up the most unearthly howling whenever any other dog approached him, especially if that other dog had designs on something he was engaged in eating or trying to eat—a tin can, for instance. At the end of a march, when the pemmican was being cut up, and he, with the rest, was awaiting his opportunity to make a general rush, his howling became almost unendurable. But he was especially despicable, because he allowed any and every dog of the team to jump on and bite him. His only redeeming trait was his earnestness in pulling, for, when the sledge stuck in deep snow or rubble-ice, he was the last of the dogs to sit on his haunches and look while *you* got it out. On several occasions when Ritenbank was making efforts to get inside the tent and steal the meat while all were asleep, Howler had given the alarm by his unearthly howling. His place in the team was on the right flank, and he kept it all the time, never dropping back and coming up in the wrong place, as did the other dogs. Next to Howler was the "Woolly dog," a dirty-looking cur with long white hair, which made Howler's life a burden all the time by snapping at him as he hauled by his side. Next came the "kooneys," signifying in Esquimaux mother-dogs. They were called "Black Kooney" and "White Kooney," and were both good workers. Then came "Ask-him," a pup when brought on board in Greenland, but now *of age*, and bearing the airs of a veteran. He brooked insult from no dog but Ritenbank, and evidently bided his time to contest the throne with him. He had even taken upon himself the kingly custom of biting the adjoining dog whenever he felt the whip. On his left were two dogs already named, "Major" and the "Boss." On the left flank was "Gypsy," a little fat kooney dog which pulled only under the lash, and yet by foraging and stealing managed to get twice the rations of any of the rest, and was always plump and fat.

The advance party reached Depot "A" in good time, and took on five sacks (five hundred pounds) of dog pemmican and some cans of corned beef, which made their load very heavy.

On the 5th of April, Lockwood reached the snow-house, and there found Brainard and the rest, making thirteen altogether. They completely filled the house, and also the dug-out in the snow-bank adjoining, so that Lockwood and Jewell moved the provisions out of the tent, and slept there, and Frederick in the tunnel. The tent being snowed in to the ridge-pole, and connected with the tunnel, they were quite comfortable. On the same day they saw an eagle on a floe-berg, which was considered a good omen. After needed rest all hands took their departure. The snow on the ice-floe was somewhat deep, and the loads very heavy. The route across the straits, previously determined on, was from Cape Beechy to within five or six miles of the east shore, and then as direct as possible to Cape Sumner. On reaching the tent on the straits, about four and one half miles out, Lockwood dropped his load, and went back to look after the sledges, then out of sight. He found Whistler sick and unable to pull, and Biederbick and Connell trying to pull the load without him—not an encouraging commencement of a long journey. Aided by the dog-sledge, all soon reached the tent and camped for the night. Lockwood, Jewell, and Frederick slept in the wall-tent, pitched there some weeks before. Lockwood writes at this point: "Finding it very cold, I was glad to get up and out, leaving Jewell to the unhappy work of getting breakfast. (Breakfast! what a misnomer in such cases!) I then went to the two tents occupied by the others to inquire for healths. Mr. Henry, correspondent of the 'Chicago Times' (as he called himself), the same who had written on the side of a large iceberg, 'Ho! for Cape Britannia,' said he could go no farther, as he had been suffering dreadfully all night with rheumatism; or, if he did go farther, we would have to haul him back, while from here he thought he could manage to hobble by himself to the snow-house, and, after resting there and again at Depot 'A,' reach the station. Henry is a big fellow, over six feet in height, with apparently the strength and physique of Hercules. It was a bad omen for the rest of us when *he* broke down. Connell had frozen his feet the previous day quite badly, and only discovered the extent of the injury after getting into camp, but thought *he* could go on, or at least was determined to try. All hands looked very forlorn, but generally were resolute and determined. Finally, Jewell had the tea and canned meat warmed sufficiently, and we stuffed ourselves with all there was to stuff, and prepared to follow the others who had already started. We overtook Fredericks (the saddler) struggling along in the snow with a sledge all by himself. He was a dwarf by the side of the giant Henry. It was necessary to do something, and so I told Jewell he must join Fredericks, and leave the Esquimaux and me to manage the dog-sledge. I overtook the main party about a mile and a half from camp, doing their best. Connell could hardly walk at all, and it was utterly impossible for him to pull. He was very reluctant to go back, but there was no alternative; so, throwing off the load, I took him on the dog-sledge as far as Cape Beechy, whence he thought he could get along by himself. On returning I picked up the load, and proceeded to follow the trail of the others. The snow soon became worse, and the sledge so often stuck that I determined to double up—take half the load at a time. The Esquimaux dogs can pull a very heavy load, and through bad places, but the moment the sledge comes to a dead halt they sit on their haunches, turn complacently round, and wait till the sledge is extricated. If not fully started, they will pull at random, or not at all. On these occasions the hard work comes upon the driver and others with the sledge."

On the 7th, they joined the other wing of the expedition, finding them in camp some miles south-west of the gap. The wind had been blowing and snow drifting for some hours, and everything indicated a storm. Lockwood and Frederick pitched tent and went into camp, first bringing up the rest of the load.

While the storm was still raging, they got off with half the load, leaving the rest making preparations for a move, and took a course for Cape Sumner, whose steep, rocky face loomed up in the distance, terminated by a line of magnificent cliffs, which extended unbroken, except by "the Gap," as far south as Cape Lupton of Polaris fame. They traveled upon level floes interrupted by ridges of hummocky ice, over which they had to get the sledge as best they could, and with frequent use of the axe. The wind blowing stronger, and the air being obscured with driving snow, they could with difficulty pick their way. Traveling over the straits was like navigating a ship in a tortuous channel. They soon found themselves in the midst of a mass of rubble-ice of the worst description; gaps and chasms between the crags and blocks of ice, often filled with loose snow, or entirely obscured by that flying through the air. They could barely see the cliffs on their right, and could not recognize their position. The dogs became very much discouraged, Frederick also, and Lockwood himself felt in no very enviable frame of mind. After many ineffectual efforts, and unloading and reloading repeatedly, they left the load and attempted to explore a route to shore. Not succeeding, they hunted for some suitable snow-drift in which to burrow, and there await better weather; but saw none. Finally, the storm letting up for a moment, they found a level floe, and, with the use of the axe, Lockwood and Frederick got the sledge upon it.

On the 8th, at 3 A. M., they arrived at Cape Sumner, and, getting through the rubble-ice near the shore, gained the steep snow-slope which lay between the foot of the cliffs and the line of immense floe-bergs along the shore, stranded and pressed close up to the snow-slope. Between the bergs and the slope, the wind had made great gaps, deep and tortuous. The only way to get along was either through these gaps—often like pits—or to take the slope above and run the risk of tumbling down into them, sledge and all, sometimes fifteen or twenty feet. There was often no alternative but the latter. Lockwood expected to find it calm there by reason of the protection of the bluffs, but, on the contrary, the wind came down from above in gusts and whirlwinds, filling the air with eddying columns of snow. When about a mile from the Polaris Boat Camp, they encountered an immense mass of snow entirely filling up the ravine from top to bottom. Leaving the sledge, Lockwood went on to see if he could reach the Boat Camp, but could hardly keep his feet on account of the wind. Returning, he and Frederick made a small hole in the side of a large drift, and, pulling in everything the dogs could possibly eat, prepared to "weather the storm." By 9 A. M., *supper* had been eaten in darkness, for they had no candles, and Frederick, wedged close up to him in the frozen sleeping-bag, was snorting away like a steam-engine. Lockwood soon fell asleep too, but woke up to find the sleeping-bag and his footgear and clothes wet with the moisture such close quarters produced. Everything inside was thawing. Soon after, masses of snow falling down through a number of rents in the side and roof of the excavation, he began to think they would be smothered alive. But while thinking about it, he went to sleep again, leaving Frederick snorting as before. Just how long they slept in that snow-bank, they did not know, but when they did wake up and try to emerge, they found themselves completely snowed in, and only got out by vigorous use of their knives, so hard and compact had the ice and snow become. Frederick being able to understand only signs and a very few words chiefly referring to food, their conversation was very limited.

They found the dogs and sledge almost buried in snow. Hastily harnessing up, they reached the Boat Camp on Newman's Bay at noon. Here they again went into camp by digging into a snow-bank and covering the hole with the tent. "Skaffer," or eating, being first in order, they supplied themselves by thawing their prepared roast. Then they had a smoke—that great solace of the traveler in every clime. Snow-houses and snow-holes, they concluded, have many objections, but they always have the merit of being warm. Feeling uneasy about Brainard and his party, imagining all manner of things about them, at 9 P.M., Lockwood left everything behind and went forth with dogs and sledge to hunt them up, and at midnight met them valiantly struggling along toward the Boat Camp. They had found shelter from the storm behind a large, friendly floe-berg, where the tent could stand. On the 10th, preceding them, he picked up the bags of pemmican he had put off, and returned to Boat Camp, where they came also and burrowed in the snow. All thus found themselves at their first station. Jewell, being originally of the party of the dog-sledge, lodged and fed with them when together, he sleeping in a single bag, and Lockwood and Frederick together. "It was," Lockwood remarks, "a choice of evils which to prefer—Frederick groaning like a piece of machinery, or Jewell always getting the stockings and wraps mixed up, and invariably laying hold of the dry ones as his own."

"Snow-holes," he again says, "having the insuperable objection of asphyxiation, we repaired the tents and returned to civilization—that is, went really into camp. Whistler and Bender were found completely done up this morning both in flesh and spirits—all kinds of pains, shortness of breath, spitting of blood, faintness. Not being enthusiastic about going farther, I deemed it best to send them back, and they left at once for the station."

They now had several things to look to before going farther—to bring up the rations sent across to the Gap, also to bring over those left at the tent on the straits.

At midnight, Brainard and party, with three Hudson Bay sledges, started on this work, and Lockwood left two hours after, with a dog-sledge and Frederick, for the same purpose. Taking advantage of smooth ice, interrupted now and then outside the pack near shore, he soon overhauled Brainard, and they reached the Gap together. There they found the boat, which had been sent over with so much labor, a complete wreck. They, however, placed it out of reach of further damage, as it might yet become important to them. They then went into camp by going into a snow-burrow prepared there some weeks before when the boat had been brought over, and proceeded to have a feast, which possessed at least one merit, that of being *enough*, for Lockwood did not deem it necessary to adhere strictly to sledge rations till they had left their base of supplies. Leaving the others to load up and return to Boat Camp, he and Frederick left with the dog-sledge for the food put out on the straits *en route*. Part of this they took up and then joined the others at Boat Camp, men and dogs well spent and tired; but a good meal, a good smoke, and a snooze in their bags, set them all right.

Their number was now reduced to nine, two having been sent back soon after leaving the snow-house (Depot "B"), and two from Boat Camp. The Hudson Bay sledges were much worn, and likely to become useless. Lockwood now determined to return to the main station for new runners, leaving the men under Brainard to bring up the supplies still out, and otherwise make ready for the advance. The round trip would be one hundred miles, and would add much to the labor of the dogs, but there was no help for it, as he could take no chances on the threshold of the long journey before them.

Soon after making this resolve, he and Frederick got off with their team, carrying nothing but an axe and half a pound of tobacco. The dogs were in fine condition, notwithstanding their recent hard work. True, they supplemented their rations and thus added to their strength by stealing thirty-five pounds of bacon! "It is wonderful," Lockwood here remarks, "what these Esquimaux dogs can do. This team, which was regarded as a scrub affair—Dr. Pavy having had his pick of dogs—hauled ice all through the winter, made a trip beyond Cape Beechy in February, another to Thank-God-Harbor and Newman's Bay in March, and then hauled a load to Lincoln Bay and four days after started on this present trip; yet now they travel along as lively as ever—so lively that the driver finds it difficult to keep up."

They duly reached the station, and, of course, Greely and all were surprised to see them, probably taking them for another cargo of cripples. After a good sleep and a feast, they were off on their return at 10 P. M. of the 14th. They took on the runners, a feed of walrus-meat, a few other trifles, and also a heliograph, the last to open communication in case of delay or disaster. Stopping six hours at the snow-house to rest and feed, they started across the strait with a small load of meat, and, notwithstanding some rubble-ice which delayed them, reached the Boat Camp at 5.30 P. M., very tired and very sleepy, too, having accomplished this remarkable journey of one hundred miles in fifty-four hours. During their absence, Brainard had brought in everything, and all was ready for the advance as soon as they could repair the sledges.

After repairing and rebuilding, they had for the trip:

1. Dog-sledge, Lieutenant Lockwood and Esquimaux Frederick; total weight, 743 pounds.

2. Large sledge (the "Nares"), drawn by Sergeants Brainard and Ralston and Corporal Saler; estimated total weight, 651 pounds.

3. Hudson Bay sledge ("Hall"), drawn by Sergeant Jewell and private Fredericks; estimated total weight, 300 pounds.

4. Hudson Bay sledge ("Hayes"), drawn by Sergeant Lynn and Corporal Ellison; estimated total weight, 300 pounds.

Of this weight, 225 pounds was of equipments, independent of weight of sledges, and 900 pounds, of food for men and dogs.

At 10.30 P. M., they left the Boat Camp and crossed Newman's Bay, to a ravine, or narrow valley, directly opposite, which the lieutenant called Gorge Creek after finding it was not the route he had taken it for—that of Beaumont's return. The others being far behind, he left the sledge and proceeded on alone to explore. Passing through a narrow gap, the valley widened out as before, in some places the exposed stones offering a serious obstacle to heavily laden sledges. Returning, he and Frederick went back with the team and assisted in bringing up the foot-sledges. Then, after an advance of ten miles in eight hours, all went into camp again. Leaving the camp at 10 P. M., and doubling up from the start, they made their way up the valley, through the gap, and to the head of the valley beyond. They found the exposed stones so annoying that Lockwood regretted often he had not taken the route round Cape Brevoort, notwithstanding the rubble-ice. Though Lockwood felt confident he had reached the divide, yet, throwing off the load, he sent Frederick with the team back to assist the others, while he went ahead to further reconnoitre. Although he ascended a high hill, he could see little encouraging beyond. He returned to the load and continued down-stream until he met the others painfully advancing, when all went into camp, after making an advance of six miles in eight hours.

Got off again with half-load at 10 P. M. Preceding the others, Lockwood and Frederick made their way over slightly undulating plains, keeping as far as possible northward until they came to a decided depression in that direction, sometimes following blind leads, and then returning and continuing on their former way. Lockwood finally saw before him the crest of the bluff of a water-course, gaining which he found to his joy a stream running north, which he entered. Though filled with snow, it afforded good traveling for the dog team. Continuing down this stream, he passed between two large masses of rock like a gateway. Here was a regular cañon as straight as a street and nearly level, whose sides were almost perpendicular and extremely picturesque. Seeing no signs of the sea, he resolved to camp here. To this end, throwing off the half load, he went back for that left behind, expecting to meet the foot-sledges on the way. Disappointed in this, he returned to the ravine, and at 6 P. M. he and Frederick were into their sleeping-bags, feeling much uneasiness about their route, for they had already traveled a much greater distance than the English maps called for as lying between Newman's Bay and the north coast.

Although the men with the drag-sledges had not come up, Lockwood resolved to leave everything behind and go ahead down the cañon with the empty sledge till assured that he was *en route* to the sea by finding the sea itself. Carrying out this resolve at 10 A. M., the cañon soon widened into a valley, with deep, soft snow-bed or stones, and inclosed by lofty mountains. He crossed this, and came to a gorge like a railroad-cutting, through which the stream ran. Ascending an adjacent hill, before him lay what seemed an extended plain, which he recognized as the sea, from a line of floe-bergs marking the coast.

Just where they were, he did not know, nor did he find out till their return. The sea had been found, so now they were to find and bring up the men and sledges. Lockwood and Frederick, with the wearied team, rapidly went back and happily found the absent ones, safely, if not comfortably, camped alongside their load.

All broke camp at 7 P. M. and proceeded to bring up such of the impedimenta as had been left behind; after which they made their way with great labor through the cañon, valley, and gorge to the sea, reaching there, at 4 A. M. of the 22d, with everything except a seal-skin mit, which got adrift and went flying before the wind over the hills like a bird; for a terrific snow-storm was then raging. They found great difficulty in making the tents stand, and, indeed, abandoned the attempt except as to one, into which they all huddled to weather out the storm. The cooking was confined to making a little tepid tea. They remained in their bags, sleeping at intervals, and even going without food and water rather than venture out.

Finally, on the morning of the 23d, the storm had abated, and they ventured out, to find that the dogs had taken advantage of the circumstances to eat up twenty pounds of bacon and twelve pounds of beef, although these had been secured, as was supposed, at the bottom of a sledge. They had also eaten a seal-skin mitten. After some repairs to the sledges, which had suffered by the stony route passed over, they proceeded on their way along the coast, keeping on the ice-foot which here ran along a low, sloping shore backed by a range of hills. At Drift Point, the snow formed steep slopes, extending from the bluffs (now near the sea) to the tops of the line of floe-bergs along shore. There, the sledge "Nares" breaking down, it was necessary to abandon it and increase the loads on the other sledges, carrying along the good parts of the "Nares" to repair the others when needful. Doubling up, they made their way along those steep slopes until near Black Horn Cliffs. Here the slopes became so abrupt that they were driven on to the rubble-ice near the shore. So difficult was their way over this with the heavily loaded sledges, that in many places by standing pulls only could progress be made. Near these cliffs they went into camp after bringing up the half-loads left behind, having advanced five miles in eight and a half hours. Leaving half their stuff, they then made their way over the rubble-ice, frequently using the axe, till they came to the end of the cliffs, when the sledges went back for the rest of the stuff, while Lockwood looked for a more practicable route. Off shore, half a mile seaward, he found a fair route, following which he reached Cape Stanton. He thought Stanton Gorge, where Beaumont had left forty rations, to be near. These, however, he failed to find. After taking a short nap in the lee of a hummock, he returned to find Frederick and the dog-sledge. The others coming up, all went into camp fully tired out, for, besides the roughness of the ice, they had encountered a stiff wind. Two ptarmigans were seen near Cape Stanton.

On the 25th of April Frederick declined breakfast—evidence of something wrong with him. Lockwood, therefore, resolved to go up to a gorge he had seen the previous day, and there go into camp and lie over a day. Frederick could hardly walk, and hence rode when it was possible. Finding a snow-slope inside the hummocks, they made good progress and reached "Gorge Rest" in one hour. In the mean while the sun came out, and the air became calm and warm, affording a good opportunity for drying wet clothes and bags. Lockwood gave a drink of brandy to Frederick, and then displayed Mrs. Greely's silk flag, as they had now attained a point higher than any American had before reached. In the afternoon, Jewell and Ralston succeeded in finding Beaumont's *cache* farther on, and, as proof of their discovery, brought back a can of rum marked "Bloodhound," the name of his sledge. It was about there that his first man was sent back with the scurvy. Afterward, when all but two had the disease, they had to go on or die in the traces.

On the 26th, Frederick was well, otherwise he would have been sent back. They built a *cache* and left one day's ration for men and dogs; also, to lighten load, snow-shoes, head and foot gear, blankets, indeed everything they could do without. They reached Stanton Gorge, dropped load, and Frederick was sent back with the team for the rest of their stuff. The men came in without doubling, having also found Beaumont's *cache* on a high hill. They all agreed that such unnecessary labor was enough to bring on the scurvy. They found there fifty-six pounds of pemmican, ten pounds of bacon, and a large box containing bread, potatoes, chocolate, tea, sugar, onion-powder, and stearine used for fuel, all of which were taken on to Cape Bryant. Beyond this point, to Cape Stanton, their route lay along the foot of steep snow-slopes beneath the cliffs, with lines of floe-bergs and hummocks outside, and was exceedingly rough. Lockwood and Frederick, after crossing Hand Bay, passed the men moving slowly and laboriously. Their troubles were increased by frequent upsettings of the sledges along the slope and by the friction of the splintered bottoms owing to the runners cutting through.

It was not till 8 P.M. that they all reached Frankfield Bay, and, thoroughly tired out, went into camp, after an advance of nine miles in thirteen hours.

Here they cached one day's rations for all, and then traveled along the low shore which skirted the base of Mount Lowe, and came upon the snow-covered surface of Frankfield Bay, a small and pretty harbor surrounded by steep mountains. Beyond this bay, they crossed a spit of land, going up a steep slope, and down another equally steep at a run. There they threw off a half load and went back for the rest. Afterward all proceeded with half-loads, Lockwood taking his post at the traces and pulling with the men. After a while he dropped off to help Frederick, while the men went on to Cape Bryant. Taking advantage of an interval of leisure, he got out the lamp and made just two pint-cups of tea for Frederick and himself. "Of all the occasions," he says, "when a draught of tea tasted particularly good, none like this lingers in my memory. Though without milk and with very little sugar, it tasted like nectar. In fact, as the gods never undertook any Arctic sledge-journeys, their nectar was not half so delicious."

On the 27th, Lockwood shot five ptarmigans or Arctic quails. Sitting on a floe-berg, they were scarcely distinguishable from the snow. The traveling on that day was on the whole fair; yet so heavily were the sledges loaded, and so much worn, that when, after making fifteen miles in twelve hours, they reached Cape Bryant at 8.30 P. M., both men and dogs were nearly exhausted. To add to their joylessness, they had to be very sparing of their rations. Cracker-dust was with them the grand panacea for short rations. This went into every stew, was mixed with their tea, and was even taken alone, and found to be very *filling*. By its aid, they persuaded themselves that the short allowance was a hearty repast.

On the 28th, Brainard and others made an unsuccessful search for a *cache* left there by Beaumont, but got a good view of Cape Britannia from a high cliff. Lockwood and Jewell also saw it from a height back of the camp. Beaumont had seen Cape Britannia, but never reached it. He got only thirty miles farther than Cape Bryant; that is, to the opposite side of the fiord which here appears, and which they called "Beaumont's Fiord." While Frederick brought up some stores left behind, Lockwood busied himself with many details connected with his further advance toward the north, for now his supports were to leave him and return to the Boat Camp, while Brainard, Frederick, and himself, with the dog-sledge, were to proceed alone.

Lockwood now satisfied himself by a careful inspection of the sledges that the supporting party could go no farther, especially as some of the men were suffering with snow-blindness. He therefore broke up one of the sledges, and with it repaired the remaining drag-sledge and the dog-sledge. Brainard, also suffering with snow-blindness, remained in the tent, while Lockwood with the others built a *cache* and deposited therein the Beaumont stores and such others as they could not take on. Food for the return party to Boat Camp having been dropped *en route*, he decided to take with him twenty-five days' rations. Hence their advance must be limited to the time these rations would feed them, going northeast and returning to Cape Bryant.

He started, therefore, with—

Men-rations, weighing 230 pounds.
Dog-pemmican, weighing 300 ”
Equipments, weighing   176   ”
Dog-sledge, weighing   <u>80</u>   ”
Total   786   ”

or about 98 pounds to each dog.

The weather, though cold, causing some frost-bites, had been beautiful during their stay here. The men had done their parts well, and had endured uncomplainingly much hard work, hardship, and exposure. The supporting party left at 4 P. M., after hearty hand-shaking and wishing good luck to Lockwood, Brainard, and Frederick, leaving the three lonely and depressed on that desolate shore.

And now, as the returning party disappeared in the distance, the explorers turned toward Cape Britannia. Although they started with a very heavy load, yet the traveling was fine, and, all three pushing, they made rapid progress, having Cape May directly ahead and across the fiord. The dogs seemed to object to going over the sea, and kept deflecting constantly to the right, the only difficulty arising from the deepening of the snow and its becoming soft. When they got stuck, Brainard would pull at the traces, while Lockwood would push at the upstand, and Frederick divide his energies between helping them and inducing the dogs to do so.

At 1 A. M. on April 30th, they camped on the fiord, well satisfied with their advance of sixteen miles in eight hours without once doubling.

Moving off at 5 P. M. with full load, they had not gone far before they were forced to throw off half of it, and soon with this half they found it difficult to get along, for the sledge would sink down to the slats and the men to their knees through the deep, soft snow. Lockwood could fully appreciate poor Brainard's efforts and labors in a fiord at the southwest, when he crawled through snow waist-deep, and on hands and knees, for two hundred yards. At 9 P. M. they came to hummocks, pitched tent, threw off load, and, while Lockwood prepared supper, the others went back with the team to bring up what they had thrown off. They had to adhere strictly to the allowance, for they had rations for just so many days. They had advanced six miles in seven hours and three quarters.

They started again the next morning with full load, but soon had to pitch off again. Had better traveling, on the whole, than on the previous day, though meeting with ranges of old floes and hummocks filled in with snow. Shortly after midnight, they came abreast Cape May, the desire of Beaumont, but which, with his crew broken down with scurvy, and with heavy sledges loaded down with all kinds of equipments, he never attained. The party pitched tent near an immense floe extending as far back as the eye could reach. Brainard and Frederick went back for the dismounted stuff, while Lockwood turned cook again, the first thing being to pulverize a lot of ice and set it on the lamp to melt. Cape Britannia and Beaumont Island were very distinctly seen, the latter from refraction double. Their allowance of alcohol was a constant source of trouble. They could not afford meat for both breakfast and supper, hence their supper consisted of tea, cracker-dust, and bean-stew. Advanced twelve miles in fourteen hours.

Lockwood and Brainard now took turns in cooking, Frederick being excused. The two former did not sleep well, and, as usual, the Esquimaux blew his trumpet loudly, but not sweetly. They left at 7 P.M. with full load, but as usual threw off a portion, leaving Brainard with it. Toward midnight they came to an open crack in the ice ten feet wide, through which sea-water could be seen below, and had to follow it several hundred yards before coming to a crossing. Thinking this a favorable chance to get a deep-sea sounding, they threw off the load, and Frederick went back for Brainard and the balance of the stores, while Lockwood got into a sleeping-bag and read "King Lear" until their return. In sounding, they ran out all the line they had, then four coils of seal-thongs, then some rope, and finally Frederick's dog-whip, and got no bottom at eight hundred and twenty feet. They began to haul up after debating whether they should not risk the dog-traces, when, presto! the rope broke, and all below was lost. Leaving their treasures in the deep, they moved on with half-load over a low line of hummocky ice having the same general direction as the crack, namely, toward Beaumont's Island. Beyond was an unbroken field of snow extending apparently to Cape Britannia. Ice being required for supper, they went into camp on the hummocks, going back, however, for the stores left behind, having advanced eight miles in ten hours.

After taking bearings, they broke camp at 4 P. M., and, with a full load, proceeded over the level snowfield, broken here and there only by hummocks trending in a curve toward Cape Britannia. Until midnight the snow-crust sustained the sledge, but after that, failing to do so, they had to reduce load. Wind and snow coming on, they camped near a small ice-mound, after advancing fourteen miles in fourteen hours, and again brought up the stores left behind.

The next morning proved clear and calm, and gave them a full view of the long-desired cape, which they reached at 8 P. M., pitching tent on the ice-foot —four miles in one hour and a half. Lockwood had read so much of scurvy, deep snows, etc., as associated with sledge-journeys in the experience of the English expedition, that he had come to regard them as inseparable from such enterprises. Yet here they were, at a point which Beaumont saw only from afar, without the first and without serious difficulty from the others. Cape Britannia had been the *ultima Thule* of Beaumont's hopes, and quite as far as Lieutenant Greely expected Lockwood to reach. But he was able to go much farther, and would do so. He built a cairn, and deposited a record of their journey to date, also rations for five days for use on their return, the spare sledge-runner, and everything they could do without. Leaving Frederick to see that the dogs did not eat up the tent and everything in it, Lockwood and Brainard climbed the adjacent mountain, two thousand and fifty feet high, to view the magnificent prospect spread out before them from that point. "We seemed," Lockwood writes, "to be on an island terminating some miles to the north in a rocky headland. To the northeast, seemingly twenty miles away, was a dark promontory stretching out into the Polar Ocean, and limiting the view in that direction. Intermediate, were several islands separated by vast, dreary fiords, stretching indefinitely southward. Extending halfway round the horizon, the eye rested on nothing but the ice of the Polar Sea; in-shore, composed of level floes, but beyond, of ridges and masses of the roughest kind of ice. The whole panorama was grand, but dreary and desolate in the extreme. After erecting a monument, we were glad to escape the cold wind by returning."

While here, Lockwood took several astronomical observations. They broke camp at 7 P. M., and traveled northward over smooth ice free from snow, to the promontory, where they came in sight of the distant headland northeast, which they had seen from the mountain-top. Hearing a low, moaning sound, and looking to the north, they saw a line of hummocks, and near it their old acquaintance, the tidal crack, stretching in one direction toward Beaumont Island, and in the other, curving toward Black Cape, as Lockwood named the headland northeast of them. Repairing their sledge, which had given way, they proceeded toward this headland, having fairly good traveling though somewhat obstructed by soft and deep snow, and camped at midnight near a hummock and not far from the crack, from which Frederick tried, without success, to get a seal. This would have relieved his mortified feelings at the loss of a ptarmigan he had shot at the cape, and which Ritenbank had stolen. Took observations for latitude and longitude before turning into their sleeping-bags. Advanced eleven miles in five hours.

The observations were repeated next morning, and they then went on their course. After going a considerable distance, they halted to rest and to view the tide-crack, now near them and about one hundred yards across, filled in here and there with young ice or detached masses. This crack was incomprehensible, differing from those seen in the straits, which were near shore and so narrow as to attract little attention. Frederick gave Lockwood to understand by signs and gestures that after a while the ice outside, or north of the crack, would move oft seaward. Resuming their way, they soon after passed Blue Cape, and thence crossing a small fiord got to Black Cape, the bold, rocky headland they had seen from the mountain. Beyond Black Cape, and in the same general direction, but seen indistinctly, appeared a dark, rocky cape, which Lockwood called Distant Cape, because, seeming so near, it was yet so far, as they afterward found. At Black Cape were seen bear-tracks, also those of the fox, hare, and lemming, in great numbers. The tide-crack here came near the shore, and then extended directly across to the next cape. The ice along shore indicated having sustained enormous pressure. Great bergs and hummocks, weighing thousands of tons, had been pushed upon the ice-foot like pebbles.

The ice-foot offering better traveling, they followed that course, though it took them somewhat away from Distant Cape. Leaving it, they crossed what seemed to them a little bay, but it took them one hour and a half to reach the cape on the farther side. Seeing a large fiord intervening between them and Distant Cape which they had wished to reach before encamping, they gave up the effort and pitched their tent. Soon after, Frederick shot a hare, but only wounding him, they had to expend all their remaining strength in running him down. But food was now everything, and they spared neither the hare nor themselves. They called that point Rabbit Point, in memory of the friend who served them a good turn. Advanced seventeen miles in ten hours.

Having, on account of a snow-storm, failed to get the sun on the south meridian, Lockwood waited until it should come round to the north meridian, as this matter of observations was important, and difficult to attend to *en route*. In the mean time, they cached some rations. Saw some ptarmigans, but failed to shoot them. Left near midnight, and having crossed the hummocks thrust in against all these capes, reached the level surface of an immense bay which they were two and one quarter hours in crossing, after untold labor and fatigue, through deep snow, so wet that they seemed to be wading through soft clay. They reached the opposite shore, bathed in perspiration, Lockwood going in advance to encourage the dogs. Sometimes they went down waist-deep. The mass of hummocks came up so near the cliffs as to force the travelers outside. Still, Distant Cape was farther on, with a fiord intervening. At four o'clock, they reached this long-sought point, and looked ahead to see what lay beyond. Away off in the same general direction (northeast) was seen another headland, separated from them by a number of fiords and capes, which lay on an arc connecting Distant Cape with that in the far distance. Inclining to the right, they made their way toward one of these intermediate capes. Sometimes seeing it and sometimes not, they finally reached it at 6 A. M., and, being unable to see anything ahead, went into camp. Soon afterward a pyramidal island loomed up through the storm in the northeast. They enjoyed part of their rabbit for supper, almost raw, for they had no alcohol to waste on luxuries, and carefully laid away the other half for further indulgence. But Ritenbank saw that half rabbit stowed away, and he too liked rabbit, as will be seen. After supper Lockwood made observations, and of trials and tribulations this was not the least. Face chilled, fingers frozen, and sun so low as to require him to lie in the snow; the sun like a grease-spot in the heavens, and refusing to be reflected; snow-drifts over artificial horizon cover; sextant mirrors becoming obscure, vernier clouded, tangent-screw too stiff to work; then, when one had nearly secured a contact, some dog interposing his ugly body or stirring up the snow; such were some of the difficulties to be overcome. Still, these observations must be made, and carefully and correctly made, or otherwise the chief value of the expedition would be lost. They secured double sets of observations here, which delayed them, but got off near midnight from this cape, which Lockwood called Low Point, and made good time toward the dim headland at the northeast. In two hours and a half they reached the cape, which he named Surprise, because they came upon it unexpectedly looming up through the gloom. Beyond and to the right was seen through the storm a dome-capped island, the inevitable inlet intervening. The traveling proving good, they reached it at four, and found it to be the end of a long line of grand, high, rocky cliffs, bearing far to the south.

The ice-foot here being free from snow, the dogs took the sledge along at a trot, and the explorers rode by turns—the first time since leaving Boat Camp. The trend of the coast-line becoming nearly east, Lockwood began to think the time had come for leaving the coast and striking off directly toward the pole, as arranged for in his orders. As this was a matter requiring full consideration, he stopped to get an observation, but, defeated in this by the drifting snow, they went into camp at 6 A. M., having advanced seventeen miles in less than seven hours.

After sleeping, Lockwood rose to take observations. While so doing, and hence out of the tent, he heard a noise in it, and suspected mischief. Sure enough, there was that old thief, Ritenbank, coolly eating up the remains of the rabbit they had kept for a second feast. A dash and a blow, and the dog scampered off, dropping part of the animal in his flight. They had reached the state of not being particular about what they ate, so they gathered up the remains and ate them on the spot.

Resuming their journey at 1 A. M., they traveled under a long line of high cliffs, with hills in the rear. The travel was excellent, but the weather abominable—high winds, with falling and drifting snow. After three hours of progress in an easterly course, a headland was seen obliquely to their left, between which and themselves lay a wide fiord. After an observation of the sun, they struck directly across this fiord for the headland in question, which they finally reached after repeatedly losing themselves in the mist and gloom. Here they stopped awhile to eat pemmican and view the surroundings. Found many rabbit-tracks, but saw none of the animals. In Arctic traveling, one craves warm meat, but seldom gets any but that which is frozen. Continuing along this coast over a good ice-foot, they were pleased to see on their left a small island with a high, narrow ledge, a few hundred yards long. This they reached and went to the north side or end of it. Mist and snow shutting in the land farther on, and also that already passed, they camped, having advanced twenty-two miles in nine and a half hours.

Finding traveling so troublesome in the storm, and much difficulty in getting observations, Lockwood resolved to remain there for better weather, all sleeping as much and eating as little as possible. Indeed, Brainard agreed with Lockwood that, if the easterly trend of the coast should continue, they had better spend their time in going directly north over the sea. On the 11th, it being still stormy and no other land in sight, they remained in their sleeping-bags on the island, which from its shape was first called "Shoe Island," but afterward "Mary Murray." All of them suffered greatly with cold feet in the mean while; and, although Lockwood's feet were wrapped in blankets, furs, and socks, they were like lumps of ice. To husband their few rations, they had eaten very little of late, and doubtless to this may be attributed their cold feet. The dogs were ravenous for food. When feeding-time came, it was amid blows from the men and fights among the dogs that the distribution was made. Old Howler was conspicuous on these occasions. That he might secure all he could, he bolted ball after ball of the frozen mass, and then would wander around, uttering the most unearthly howls while the mass was melting in his stomach. He was, indeed, a character. He had an air of utter weariness and dejection, as well he might, for who can be more miserable than the dethroned monarch, jeered, cuffed, and condemned by his late subjects? One day one of the dogs swallowed a live lemming, and the little animal went squealing all the way down to the corporation.

The weather clearing up a little the next morning, Lockwood took sun observations, and soon after saw a cape with very high land behind it, at the northeast. But the storm setting in again, they could not attempt to cross the mouth of the deep fiord intervening between them and the cape until nearly two hours after midnight. The traveling being good, and aided by a high wind, they made good time across the fiord toward the cape, alternately visible and invisible, and reached it in two hours. This cape proved to be the extremity of a line of high, rocky cliffs, stretching toward the southeast. Here they found the ice-foot entirely obstructed by lines of floe-bergs and hummocks pressed up nearly to the foot of the cliff, and to add to their difficulty, the tide-crack ran here close to the cape. With great labor they got the dogs and sledge upon a hummock, thence along its surface, using the axe, and finally lowered them down again, and, by a bridge over the crack, gained a level floe half a mile beyond the cape. There, finding a branch crack twelve or fifteen feet wide, Frederick went forth to seek a crossing, while Lockwood and Brainard obtained a peep at the sun for position. The fog rising, the grandest view they had yet seen was suddenly disclosed. To their right were seen the high cliffs connected with the cape just passed, bending to the southeast to form an inlet. Away beyond and across this inlet, and east of them, was the farther shore—a line of very high cliffs, terminating in a bold headland northeast of their position. Back of the cape and cliffs, the land became higher and higher, till, just east of the travelers, stood a peak apparently four thousand feet high. Between them and the cliffs below the peak was seen an island of pyramidal shape and quite high. The explorers made good time toward it, over a level floe, as some hummocks and tide-cracks at the mouth of the inlet prevented them from going direct to the cape. Thence, after a short rest and a relish of pemmican, they took their way toward the cape, now standing nearly north of them. Soon the snow became so deep and soft that the sledge often sank below the slats, the dogs to their bellies, and the men to their knees. Fortunately, the load was very light, and yet, had not the deep snow soon after become dry and feathery, they could not have proceeded. It was then that Lockwood promised himself never to undertake another sledge-journey, a resolve afterward easily forgotten when in camp with a full stomach. Time, rest, plenty to eat, and a good smoke, sometimes make philosophers, was the reflection recorded. About noon, after changing their course around an easterly bend of the cliff, they came to what might be regarded as the northern extremity of the cape, beyond which lay the inevitable fiord. Here they camped on the ice-foot, below a mass of picturesquely colored rocky cliffs, and essayed, but failed, to get observations. Their advance was sixteen miles in ten hours.

On the 14th of May, occurred a storm so violent that it seemed as if the tent must be blown down. Ritenbank took advantage of it to burrow under the tent and lay hold of a bag of pemmican, but a timely blow on his snout "saved their bacon." After discussion with Brainard, Lockwood concluded to go no farther, as their remaining rations would hardly suffice to enable them satisfactorily to determine their present position. While waiting for the sun that this might be done, they improvised a checker-board from the chopping-board, and played some games. After a while, finding that the cliffs somewhat interfered with the observations, they moved the tent farther west, stopping to build a cairn, large and conspicuous, and depositing a full record of their journey and a thermometer. This cairn stood on a little shelf or terrace below the top of the cliff. Brainard also cut "XXX Bitters" on the highest rock of the cliff he could reach, Lockwood telling him he only wanted to get a bottle for nothing on the strength of his advertisement. They were engaged until midnight, chiefly in taking observations and in collecting specimens of rocks and vegetation. Some snow-birds were seen.

The next morning the weather became warm, beautiful, and delightful, the sun bright and sky clear, and there was no wind—surely a bit of sunshine in a shady place.

Taking Observations at Lockwood Island.

They took advantage of this to bring out hand-gear, foot-gear, bags, and rubber blankets to dry, everything having been damp or wet for nearly a week. Lockwood and Brainard got but a few short naps after supper, for it was necessary for one of them to be awake to insure their getting up at the right time to take "double altitudes," etc. They secured a complete set of observations, thirty-six in all. A few hours later, Lockwood and Brainard started to make the ascent of the cliffs and of the height beyond. They gained a considerable elevation, and stood on a little plateau overlooking both sides of the promontory, the sea, and a large extent of mountainous country to the south thickly covered with snow. Lockwood unfurled Mrs. Greely's pretty little silk flag to the breeze, and felt very proud that, on the 15th day of May, 1882, it waved in a higher latitude than was ever before reached by man. By careful astronomical observations under peculiarly favorable circumstances, they found themselves in LATITUDE EIGHTY-THREE DEGREES AND TWENTY-FOUR AND A HALF MINUTES NORTH, LONGITUDE FORTY DEGREES AND FORTY-SIX AND A HALF MINUTES WEST OF GREENWICH, thus surpassing the English, who sent the Nares Expedition of 1875-'76, costing upward of a million dollars, for the express purpose of reaching the north pole, and which expedition sent its chief sledge-party directly north over the ice for the purpose of making *latitude alone*. The view from their lofty station was grand beyond description. At their feet, toward the east, was another of those innumerable fiords, a bald headland forming its farther cape, bearing northeast. Seemingly projecting from its foot was a low point of land, doubtless separated from another by still another fiord. This was as far as Lockwood could see in that direction—probably fifteen miles. Thence round toward the north and in the direction of Cape Britannia lay the vast Polar Sea, covered with ice and desolate in the extreme. Toward the south lay a vast panorama of snow-capped mountains, so overlapping and merging one into another that it was impossible to distinguish the topography of the country. They stayed on the top only twenty minutes, and at 4.50 reached camp again, greatly to the delight of Frederick. He had seemed a good deal "down at the mouth" of late, which Brainard thought was caused by their long distance from home and the absence of dog-food and "skaffer." Hastily packing up their small load, they started on their return at 5.30 P. M. Though taking a more direct course across the first fiord, they met with soft snow, which was very tiresome to pass through. The weather now commenced to cloud up again, threatening another storm. It was very fortunate that they reached their farthest just in time to take advantage of the thirty hours of fine weather. However, they were now homeward bound, and did not care for storms or anything else, provided they could "*move on*," nor did they require any policeman to help them in that particular.

And now that Lockwood is returning from his special expedition in safety and good health, a few additional facts and a passing reflection on his exploit will not be out of place. Lieutenant Lockwood's motives in undertaking this special expedition, in which he was so successful, he explained in these words: "My great wish is to accomplish something on the north coast of Greenland which will reflect credit on myself and on the expedition. But there are many ifs in the way—many visible contingencies on which success depends, as well as many invisible ones which have never suggested themselves. Among the former, scurvy stands like a giant, and if this giant attacks us, far from accomplishing anything, we may not ourselves get back." As we think of Lockwood, at the end of his journey, with only two companions, in that land of utter desolation, we are struck with admiration at the courage and manly spirit by which he was inspired. Biting cold, fearful storms, gloomy darkness, the dangers of starvation and sickness, all combined to block his icy pathway, and yet he persevered and accomplished his heroic purpose, thereby winning a place in history of which his countrymen may well, and will be, proud to the end of time. Of all the heroic names that have blossomed on the charts of the Arctic seas during the present century, there is not one that will hereafter be mentioned with more pride and enthusiasm than that identified with Lockwood Island, memorable as the nearest point to the north pole ever reached by man.

XII
FROM LOCKWOOD ISLAND TO LADY FRANKLIN BAY.

When returning to Lady Franklin Bay, Lockwood and his companions reached Shoe Island shortly after midnight. They deposited a record in the cairn there, and proceeded to the cape west of the island, where they went into camp, after a retreat of twenty miles in eight hours. Lockwood suffered much from his eyes, having evidently strained them while endeavoring to see the sun during the late stormy weather. The cold food, upon which alone they could depend, seemed to weaken the stomachs of all the party, and yet they plodded on. At Storm Cape, they left the grand line of cliffs behind, and took a compass course across the great fiord, amid a storm as before when they crossed that inlet. As usual, the dogs thought they knew best, and Frederick thought he knew best, so the compass received little consideration, and they inclined too much to the left, being three hours and twenty minutes in crossing. They stopped at a cairn and deposited a record. In another hour they reached Pocket Bay, and in another, Dome Cape, and then, crossing the inlet, went into camp. "Skaffer" was soon ready, cold chocolate, and a stew with lumps of ice floating round in it, particularly unfortunate after a march which was perhaps the most uncomfortable of the trip. It had been blowing and snowing all day directly in their faces—very severe on snow-blind eyes, which it was necessary in crossing the fiords to keep open in order to see the way. In addition to this, strange to say, Lockwood suffered with cold hands. Generally, while traveling, they were warm enough, and only got cold when stopping; but on that day they were aching with cold a great part of the time. The dogs had eaten up his seal-skin mits some time before, and the woolen ones gave little protection against the storm, with the mercury 30° below zero. They found the ice-foot now generally covered with snow, but they retreated twenty-seven miles in eight hours and forty minutes. Left camp shortly after 5 P. M., and, passing Cape Surprise, struck directly across the fiord for Distant Cape. When opposite their old camp at Low Point, a glacier was seen in the interior, a green wall of ice lying at the foot of what looked like a low, dome-shaped hill, but which must have been a mass of ice covered with snow, as is all the interior of this country. The travel over the floe was quite good, but when just beyond Distant Cape, they found themselves in the deep snow of the wide fiord to the west of it, a part of the route they had been dreading for some time. They finally, however, reached the farther side. The dogs must have smelled the pemmican in *cache* there, for, during the last two hundred yards, they bent all their energies to the work and seemed wild to get ashore. They pulled the sledge through a fringe of hummocky ice at the coast in a way that proved how they *could* pull when they set their hearts on business. The weather during the day was variable. When they started, it was quite thick, and the wind blew strongly in their faces, making the traveling very disagreeable; but toward the latter part of the march, the wind died away and the sun appeared. The traveling was better than when outward bound, the late storm having improved it very much. Brainard did all the cooking, Lockwood chopping the ice and assisting in various ways. They got off a little after six, and in two hours were at Black Cape. Here they stopped awhile and built a cairn, and at Blue Cape stopped again. The next four and a half hours they pursued their monotonous course across the floe, Lockwood indulging in these reflections: "What thoughts one has when thus plodding along! Home and everything there, and the scenes and incidents of early youth! Home, again, when this Arctic experience shall be a thing of the past! But it must be confessed, and lamentable, it is, as well as true, that the reminiscences to which my thoughts oftenest recur on these occasions are connected with eating—the favorite dishes I have enjoyed—while in dreams of the future, my thoughts turn from other contemplations to the discussion of a beefsteak, and, equally absurd, to whether the stew and tea at our next supper will be hot or cold."

They next camped some miles from North Cape, opposite the immense fiord there, which runs inland an interminable distance without visible land at its head. Lockwood had intended going up this fiord to what seemed like the opening of a channel on the south side of Cape Britannia, but the uncertainty and their fatigue finally induced him to continue the way they had come, the weather being delightful. Ritenbank went about all day with his head and tail down, perhaps repenting his numerous thefts. Advanced seventeen miles in eight hours.

Left camp at 6 P.M., and in about three hours reached North Cape, where they stopped some time to take a sub-polar observation, making its latitude 82° 51'. Cape Britannia was reached without event, and there they stopped long enough to get the rations left in *cache*, and deposit a record in the cairn; then continued on the floe a half-mile to get out of the shadow of the mountain. At the cairn they got the snow-shoes left there, and the spare sledge-runner. They also collected some specimens of the vegetation and rocks, and saw traces of the musk-ox, showing that these animals wander even this far north. They saw also some snow-birds. They had thought that when they reached Cape Britannia they would feel near home; but now having reached it, the station seemed as far off as at any point they had left behind, and they could not rest until Cape Bryant was reached.

The sun was very bright and warm when they left camp at 9.50 P.M., but a heavy fog hung like a curtain on the horizon, and shut out the land all around. They were, in fact, traveling on the Polar Sea, out of sight of land. Shortly after starting, Lockwood put on snow-shoes to try them, and found immense relief at once. He blamed himself every day for a week for not having tried them during the journey out, and thus saved himself many hours of the most fatiguing travel through deep snow. Brainard, seeing the advantage, put on the other pair, and from that time there was nothing about which they were so enthusiastic as the snow-shoes. They afterward wore them more or less every day. At 6 A. M. they went into camp on the floe. The fog by this time had disappeared, and everything was singularly bright and clear. Advanced sixteen miles in eight hours, and got off again a little after 8 A. M.

It was a beautiful day, calm and clear, and the sun was really too warm for dogs and men. They got along very well, however, on the snow-shoes, and one of the men keeping ahead to encourage the dogs and make a straight course, they finally reached, at the place they had crossed before, their old friend, the tidal crack, now frozen over. They lunched regularly every day on pemmican and hard bread, and rested whenever tired. A beautiful parhelion was seen, one of the most complete yet observed, in the perfection of its circles and the brightness of its colors. The blue, yellow, and orange were very distinct. They went into camp after four, the weather cloudy and threatening snow, having advanced sixteen miles in eight hours. They left again at 8.40 P. M. Snow falling, and no land being in sight, they kept near the right course by means of the compass. Their course was north-west (magnetic), the variation being in the neighborhood of ninety degrees. Went into camp near St. George's Fiord at 4.40 A. M., suffering a good deal from snow-blindness afterward. During the march were troubled very little, strange to say. Rations were now getting low. The snow was very soft, and, owing to this and the warm sun, the dogs "complained" a good deal. Advanced sixteen miles in eight hours. Started off again at 8.40 P.M., reached shore shortly after twelve, about three quarters of a mile short of Cape Bryant, and, following the coast, pitched tent at the old camping-ground. After visiting the cairn on the hill, they determined to make up arrears by having a royal feast—anticipated for many days. "How nice that English bacon must be! How superior that English pemmican to the abominable lime-juice pemmican!" Brainard made a generous stew out of the aforesaid, with a liberal allowance of desiccated potatoes, etc., and they "pitched in!" But oh! what disappointment! Before eating a half-dozen spoonfuls they came to a dead halt, and looked at each other. Even Frederick stopped and gazed. The dish was absolutely nauseating. "Oft expectation fails, and most where most it promises." Fortunately, there was left there a tin of frozen musk-ox meat, with other stores rendered surplus by the supporting party being able to go no farther. After this *feast* on the

English stores, they confined themselves to the musk-ox. The English pemmican, though a little musty, when eaten cold was quite palatable. This and the bacon were each put up in metallic cases. The bacon they subsequently found to be inclosed in *tallow*, and this it was that made their feast so disappointing. After this they all went to look for Lieutenant Beaumont's *cache*, left here when his party was disabled by scurvy. The search was unsuccessful, although they traveled the coast for two miles and a half, advancing twelve miles in four hours. Getting up at twelve, Lockwood and Brainard went out to the tide-crack about half a mile from shore, and, by means of a rope and stone, undertook to get a set of tidal observations. They kept up the observations for nearly twelve hours, and then becoming satisfied that their arrangements did not register the tide, owing to the depth, currents, etc., gave it up, much disappointed. All their work went for nothing. These observations made their eyes much worse, and both suffered with snow-blindness all the rest of the way.

While thus occupied, the dogs took advantage of their absence to visit the *cache* and eat up part of a sack of hard bread and half a dozen shot-gun cartridges—the shot and the brass being rather indigestible. They left camp after midnight and a beautiful morning followed, calm and clear, the sun unpleasantly warm; and no wonder, since Lockwood was wearing three heavy flannel shirts, a chamois-skin vest, a vest of two thicknesses of blanket (double all round), a knitted guernsey and canvas frock, besides two or three pairs of drawers, etc.

They tramped along on snow-shoes, and a couple of hours after starting, Brainard, who was on the hill-side to the left, discovered, with his one unbandaged eye, relics of Beaumont—an old Enfield rifle, a pole shod with iron, a cross-piece of a sledge, three or four articles of underwear, some cartridges, sewing-thread and thimble, and the remains of a shoe with a wooden sole about an inch thick. Other articles mentioned by Lieutenant Beaumont in his journal were not to be found. They may have been carried off by animals or buried in the snow near by. The articles found were in a little bare mound near the ice-foot. "Poor Beaumont! how badly he must have felt when he passed along there with most of his party down with scurvy, dragging their heavy sledge and heavier equipments!" Farther on, Lockwood shot a ptarmigan on top of a large floe-berg thirty feet high, and, by taking advantage of a snow-drift and doing some "boosting," they secured the bird. They stopped at *cache* No. 3 (near Frankfield Bay) and took out what the supporting party had left there. Gave the dogs the lime-juice pemmican and ground beans, but it was only by seeming to favor first one dog and then another that they were induced to eat it, thus illustrating the advantage of their "dog-in-the-manger" spirit. Went into camp on the east shore of Hand Bay.

Their buffalo sleeping-bag now began to feel too warm, but was always delightfully soft and dry. Eyes painful. Advanced twelve miles in ten hours. After crossing Hand Bay they made a short stop at Cape Stanton. The Grinnell coast now became very distinct, and seemed home-like. They could see Cape Joseph Henry, or what they took for that headland. The floes off shore, consisting of alternate floes crossed by ridges of hummocks, made very laborious traveling. On reaching the *cache* near Stanton Gorge, they got the rations left there. The traveling continued very difficult and tiresome. On reaching the Black Horn Cliffs, they decided, as their old tracks were entirely obliterated, to follow along under the cliffs, instead of taking the wide *détour* they had made going out. They got along pretty well for a while, and then reached a mass of hummocks and rubble-ice. There they found a relic of the past—a towel which the men had used to wipe the dishes, and had lost or abandoned. By dint of hard work they got through this bad ice, crossed the smooth, level floe adjoining, and then came to the next patch of rubble-ice. After proceeding through this some distance, the sledge needing relashing, Lockwood went on alone with the axe, making a road as he went. Found the site of their old camp on the shore, but, as the snow slope there had become impassable, he kept along the coast on the floe and finally found a landing several miles to the west. Sledge and all got here at eight o'clock, and they continued on over the snow slopes, passing the remains of the "Nares" sledge and reaching Drift Point, where they went into camp alongside a big floe-berg, with lots of icicles upon it waiting for them, having advanced twenty-two and a half miles in ten hours. Finding strong winds and snow from the west, they delayed starting till almost midnight. The ice-foot along this low, sloping shore being excellent, they made good time, in an hour reaching the place of their first camp on this coast. The melting of the floe-bergs and the fall of the snow had so changed the general aspect, that the place was hardly recognizable. At 2 A. M. they came opposite the break in the cliff where they had entered on the coast in April. They soon made out the dark object seen previously from this point to be a cairn, and discovered a small bay which they knew must be Repulse Harbor. Crossing this bay, they reached the cairn at three o'clock. It was a tremendous affair, and the tin can inside was full of papers by Beaumont, Dr. Coppinger, and others. As a cold wind was blowing, Lockwood made a short-hand copy of the documents and left the originals.

Lockwood's eyes filled with tears as he read the last postscript of the several which followed the main record of poor Beaumont. Sitting on these bare rocks amid snow and wind, with a desolate coast-line on one side, and the wide, dreary straits on the other, he could well appreciate what Beaumont's feelings must have been when he reached here with his party all broken down with scurvy, and, after trying to cross the straits and failing on account of open water, had no other recourse but to try and reach Thank-God Harbor. His last postscript reads thus:

"Repulse Harbor Depot, June 13, 1876.—Three of us have returned from my camp, half a mile south, to fetch the remainder of the provisions. D —— has failed altogether this morning. Jones is much worse, and can't last more than two or three days. Craig is nearly helpless. Therefore we can't hope to reach Polaris Bay without assistance. Two men can't do it. So will go as far as we can and live as long as we can. God help us!
(Signed)   "L. A. BEAUMONT."

He and Gray were the only ones left, and both shortly discovered scorbutic symptoms.

Chilled through, Lockwood now continued along the coast to the west, following the ice-foot under a grand line of cliffs. After a while, they came to a narrow break or cleft in the cliffs, the gateway of a small mountain-torrent. It was like a winding and dark alley in a city, with vertical sides rising to the height of several hundred feet. Entering it, they presently came to an immense snow-drift, probably fifty or more feet high and filling up the gorge like a barricade, with another a little beyond. They returned to the sledge, thoroughly satisfied that Beaumont never went through that place. About seven they came to what seemed to be the "Gap Valley" of the English, a wide, broad valley, extending due south about three miles to a ravine. They therefore turned off from the coast and followed it, encountering a good deal of deep snow and bare, stony spots. At 11 A. M. they camped in the ravine near its head, thoroughly tired out. They now had only one day's food left, and it behooved them to make Boat Camp in another march, even though fifty miles off. Advanced seventeen miles in eleven hours. The dogs for several days had been on short allowance, and during their sleep tore open the bag of specimen rocks and stones, but fortunately did not chew them up as they had done the cartridges.

Getting off at 3.29 and crossing the table-land, they struck a narrow gorge running precipitately down to Newman's Bay. At its head was a mountainous drift of snow, which they descended on the run; then came a number of smaller drifts, completely blocking up the gorge, over which they had to lower the sledge by hand. Near the bay, they discovered a singular snow-cave one hundred feet long, and occupying the entire bed of the stream, arched through its whole length by beautiful ribs of snow, from which depended delicate snow-crystals. The entrance was quite small, but inside, the roof was far above their heads. They lost sight of its picturesqueness in the thought of its fitness for the burrow of a sledge-party. This brought them on the smooth surface of the bay, with familiar landmarks before and around them—Cape Sumner, Cape Beechy, and far in the distance, Distant Point and the land near Franklin Bay. Looking back at the ravine from the bay, Lockwood felt sure no one would ever take this little, insignificant, narrow gully for the route of a sledge-party, and that no one traveling this, or the one they took going out, would ever take either again in preference to going round Cape Brevoort. They delayed along the shore of the bay almost an hour, leisurely building a cairn and viewing the scenery, and then going on, reached the farther side at eight o'clock, making their last final retreat of ten miles in five hours and a half. There was the whale-boat, and pitched alongside it, anchored down by stones and held by ropes, the six-man tent of the supporting party. Inside were Sergeants Lynn and Ralston, and Corporal Ellison, fast asleep. Lockwood had told Lynn to send back to Conger three of his party on reaching Boat Camp. The remaining three awaited his return. The work of pitching tent woke up the other party, and soon they heard the sound of the Polaris fog-horn (picked up near by), and saw three heads projecting from the tent, whose owners gave them a warm welcome, as well they might, after awaiting their return nearly a month at this place, the dreariest of all in that dreary region. The remaining stores were ransacked for a big feast, without regard to the rations. Corned and boiled beef, canned potatoes and beans, butter, milk, and canned peaches, made a meal fit for a king or for gods that had just experienced an Arctic sledge-journey. The monotonous life of these men had been varied only by a visit from two bears, and the arrival of Dr. Pavy—sent by Lieutenant Greely with some rations.

The news from the station was that Dr. Pavy with Sergeant Rice and Esquimaux Jans had got only as far as Cape Joseph Henry, when they were stopped by open water. Lockwood had taken it for granted that the doctor would attain Markham's latitude and excel his own. Lieutenant Greely had been west from Fort Conger on a trip of twelve days in the mountains, and had discovered a large lake with a river flowing out of it, which had no ice on its surface—something very wonderful. The vegetation had also shown a much milder atmosphere than anywhere else in these latitudes. Numerous Esquimaux relics had been found, and many musk-oxen seen.

Turning their backs on the Boat Camp, and with many loud blasts on the Polaris fog-horn, they started at 11.25 P. M. for Fort Conger.

The snow along the snow-slopes was badly drifted, but with so many to help, they got along without much delay and soon reached Cape Sumner. They found the rubble-ice south of that point worse than before, and here and there were little pools of water. The weather was very thick, the wind blowing and snow falling, and the farther side of the straits completely hidden, so that they went *via* the Gap, but there had to leave the shore and direct their course as well as possible by compass. Presently they could see neither shore, and got into a mass of rubble-ice, mixed with soft snow-drifts. Lynn and party (Ralston and Ellison) had not traveled any for so long that they began to get very much fatigued, and could not keep up with the sledge. They had not slept since the arrival at the Boat Camp, owing to the excitement of the occasion. The driving snow hurt their eyes, and they were a very sorry party. However, they kept on, and finally came in sight of the west coast, and some hours afterward, finding good floes to travel over, a little before noon reached the "tent on the straits"—about five miles from Cape Beechy—Ellison and Ralston completely exhausted.

En route again, they spread the American flag on a long pole and carried it thus till they reached the station. At the snow-house, where they remained some hours to rest and get something to eat, they found Ellis and Whistler, who had come up from Fort Conger to look out for the party.

All found their eyes more or less affected excepting Frederick. Ralston's were so bad that he was sent on in advance, led by Ellis. He walked almost the whole way with his eyes closed. Lynn held on to the upstanders of the sledge, and thus found his way.

On the first day of June, Ralston and Lynn went in advance, led by Ellis and Ellison. They could not see at all, and, as their guides carried the guns and each had his man made fast by a strap, they looked very much like a party of prisoners. At Watercourse Bay they met Lieutenant Greely, who had come out to meet them, and was well satisfied with the result of the expedition, and soon after they reached Fort Conger.

Lieutenant Lockwood not only received many hearty congratulations from his companions, but even the weather, as if in sympathy with the general gladness, became bright and cheerful. The important business of working out the latitude that had been attained was now proceeded with. Efforts were made to verify the prismatic compass which was serviceable, but had a limited range. Much of the ground around the station was bare of snow, and, as the temperature was rising rapidly, Lockwood felt as if he would like to be off again on a wild tramp. When he said something about certain sledge operations in the future, Greely replied, "If you are content to go, I will give you all the help I can."

XIII.
WAITING AND WATCHING.

To a man of Lockwood's character, the return to the station did not mean that idleness was to be the order of the day, and while yet suffering from rheumatic pains in his back, shoulders, legs, feet, and joints, he began to mark out a trip for himself through Lady Franklin Bay. In the mean time, some of the men were off trying to obtain fresh meat, Frederick killing a hare and Jans a seal weighing over five hundred pounds. Kislingbury amused himself with a pet owl, which delighted him with a present of eggs. On the 9th of June, the people at the station celebrated the birthday of their companion Long by a good dinner, and on the following day Lockwood, accompanied by his friends Brainard and Frederick, started with a dog-train for his proposed tramp. They made their first halts at Basil Norris Bay and at Sun Bay, and traveling over a level bed of what had once been a fiord, thence passed on to Stony Point, and then to Miller's Island, where they encamped. Although they saw a number of seals, they succeeded in killing only a couple of hares and a brace of brants. Their next stopping-place was Keppel's Head, the route being very wet, in fact, almost a continuous lake. Having nothing to wear but his moccasins, Lockwood's feet were saturated three minutes after starting, and became so cold that he thought they would freeze. The pools were sometimes so deep as to wet the load on the sledge. However, the dogs made good time, and they reached Keppel's Head at 11 P. M. Here the traveling became much better, and they were able to avoid a good many of the pools.

Passing Keppel's Head, they kept a sharp lookout for Hillock Depot, where Lieutenant Archer, R. N., had left a large number of rations. They searched for some time before finding any signs, but finally found the *cache*, and near by some pieces of United States hard bread, and a little bag of American tea. This was interesting, as proving that to have been the farthest that Long attained, although he claimed to have reached the head of the fiord. The unpleasant task then devolved on Lockwood of taking him down a peg or two. Lieutenant Archer was a week reaching this place, Hillock Depot, half-way up the fiord, which is about sixty miles long. The scenery is grand. High cliffs, generally nearly vertical, ran along the shores everywhere. Whenever they looked inland they saw a lofty mass of snow-covered mountains. All this was so common, however, in all the region, that it was only when *new* that it was appreciated. Lockwood and Brainard had a good laugh at Long's expense, and then turned into the two-man summer sleeping-bag, made of two blankets, trimmed off so as to weigh no more than necessary, and inclosed in another bag of light canvas. Their breakfast consisted of corned beef, baked beans, tea, hard bread, and butter—a very fine repast. Lockwood and Brainard both thought that this kind of traveling did not pay on a "picnic" excursion, but, as they had started to go to the head of the fiord, they did not like to turn back. The ice promised to be worse on their return, and this, and Lockwood's lame foot, and the lameness of one of the dogs, decided him to return. Leaving camp on return, they soon reached Keppel's Head, and afterward Basil Norris Bay, where they camped, and decided to remain a day or two and have a hunt for musk-oxen. Mud, water, and "sludge," as well as Lockwood's lameness, proved a drawback to his success; but Frederick returned from his tramp, bringing along a quarter of a musk-ox, having killed two and wounded a third, he said. They seemed to have cost two dozen cartridges, and he had probably stood off at a distance and bombarded them.

Brainard returned after him. He had been up the vale as far as the lake, and had seen a few geese and a rabbit. He brought back a "skua" bird and some Esquimaux relics; had seen several circles of stone, marking the summer camps of these people, and picked up a good many bones, etc. All had something to eat, when the two started out with the dog-team for the musk-oxen killed by Frederick. Then came on a heavy rain, lasting for several hours, while the snow and ice were fast disappearing. This was the first rain they had seen in the country.

During their absence from the station, to which they returned with their game, seven musk-oxen had been killed and four calves caught alive. The men had had an exciting time. The animals formed a hollow square with the calves inside, and did some charging before they were all down.

The calves had been put in a pen a short distance from the house, were very tame, and it was supposed little difficulty would be found in raising them. They ate almost anything.

On the 17th, Lockwood expressed his feelings as follows: "I find myself oppressed with *ennui*, caused, I suppose, by the present monotonous existence following the activity of my life since the early spring."

On the 22d of June, a "turn-stone" (a bird of the snipe species) and two or three ducks were shot. The little stream back of the house was babbling along at a great rate, the snow fast disappearing. Temperature 44°, which was about as high as it was likely to be, the sun having reached its greatest northern declination, and the temperature not having gone above this during the previous August.

On the 24th, Lieutenant Greely and a party left for Hazen Lake and beyond, to visit the western coast of the country if possible. In the mean time, the dogs having attacked the young musk-oxen, came near killing one of them. The dog King and two others were found on top of "John Henry," the smallest of the calves, and, but for Frederick happening to see them and going to the rescue, "John Henry" would soon have surrendered his ghost.

During a walk on the 28th, Lockwood found North Valley River quite full, and rushing along like a mountain-torrent. Open water-pools were numerous near the shore. Had a fine view from Cairn Hill, two thousand feet high, seeing extensive lanes of open water toward Petermann's Fiord. Weather delightful.

On the 1st of July they had the second rain of the season, and Lockwood was gloomy; existence extremely monotonous; he was almost ashamed to confess how "blue" he felt. Ducks and other fowl brought in almost daily; also Esquimaux relics frequently brought in. Men arrived from Lieutenant Greely's party on Lake Hazen and reported all well there. He had found many interesting relics, and had seen large droves of musk-oxen—between two and three hundred—in Black Vale. On the 4th the men at the station celebrated the day by displays of flags, shooting and other matches, and a base-ball game. They succeeded in getting the Lady Greely afloat, and Cross repaired pipes found to be out of order. They found that the flies were blowing their fresh meat badly. Fearing that it might be lost, it was ordered to be served more frequently. Long and Ellis, who had returned from St. Patrick's Bay, reported it as open.

Lieutenant Greely and party returned on the 10th from Lake Hazen. They had a good view westward for fifty miles from a mountain four thousand feet high; saw no sea, but many glaciers. Found a large river entering the lake at its southwestern extremity.

Lockwood took the launch down to Dutch Island, giving all the men an excursion. But for entertainments of this sort he was afraid he should forget how to talk. The officers often went through a meal without exchanging a word; so also through the day. He could not say who was in fault.

Loose ice was still filling the harbor and bay—paleocrystic floes that had floated in.

Brainard and Cross brought in eleven ducks killed at Breakwater Point, having to swim in order to get them.

Weather now mild, ice in harbor much broken up, and channel outside open. Lieutenant Greely thought there was every reason for expecting a relief-ship soon. It was very desirable on many accounts that she should come. A false alarm of her approach created great excitement. Some one said he saw her smoke in the distance.

The hunters brought in ducks or other game almost daily. A weasel was shot near the house—a beautiful little animal, yellow with black tail. Dead wolves were sometimes found—probably those poisoned in the winter. Brainard, Cross, and Ellis returned from Beechy, where they killed three musk-oxen, two dozen geese, and some ducks.

Lockwood occupied himself on his maps of the Greenland coast, adding pictures of scenery from sketches taken *en route*.

Jans, desiring to capture seals, tried to approach them by interposing a cotton screen. But the seal had too much sense to wait for him, and slipped off the ice into the water.

On the 31st, Lockwood measured some ice-floes aground in the harbor, finding them to be fourteen feet thick. He had seen many on his northern trip which, by Nares's rule of one seventh above water, would have been thirty-five to forty-five feet thick. Of course, these were paleocrystic floes, the accumulation of years.

On the 7th of August, Lockwood went with Lieutenant Greely and a party in the launch to Cape Lieber, finding the bay very free from ice. Left near the cape some provisions for use in case of having to retreat next year in boats, a subject which, from the non-arrival of the ship, was then agitated. They got many Esquimaux relics. The straits away down as far as Franklin Island and Cape Constitution, as seen from an elevation, were free from ice. They could see nothing to prevent the ship from coming. Returned in the evening, landing at Proteus Point, because a large floe-berg had floated in during their absence and occupied their harbor.

Lieutenant Greely did not expect the ship before the 15th. Many eyes were daily fixed on the bold profile of Cape Lieber, from behind whose rocky face she must emerge, if she came at all.

On the 13th, Lockwood, with Brainard, Lynn, Cross, Ralston, and Fredericks, started in the launch on an excursion up Lady Franklin Bay to the head of Archer Fiord, having in tow the boat Valorous with Rice and crew as far as Musk-ox Bay. There they left Rice and his boat and proceeded up the Archer Fiord, somewhat annoyed by scattered ice and by some large bergs which they had to go around. They had not gone far up the fiord before they saw, on a gentle slope of the southern shore, a herd of musk-oxen grazing a few hundred yards from the water. Though strategy was employed to approach without being seen, the herd took the alarm and scampered over the hills which terminated the slope. Lynn, anticipating this, had gone some way up these heights, but the animals by a *détour* avoided him and soon passed over the crest of the heights. The slope along there was sufficiently gentle to afford foothold to grass and willows, and thus presented a landscape charming to those who had gazed on little other than rocks and ice for so many months. Seeing two other oxen some time after, near a steep hill overlooking a rocky gorge, Lockwood, Brainard, and Frederick went for them, Fredericks approaching in front, and Lockwood and Brainard, by a flank movement, cutting off retreat. This resulted in the slaying of both animals. But how to get them to the launch was the question, as they were then a mile inland. Finally, cutting off the heads, they gave the bodies an impetus down-hill. They went from steep to steep like comets, leaving clouds of dust behind. Once or twice they lodged on steps or terraces, from which they were dislodged, thence to renew their journey downward. Afterward several other musk-oxen and some ptarmigans were shot, thus providing abundant food for all hands, with a large surplus to carry back to the station.

As they progressed up the fiord, the scenery became more and more grand and interesting. A glacier was seen some distance inland, at the head of a stream bordered by vertical cliffs curiously colored and of fantastic shapes. One pinnacle was apparently surmounted by an old dilapidated castle. Though the fiord was not wide at Bulley's Lump, nor the cliffs very high, yet they encountered a furious wind, as though blowing vertically. Toward the head of the fiord, they saw numerous ducks and flocks of geese on shore, apparently overcome by the force of the wind. Many of these they added to their abundant stores. Here, too, they found Esquimaux relics, indicating the abodes of men long years ago—circles of stones, very old; also pieces of drift-wood, whence coming they marveled. Reaching the head of the fiord, where the water became shallow, they landed, spread their sleeping-bags on the rocks, and made amends for their twenty-five hours' want of sleep.

Waking up, they found that the receding tide had left them high and dry by one quarter of a mile. This rendered Lockwood very uneasy, and induced him to give up his intended journey of half a dozen miles into the interior. He went, however, a mile or so inland, and from a height saw a lake, and several miles above it a glacier, apparently very large. Vast cliffs, three thousand feet high, bordered the valley or ravine he followed, and beyond these were snow and ice clad summits of vast elevation. Yet here, in this desolate region, were seen proofs of the abode of man—circles of stones covered with lichens, a proof of their antiquity. Here, also, he found the hip-bone of some immense mammal, and afterward added it to his museum. He returned to the launch near the time of high tide, and after lightening, they got the launch into deep water, with much labor, but greatly to their relief. On their return they visited Record Point, left a short account of their visit, and copied that of Lieutenant Archer. He had explored this fiord in 1876, occupying one month, but they did it in sixty-nine hours. He traveled with sledges and a supporting party—

they with a steam-launch, all being on board. Their coal getting low, they made few other stops *en route* except to pick up their meat and game, returning direct to the station. The result of the expedition, as to game, was, twelve musk-oxen, three hares, twenty-four geese, thirty-six turn-stones, six knots, three terns, and twenty ptarmigans. Distance made, going and returning, one hundred and forty miles. Long and others killed numbers of musk-oxen during their absence, so that they now had on hand about eight thousand pounds of fresh beef. Another musk-ox was killed, soon after their return, in full view of the house, and thus four hundred and thirty pounds were added to their stock. This was the eightieth musk-ox shot since their arrival, the year before. They had a good view of the bay and straits, both of which seemed open, offering no obstacle whatever to the passage of the ship. They were all very much disappointed at her non-appearance.

Lieutenant Greely, wanting Howgate's Fiord explored and surveyed, and Dr. Pavy wishing to make an excursion from Cape Baird, Lockwood, on the 21st, left in the launch, with Rice, Cross, Lynn, Fredericks, Snyder, and Israel, and with Dr. Pavy and Ellison as passengers, to land the doctor on the south shore, and thence proceed westward to Howgate's Fiord. Following a lead westward, they finally found open water, which enabled them to reach the south shore of the bay some five miles above Cape Baird, where they landed the doctor and Ellison, with their rations, etc. In crossing the open water, they had strong south winds, and heavy seas which boarded the launch and washed her from stem to stern. Though much strengthened against ice, when heavily laden she sat too near the water to be a comfortable sea-boat. Thence they proceeded to Miller Island, where they had smooth water, and were enabled to cook their food and enjoy an excellent meal. They found much ice in Howgate's Fiord, yet, after trying to kill a musk-ox seen on shore, made their way to Ida Bay, at its head, and proceeded to the north shore, for Israel to lay out his base-line and take angles, and Rice to take photographs of prominent objects. While they were so doing, the others started in pursuit of a musk-ox some distance from the shore. The animal, seeing them, went up the valley at a rapid rate, leaving behind him so strong a musk odor as to mark his wake as distinctly by the smell as that of a steamboat is marked by the eye. Lockwood abandoned the chase for other duties, but the men kept on, and afterward brought in the animal's carcass. These having returned, and Israel and Rice having finished their work, all proceeded toward a very high, and conspicuous promontory, marking the entrance to the bay, which Lieutenant Greely wished Lockwood to ascend, and afterward go up the northern arm of the fiord; but they were unable to do either, having been brought to a full stop in the narrow channel by an immense floe of old ice. They therefore returned out of this *cul-de-sac* to the south shore, where Israel wanted to take other angles. Here they found traces of Esquimaux habitations—meat *caches*, and various bone implements, all very old. Thence, *via* Miller's Cape, they made their way to Stony Cape, not, however, without great difficulty because of moving ice, which sometimes forced them too close to the island, and compelled them to make *détours*. The weather threatening, they did not stop to take other angles, but crossed to the head of the bay, near the Bellows, and cast anchor; and, while the others slept, Lockwood walked up the Bellows in quest of game, but saw none.

The vegetation was just sufficient to remind him of the glorious trees and grasses of another zone far, far away. Still, with all its desolation, Lockwood thought it a very picturesque region, and that perhaps the moon, to one on its surface, presents a similar aspect. They left for the station on the 25th, encountering much ice all the way. Off Cape Clear it whirled about in such a manner as to threaten to crush the launch. At one time a large piece of ice— larger than the launch itself—was caught between the moving pack and the grounded ice and thrown up into the air fifteen feet. Finally, they reached the station, sadly disappointed not to see the masts of the hoped-for ship. They could not divine the reason for her non-appearance. Dr. Pavy thought that it never started, for want of an appropriation. Lieutenant Greely thought otherwise. It looked then as though they would have to retreat in boats during the next summer, and might fail to meet the ship in the channel; or, on reaching Littleton Island, find she had not been there, and then undoubtedly all of them would perish.

A fine salmon-trout of three pounds and three quarters was caught in a net about this time, and, while Rice tried to obtain more, Brainard went to Depot "B" on a hunt for musk-oxen and other game.

On the 26th, Lockwood went across Lady Franklin Bay in the launch after Dr. Pavy. Saw many seals, but failed to secure any. Found the doctor and Ellison awaiting them, forlorn enough. They had reached Carl Ritter Bay, seen musk-oxen, and discovered some lakes. Lockwood left more stores over the bay, and returned through much ice. It was pleasant to see how readily the launch cut through the young ice then forming in the midst of falling snow.

On the 28th, Lieutenant Greely, desiring some further exploration up Ella Bay, and inland from its head, Lockwood and a select party made several attempts in the launch to accomplish it; but the young ice was forming so rapidly, there was so much pack-ice, and the snow was obscuring the atmosphere so badly, that Lieutenant Greely, after some hesitation, decided they had better not go, and, instead, requested them to take the long-boat Valorous to Cape Baird and leave her there, and then lay up the steam-launch for the winter.

This they attempted to do, but, on reaching Dutch Island, had to give it up, as the entire harbor, bay, and straits were full of drifting ice, many of the floes standing five feet out of water. The launch having been left at anchor near the island, the next morning Lieutenant Greely ordered all hands down to the island to rescue her from impending peril. They found her very much careened and half full of water. She had been anchored in shoal water, and, heeling over at ebb-tide, had filled at the next flood. Fortunately, no harm was done to the boat, which might yet prove to be their salvation, and should be got into safe winter quarters, as that season was evidently already setting in. It was after this boat excitement that Lockwood indulged in these reflections: "I find myself constantly reading over old letters brought with me and received at St. John's, though read before again and again. The effect is depressing, bringing too strongly into view home and the dear ones there. I am oppressed with *ennui* and low spirits, and can't shake off this feeling, partly induced by the cruel disappointment of *no ship*."

Subsequently he wrote, "Have been reading of Kane and his travels. He is my *beau idéal* of an Arctic traveler. How pitiful that so bold a spirit was incased in so feeble a frame! Why is Nature inconsistent? In the Arctic his health seems to have been fair. He of all his advance party escaped the scurvy. It was his spirit, doubtless, that kept him up. Hayes does not compare with him. Though beautifully written, there is an air of exaggeration about Hayes' book, which destroys its interest. Doctor Pavy, who has hitherto been the advocate of Hayes, since his return from Carl Ritter Bay seems to have changed his mind about him, and now agrees with Greely and me that Hayes never reached Cape Lieber. To have done so, he must have performed in part of his journey ninety-six miles in fourteen hours—an impossibility.

"The life we are now leading is somewhat similar to that of a prisoner in the Bastile: no amusements, no recreations, no event to break the monotony or dispel *ennui*. I take a long walk every day along shore to North Valley with that view, study French a little, or do some tailoring, now doubly necessary, as our supply of clothing is getting low. Our stock of reading matter, unfortunately, is limited except in Arctic books. One must live up here within himself, and is unfortunate if dependent on others for happiness. The others are as moody as I am—Greely sometimes, Kislingbury always, and as to the doctor, to say he is not congenial is to put it in a very mild way indeed. But why not study? Well, the atmosphere is not conducive to it. I must go on another sledge-journey to dispel this gloom. Lieutenant Greely was thinking of sending me to Lake Hazen to continue his explorations, but thinks the snow too deep. I will make a trip to the Bellows, and follow up the cañon at its head.

"The hilarity in the other room is in marked contrast to the gloom in this. For several days the skating on the young ice of the harbor, now three inches thick, has afforded pleasure to the men. Israel broke in some distance from shore, and, being unable to get out by himself, would have perished but for the aid of others who saw him after he had been in the cold water fifteen minutes. Biederbick is constantly chaffed by the men for his persistent gunning expeditions, from which he always returns empty-handed. He takes everything seriously, and hence resents with warmth any insinuations against Germany, particularly if his own little principality of Waldeck be assailed. Biederbick tried to poison some foxes, and boasted of his plans. A fox having been caught by some one else and killed, Henry placed the body near Biederbick's poison, first placing within its mouth a paper stating (as though written by the fox) how and where he met his death. Soon after Biederbick inspected his poison, and finding the fox, brought him home in triumph. Henry gravely declared the fox had not been poisoned, much to Biederbick's amazement. They proceeded to examine the fox, and Henry pulled from its throat the certificate that had been placed there. The men around laughed at Biederbick's expense, and he wilted."

The foregoing allusion to Dr. Kane can not but be read with special interest, as it gives one an insight into the noble character of Lockwood, who had the heart to appreciate a man like the discoverer of Grinnell Land. Both, indeed, were men of rare and exalted qualities, whose memories will always be treasured with respect and affection by the whole American people.

An effort was made under Lieutenant Kislingbury to raise, from calves caught, a herd of tame musk-oxen. They became very docile and tractable, even to the extent of hauling in teams. The chief difficulty was to keep the dogs from them. One of these calves was seriously wounded by them, and was therefore killed. It was rumored that its meat would be served for dinner, and some of the men, to carry out the joke, hung the quarters on the meat-rack near the house. When other meat was served for dinner, Fredericks, who had cared for the calf and named it John Henry, ate nothing—very proper conduct for a man of feeling and a hater of jokes.

Lockwood frequently went to the observatory with Israel to get some insight into the workings of the magnetic instruments. On "term-day," the instruments were read every five minutes during the twenty-four hours, and for one hour every twenty seconds. "Poets write of the constancy of the magnetic needle," said Lockwood, "while in fact it is the most inconstant thing known. Not only does it vary yearly, but monthly, daily, hourly, yea, every minute and second. Here the magnetic disturbances are very pronounced, and at times the magnetic needle is apparently almost beside itself. The aurora, too, has frequently a very noticeable effect upon it."

It was now becoming a matter for discussion that, should they be so unfortunate as to have to spend a third winter in this region, they would have to live on salt meat and hard bread. Dr. Pavy said they were already getting short of many articles of food, and of some they were entirely out—short of sugar and also of candles and foot-gear, of the latter, only a few pairs of cork-soled boots, unfitted for use in these parts, remaining. Lockwood felt that he would rather take any risks in boats than stay there another winter.

The weather, which had been variable, having settled calm and clear, Lockwood started on his proposed sledge trip up the "Bellows" with Jewell, the Esquimaux Frederick, and an eight-dog team. Having young ice most of the way and no load, they made rapid progress to the tent at Basil Norris Bay. The dogs moved at a gallop, giving to all the rare opportunity of a ride. Here they found sleeping-bags and provisions. The next morning they reached Black Rock Vale and followed the windings of its stream-bed until they came to Lake Heintzelman, a beautiful body of water, or rather ice, perfectly smooth and free from snow, filling the whole valley, some three miles wide, to towering cliffs, and extending about five miles. So smooth was the surface that the dogs could have pulled a ton. Feeling rather chilly, they all held on to the upright of the sledge behind, and were dragged along on the soles of their shoes. Reaching the head of the lake, and finding the way so rough as to endanger the sledge-runners, they deemed it best to go into camp and reconnoitre before proceeding farther. While Lockwood and Jewell got supper, Frederick went on a hunt for musk-oxen. The former afterward followed with the team to bring in the game which he had killed, first skinning and cutting it up, not an easy job, as they had only a very dull hatchet and equally dull case-knives. They finally succeeded, however, after much labor, and returned to camp at a late hour. The ox killed was the only one seen, although it was there—three miles above the lake—that a hundred had been formerly seen. The following morning being chilly and the sky overcast, they returned to the tent at Basil Norris Bay, the dogs carrying the men, as well as nearly four hundred pounds of meat, over the smooth lake at a rapid rate.

While crossing they heard an unusual noise, like distant thunder, which at first they were unable to account for, but finally concluded was due to the cracking of the ice, arising probably from changes of temperature. The whole expanse of ice was marked by cracks extending in every direction, not, however, coming to the surface, but visible below.

In returning to the station, they avoided some rough places by hugging the south shore of the harbor, a rumbling noise of moving and crushing ice being heard in the direction of Dutch Island. On reaching the station, they found that a large bear had visited the house, dragging off the skeleton of a musk-ox which Dr. Pavy had hung out to dry as a specimen. Tracks of another bear were afterward seen near the house. At Lieutenant Greely's request, Lockwood with others followed these tracks, came in sight of the animal, and saw him make his way toward the middle of the straits through leads of open water and over hills of ice with seeming ease. Of course, they failed to add bear-meat to their well-stocked larder.

After enjoying a hot bath, which Lockwood commended as a grand luxury, he penned the following from his corner in the station-house:

"The men have added a bagatelle-board to their other sources of amusement, and sometimes have bagatelle tournaments. Lieutenant Greely and I often play chess, and sometimes I take a game of checkers with the Esquimaux. These, by-the-way, seem much better reconciled than they were last winter. Probably have come to understand us better, and we them.

"Much of my time has been occupied in making maps of the several launch trips and in writing out stenographic notes. Still, the monotony here is dreadful, and tells on all. It certainly does on me. Dr. Pavy and Lieutenant Kislingbury spend much of their time in the other room, and, when in here and Lieutenant Greely absent, are engaged in the most gloomy prognostications as to the future, and in adverse criticisms on the conduct of the expedition. It is really dreadful, and I sometimes think the life of an exile in Siberia preferable to this. The absence of light without keeps us within-doors, and the want of exercise and fresh air promotes restlessness. Our supply of books comprises only novels and Arctic literature. A few really solid books of history, biography, essays, etc., are much to be desired, though, under the circumstances, I suppose it would be difficult to concentrate one's mind on them.

"Our experiment with calves had to be given up. All died but one. Long took that to Dutch Island, but it would not stay. Like the human animal, the poor thing wanted sympathy and something to love, and followed him all the way back, notwithstanding all he could do to restrain it. Tame foxes and tame owls have also been given up. The former bit their keepers, the latter ate each other up. The dogs multiply rapidly, and would increase faster, but that the pups are eaten by the old ones. I saw the mother of a dead pup keeping Ritenbank from swallowing it, while she hesitated whether or not she would do the same thing herself.

"We are again building around our house with ice, which proved such an addition last winter, and the double sashes to the windows have been put in. I have added a side-board to my bunk and covered the adjacent walls with paper, thus adding to the warmth. Much may be done to mitigate the evils of this climate. The moral and social evils are what we can not meet, or rather do not repel."

Mrs. Greely's birthday was again observed, chiefly by a good dinner with wine furnished by Lieutenant Greely. Lockwood's own birthday was also celebrated in like manner, when he recorded the following: "After dinner Lieutenant Greely and I had a long talk—reminiscences of army-life, speculations as to our retreat in boats, etc. When alone, my mind turned to the dear ones at home and the many warm friends I had elsewhere, and to the happy days spent with them.

Lockwood's Corner.

"My corner, which is the coldest of all the corners, was improved by covering floor and walls with paper. I also found an improvement by adding sideboards to the bunk, and finally by converting the bed into a regular sleeping-bag. Before this was done, I sometimes became very chilly during the night after the fires went down. Our lamps now burn all day. How wearisome this constant artificial light becomes, we know from the experience of last winter. I dread it under our present social relations. Even Lieutenant Greely refers to these as intensifying what would otherwise not much distress him. My daily routine is somewhat as follows: Breakfast at half-past seven, with scarcely a word spoken by any one. Then I smoke, standing by the stove in the cook's room. Afterward, tailoring or some other work. At noon, a walk to Proteus Point if possible. Afterward, read or sleep till dinner at four. Again smoke as before. Then a few games of chess with Lieutenant Greely or checkers with the Esquimaux. Then read a little French or a good deal of whatever I find most interesting. Then to my army-bunk, to sleep till next morning, when the same routine is repeated."

On the 20th, he made a trip to Depot "B" with some of the men and two dog-sledges to bring down the musk-ox meat left there in *cache*. They found the foot-ice near shore so rough that they had to keep well out, but still they made the eighteen miles in six hours, which may be regarded as fair traveling with dogs.

They met many bear-tracks, but old, probably made by the same animals that visited the station. They found that these animals, and also foxes, had found their meat-*cache* and had done much damage, four quarters of meat and fifteen geese having been eaten by them or taken away. Returning next day with what remained, and taking in more meat at St. Patrick's Bay in still worse condition, they made their way home over a sea of rubble-ice. To show the effects of ice-movements, Lockwood observed, when crossing Watercourse Bay on their return, the sledge-tracks made the day before fifty feet in the air on top of floe-bergs!

They made a visit to some floe-bergs at the mouth of Lady Franklin Bay to get specimens of colored ice seen there on a berg. These were mostly yellow, but some specimens almost black. On melting, they gave an offensive odor, and made deposits of their color. Analysis only could determine the nature of the coloring-matter. Young ice was measured, and found to be twenty inches thick.

Lockwood would have been glad enough to be away from that cold region, and yet he seemed determined again to explore the north Greenland coast, and thought that, under favorable circumstances, he could go farther than he had already gone by at least seventy-five miles, thereby manifesting a degree of pluck almost unique in its character. Difficulties might arise to defeat his plans, but, these surmounted, all his energies and hopes would be directed to returning home. It was Lieutenant Greely's opinion, however, that his "farthest" would not be again reached in the present century.

On the 5th of November Dr. Pavy returned from an expedition to Carl Ritter Bay, which he had reached by following the valley back of Cape Lieber, as the ice-foot was found impracticable. The dog-food, or dried fish, taken, being insufficient and poor, one of the dogs died, and was immediately eaten by the others. The straits below were found quite open. They killed one musk-ox, but could not bring in the meat. On the return, so rough was the ice over the bay that twelve hours were required to cross from Cape Baird.

The doctor urged the policy of storing provisions at Cape Hawkes for their boat-journey, a thing easier to talk about than to do, as Cape Hawkes was one hundred and fifty-five miles, in a straight line, south of Lady Franklin Bay, and it would occupy a dog-sledge to go and return at least one month. If anything was to be done in that direction, all thoughts of further exploration must be abandoned. The doctor predicted that a naval expedition would be sent for them the next year, Congress having hitherto failed to provide for their relief.

In one of his tramps to Proteus Point, Lockwood's feet were again frosted, owing partly to his imperfect foot-gear, and he then became convinced that a light, flexible moccasin was the best thing to wear in that country.

For several days about the middle of November, there were magnetic disturbances of a pronounced character coincident with the storms and auroras they were experiencing. Storms were always indicated by rapid changes of barometer, but sometimes the barometer fell and no storm followed. Auroras had recently been attended with varied colors, which was unusual, as they had formerly been uniformly white. A surveyor working there would find, at times, his compass-needle almost unmanageable. Seals were seen in the most unexpected places, one of them having been killed with a hatchet in a tide-hole.

On the 21st, Lockwood was startled, when setting out on his usual walk, to see what looked like smoke coming from the roof of the house; but what he mistook for smoke was only the condensation of vapor escaping from the house. The appearance of the smoke coming from the chimney, and of the steam from the roof, projected as they were on the sides of the snow-covered mountains, was very pretty. The ice-wall around the house was a great protection, not only keeping the hot air in, but protecting the house from the furious blasts which would otherwise enter it, if, indeed, they did not destroy it.

Lieutenant Greely resumed his lectures, which had before proved so interesting. He gave one, which they all admired, on the history of his native town, Newburyport. Israel had also assumed the *rôle* of lecturer on astronomy, with which he was familiar.

When Lockwood became desperate with *ennui*, he got out his old letters and again read them, as they carried him back to his distant home and parents and sisters. He earnestly prayed that a kind Providence would restore him to them. This was the end of all his hopes.

On the 30th of November Lockwood wrote as follows: "This is the day Lieutenant Greely appointed for thanksgiving, and thankfully should we keep it; for we have not only escaped sickness and any serious discomforts, but we have had undoubted success in our efforts both scientific and geographical. We have had a royal feast of soup, beef, corn, Lima beans, pineapple-jelly, nuts, and figs."

Contrary to his resolve, a few days later he commenced reading novels. His feeling was that they withdraw one from one's self, which is something gained; but they put one up in the clouds from which it is often painful to descend. They cause the reader to live for a time in an ideal world, and bring him back to the stern reality with a sense of disappointment.

On the 8th of December, Lockwood was greatly impressed by the absence of light, and gave his views as follows: "It is now very dark, even at noon, except when we have the moon and a clear sky. Even on the floe, where the pure white snow reflects every bit of light, it is now so obscure that it is difficult to see the path at one's feet; and even the outlines of the mountains, high above the horizon, are very dim. A faint gleam of twilight over the south horizon, at noon only, shows the direction in which the sun and 'God's country' lie. So dark is it that I have several times stumbled over the dogs lying outside at the door; and when in a pathway, one has rather to feel the way than see it, requiring the use of a lantern in going from the house.

"No wonder, then, that the moon is so highly appreciated in this benighted region. How delightful it is, after a fortnight's absence, to have her with us once again! How a poet would rave over the moon could he once know a polar winter! We have her now in all her glory, lighting up this vast desert waste, which, covered with its mantle of snow and ice, now becomes a thing of beauty.

"The effect of continued absence of sunlight is very marked in the complexion of all the men, as well as in their loss of vigor. They are as blanched as potato-sprouts in a dark cellar. Blessed orb of light and life! One can hardly imagine the one without the other. The moral as well as the physical influence of sunlight is very soon seen after the sun's reappearance, the middle of February."

They still kept up birthdays, and the 24th was that of Saler, when they had a feast selected by himself. The musk-ox beef was particularly good, being young and tender, and free from the musk flavor so common with old oxen. They were now used to this, however, and it did not trouble them.

In the evening Lieutenant Greely brought out a few Christmas presents to distribute, which had not been issued the previous year, and there were some prizes of tobacco, soap, etc., raffled for. A chromo-picture of good "King Billy" of Prussia was given to Long, whose hair is somewhat red. The hair in the picture being of the same color, much mirth was elicited, as Long was sensitive about his hair, and was constantly chaffed by the men on that account. Lieutenant Greely made a few appropriate remarks, referring to the success of the expedition, and praying that their good fortune might continue, etc.

The Christmas-dinner was remarkably good—one that might have been enjoyed anywhere. The appetites of the men and of the officers were equal to the occasion. Of late some of them had shown less appetite than formerly, possibly because their supplies showing signs of failing in a few particulars, the table had shown less variety. The average weight of the men was found to be one hundred and seventy-one pounds, Lockwood's weight being one hundred and seventy-six, embodying a good deal of caloric.

On the 8th of January, 1883, after repairing some damage done to the launch by the ice, Lieutenant Greely announced his resolve to leave for home in boats not later than August 8th, and sooner, if the ice permitted.

On the 23d, efforts were made to cross the bay to Cape Baird, but without success, the difficulties being the absence of light, the intense cold, and the extremely rough ice. It was desired to open a passage to Cape Baird, and make a depot of provisions there for use on the retreat. Their first efforts carried these stores only to mid-channel, but afterward Sergeant Lynn and others carried them over to Cape Baird.

Much of Lockwood's time was of necessity occupied in tailoring, and he had become quite an expert. Service in the north not only demanded much clothing, but the garments must be strong and warm. Their supply in store being somewhat limited and not judiciously chosen, particularly in foot- and hand-gear, all were from time to time engaged in repairing old garments or making new. Rice suggested a method of doubling the supply of woolen socks by cutting off the legs of long stockings and sewing up the bottoms of the leg part. For his proposed spring trip, Lockwood was counting upon a rig consisting of two merino shirts, three flannel shirts, one chamois vest, one vest made of two thicknesses of army-blanket, one woolen Jersey, one swan-skin cloth over-shirt, one pair of merino drawers, two pairs of flannel drawers, soldier's trousers, cloth cap covering head and neck with a skirt covering the shoulders, and a pair of moccasins over heavy woolen socks—all to be worn at once, though seemingly heavy enough to weigh down an elephant. The only clothing in reserve was woolen wrappers and socks for the feet, and a seal-skin "timiak" for exceptionally cold weather. Having suffered much from cold feet, Lockwood had paid special attention to foot-gear, but without great success. Frequently he was kept awake most of the night from this cause. He noticed that the dogs suffered more in their feet than elsewhere, and might be seen at any time standing around with their feet drawn up under their bodies. The feet and the nose seemed to be the only highly sensitive parts of the Esquimaux dog, these being, indeed, the only parts not covered with long wool. Lockwood never tired of watching these animals. They were susceptible to kindness, though generally getting little of it. They followed him on his lonely walks, and seemed grateful for any notice or attention on his part. The young pups soon became docile and tractable in harness, though a little more difficult to manage than old dogs.

When the 1st of March arrived, all hands were engaged in preparing for their spring work. First in order was the supply of their depot on the eastern side, and Lockwood purposed leaving soon, to convey several hundred pounds of rations to that place. As usual in such cases, Dr. Pavy and two others of the party indulged themselves in the most gloomy prognostications as to the future, declaring that all idea of further explorations should be abandoned, and all their efforts applied to depositing provisions down the straits to secure their safe retreat in boats in August and September. Both Lieutenants Greely and Lockwood did all they could to make a success of this expedition, but the social atmosphere was not congenial, and there was little enthusiasm manifested. How different would have been this life if all had pulled together! Lockwood was impatient to be away from this trouble and at work. If he could not go farther than on his previous trip, he could at least try, and no man could do more than his best.

On the 10th of March, Lockwood left with two sledge-teams of ten dogs each for the purpose of placing supplies on the Greenland side of the straits—he, Sergeant Brainard, and Esquimaux Frederick, with one sledge; Sergeant Jewell, Corporal Ellison, and Jans, with the other. After leaving Depot A, where they added to their load, they had on each sledge about nine hundred and thirty pounds, or nearly one hundred pounds per dog. Found much rubble-ice on St. Patrick's Bay, but, generally, the route to Depot B was good, and the journey was made in eight hours from the station. Although they had a fire in the little stove of the depot tent, all passed an uncomfortable night, not only from cold, but from their cramped and crowded condition. Their feet were higher than their heads, and the head in one instance was under the edge of the damp, frost-covered canvas. "Woolly" was found to be lame, and had to be left in a hole in the snow-bank, with a supply of hard bread; Ellison was feeling badly, yet said, "All right," and insisted on proceeding. Seeing no favorable passage from Cape Beechy, they concluded to go up to Wrangell Bay and try the passage direct from there to Cape Brevoort. To reach Wrangell, they had to leave the ice-foot and move out on the straits, and soon found themselves in an awful mass of rubble-ice like a vast plain covered with bowlders. A great deal of chopping had to be done with the axe, and what progress they made, was with half-loads. They encamped on the straits, and, while the others returned for the discarded loads, Lockwood prepared supper, succeeding only in making some ice into lukewarm tea, which, with cold bread and meat, they hastily swallowed before creeping into their sleeping-bags. They secured but little sleep, as may be imagined when it is known that the thermometer registered that night -48°. Under such circumstances, they seemed never completely unconscious, and got up in the morning under the belief that they had not slept at all.

Reaching the south cape of Wrangell Bay, they turned to the right and went directly toward Cape Brevoort, still meeting with ice of the most formidable kind, over which the heavily loaded sledges had frequently to be lifted. Tired out, they camped at 5 P.M. in the midst of the strait. The first thing to be done was to look out for the foot-gear. This always had a lining of frost inside as well as out, being wet from perspiration if not from leakage. Brainard always changed his stockings for dry ones when he could do so, but Lockwood and Frederick generally let theirs go, the latter from indifference to frost-bites, and the former to escape the pain arising from tender feet and fingers. By incasing his feet in dog- or sheep-skin wrappings, he managed to pass the night comfortably.

Ellison, being really sick, was sent back to the depot to the tender care of Woolly. After moving for a time over rubble, several of the pieces of which came up to a man's shoulders, they were greatly encouraged by coming to a grand paleocrystic floe, whose gently undulating surface stretched east, north, and south as far as the eye could reach. This floe reminded Lockwood of a Western prairie, its mounds and gullies making the resemblance more complete. As an offset to this smooth way, they had to face an icy north wind with the thermometer from -35° to -48°. Frederick got one cheek and a finger frost-bitten, Brainard his face, and Lockwood his nose. Here they put off the load, and at a run with the empty sledge returned to their former encampment, where the tent was left standing, to await the return of Jewell, who had gone back to Depot B to leave Ellison with Woolly.

The next morning, packing everything on the two sledges, they soon gained the smooth floe seen the day before, whence, detaching Jewell for some stores at Lincoln Bay, which he was to leave at this point and then return to Fort Conger, Lockwood, Frederick, and Brainard proceeded across the floe with as much of the total loads as the dogs of their sledge could drag. Coming within five miles of Cape Brevoort, and seeing formidable ice in that direction, while toward Newman Bay the ice was better, Lockwood concluded to head toward that bay. They did so until 5 P.M., and then camped on the straits, completely exhausted. During the night they had a violent south wind, but they had campaigned too much not to be prepared for this with tent-pins securely driven.

In the morning they made their way over pretty good floes with some rubble, and reached at noon the whale-boat at Polaris Point, finding the rations in her intact. Thence, following the snow slope along the cliffs, and passing the point where Lockwood and Frederick had spent many hours the year before in a snow-hole, they passed round Cape Sumner through masses of ice in some places piled fifty feet high, and finally reached the Boat Camp on Newman Bay.

Having thus provisioned the Boat Camp, they took a survey of the routes back, and concluding that, all things considered, the one direct to Cape Beechy was the best, returned by it with the empty sledge, making rapid progress and reaching the west shore in just seven hours. Notwithstanding they had no load, the passage was by no means easy, for they had to pass over mountain-ridges, deep pits, and gullies in the rubble-ice, where the dogs could scarcely keep their footing. Lockwood was impressed, as often before, with the power and endurance of the dogs. Ellison had left the depot, but Woolly still remained, and there, also, they found Jewell, who had been up to Lincoln Bay, where he found that the foxes had eaten up a large part of the meat in *cache* there.

With Woolly on the sledge, they returned to the station, meeting Snyder and Whistler *en route* with a pup-team and sledge, going for Woolly. It was interesting and touching to witness the demonstrations and delight of these youngsters on meeting their elders, among which were the mothers of some of them.

Jewell said that, on his return to the depot, he put away his dog-harness in one of the empty tents, and that when he awoke the next morning he found nothing remaining but the bone buttons and the whip-handles, the dogs having eaten everything else. Another dog-story is recorded as follows:

"Milatook had pups the other day, and all were killed except one. It was discovered yesterday in a very unfortunate condition, with tail frozen hard and stiff, and legs in nearly the same condition. Some of the men soaked the tail in water, and eventually 'brought it to.' It is a sad tail."

XIV.
RESUMING A DESPERATE STRUGGLE.

On the 19th of March, fair weather came out of the north, and not only cheered the hearts of the whole colony at the station, but fired the desire of Lieutenant Lockwood for the new campaign, which he had long been contemplating. After a consultation with Lieutenant Greely, he concluded to start on the following day, or soon after. As usual, some cold water was thrown upon his plans, one of the critics declaring that they had experienced enough of that kind of business; and another, that they had better be thinking of their coming fate. But Lockwood's reasoning was as follows: "Before I go home, I must make another 'strike' on the north Greenland coast. If the conditions of the ice are no worse, I ought to be able to discover the northeast extremity of Greenland, and add several miles to my latitude, although Lieutenant Greely thinks that my present 'farthest' will not again be reached in our day. I say nothing about all this, however. *Act* first and talk afterward has always been my way."

Lockwood was both hopeful and determined, and on the 23d he received his final orders to the effect, that, should he not be able to reach a higher latitude than he did before without undue danger, or should he or any of his men break down or become dangerously ill, he was to return forthwith. To this he replied that he knew not what might happen, but he intended, if possible, to reach the eighty-fourth parallel. In anticipation of his own birthday, and to honor the explorers with a good "send-off," Lieutenant Greely gave a dinner on the 26th, and, thus fortified, they were prepared to move on the following day, rejoicing.

Lockwood had two fine teams of ten dogs each assigned for his use, and, as before, the faithful Brainard and Esquimaux Frederick were to accompany him. Everything passed off quietly, without the excitement or enthusiasm of the previous spring. They left the station at 8.30 A. M., the advance sledge bearing the silk flag of Mrs. Greely, with Brainard and Frederick the Esquimaux; the supporting sledge with Jewell, Ellis, and Esquimaux Jans; and then the pup-team and sledge driven by Snyder, and carrying Greely and Lockwood. On reaching Watercourse Bay, whence they were to take back a load of coal, Lieutenant Greely and team left them, after bidding God-speed, and telling them to be sure and bring back the north end of Greenland! Reaching Depot A in two and a quarter hours, they took on two small seals left there, and passing Depot B, where they obtained more provisions, they reached Cape Beechy at 4 P. M.—the dogs quite fresh, but the men much wearied.

When they resumed their journey, it was snowing and the Greenland shore invisible. They took a direct course by compass for Cape Sumner over rubble-ice until they reached the first floe, on whose hard, undulating surface they made rapid progress until they came to rubble-ice again. Brainard, with axe in hand, went ahead, clearing the way over impassable places, until the high cliff of Polaris Promontory came in sight. Finally, both Jewell and Ellis suffering from pain, when three miles from Cape Sumner they stopped for the night, after making twenty miles, and all went into bags.

Moving early next morning with considerable wind, they got into bad ice with cracks, down which some of the dogs fell and had to be drawn up; but finally, finding a better route, reached the Polaris Boat Camp, where, leaving some meat for the dogs when returning, they continued on toward Gap Valley, generally over rolling floes, and through rubble, requiring a good deal of cutting, tugging, and pushing.

When three miles out they went into camp again, leaving Ellis to prepare supper for all, while the others, with both sledges, returned to the Boat Camp.

Leaving Brainard to get ready the alcohol to be taken from the whale-boat, they kept on along shore to the foot of the cliffs and the *cache*. Here they found the snow-slopes much worse than on their last visit, but, the sledges being empty, they could have gone along over anything except a stone wall, and even that would have had to be very high to stop them. Fox-tracks were seen near the *cache*, but they found it intact. The ice they had piled about it was almost covered by the drifting snow. The contents of the *cache*, about one thousand pounds in all, were put on the two sledges, and soon after they went down a snow-bank so steep and hard that the sledges took entire command, though all hands tried to hold them back; but the dogs keeping out of the way, no harm was done. This was at Cape Sumner, whence they returned to the Boat Camp. Here, taking on the things prepared by Brainard, they returned to the tents. After supper some hours were spent in getting ready the rations for from twenty to forty-eight days. Jewell and Ellis were both complaining; otherwise, every thing looked very promising.

On the morning of the 30th, it was clear overhead but cloudy around the horizon, and a slight snow was falling. The loads were about eleven hundred pounds to each team, but the dogs did admirably, and good speed was made, the ice being covered with a very light depth of snow. At the mouth of the gorge by which they were to ascend and cross the Brevoort Peninsula, they reduced the load on each sledge and started up this narrow, rocky, winding cañon. The snow was hard and they were getting along well, when right before them appeared a wall of snow, so steep and hard that Lockwood had to use his big knife, to ascend. It was about thirty feet high. He went alone to view the situation. A few yards beyond was a kind of ice tunnel whose roof was about three feet high. Then came another high, steep snow-drift with a snow-cavern alongside, probably fifty yards in length; and also a few feet farther was found a deep pit formed by the snow. Climbing around this and proceeding half a mile, he found that the gorge made a bend to the east and became still more narrow and rocky; but a side ravine offered a chance to get out of this big gutter, up a long, steep slope of hard snow, three or four times the height of the preceding drifts; and then Lockwood found himself on the table-land overlooking Newman Bay.

The sledges with great difficulty gained this comparatively level divide. The landmarks not being altogether familiar to Lockwood, he took a long walk after supper to a distant ridge, where, seeing the sea-coast, his way became perfectly clear. It was a lonely and dismal walk, and the ridge seemed to get farther away as he approached it. After more than two hours' absence he returned to the tents, crawled in alongside of Sergeant Brainard, and was quickly lulled to sleep notwithstanding the snoring of Frederick. The horrid sound issuing from his bag was as loud as a brass band at a circus.

The process of getting breakfast was to be preferred to that of getting supper. When a man went into camp, after a toilsome day of travel, and had helped to pitch tent and unload the sledge, it was hard, while covered with frost, with cold and perhaps wet feet, to chop ice and meat, and handle cold metal.

After an uncomfortable night, with the temperature down to -45°, they started again. Proceeding several miles, they reached a narrow, winding ravine, and finally a gorge, which they followed until they came to the head of the wide Gap Valley, and thence to the sea-coast. Turning east, they continued on a few hundred yards, and were then stopped by the ice-wall, which crowded so closely to the shore that the sledges could not be hauled through. Lockwood and Frederick pitched the tent, while Brainard went ahead with the axe, and, after much hard work, made a passage about one eighth of a mile long through this place. They managed to worry through with half the load by three o'clock, and, leaving Brainard to get supper, Lockwood and Frederick went on with half the load for about one and a half miles. The route beyond the bad place was excellent. Dropping the load, they returned to the tent by four o'clock. Jewell came along later, he and Ellis complaining again of their difficulty in keeping up with the sledge when it went faster than a slow walk.

While approaching the cairn at Repulse Harbor, on the 1st of April, Brainard's sharp eyes discovered the site of the English depot of rations, which contained Lieutenant Beaumont's sextant, an English flag, a cooking-lamp, old clothes, and some foot-gear. The road before them was excellent, and they made good time, soon passing the route of the preceding year, which reached the coast just east of Repulse Harbor.

On coming near Drift Point, they were better able to see the northern expanse outside the ice-wall which lined the coast and had interrupted the view. Lockwood saw a good deal of young ice interspersed with holes, and leads of open water. The main pack beyond seemed permeated by leads of what had been quite recently open water. Dark, misty "water-clouds" were seen everywhere northward. The young ice extended along shore in both directions as far as they could see, and out from shore a hundred yards or more. Beyond it was the polar pack, broken into small floes and rubble-ice, which had a glistening green appearance, as though recently pushed up by the grinding of the fields about it; all this was very surprising.

They made their way over the snow-slopes of Drift Point and beyond until the near approach of the cliffs on one side and the ice-wall on the other brought them to a halt eighty miles from Fort Conger. Here they encamped with everything, having come thus far in six days.

The ice-wall along here was from forty to fifty feet high. Outside, there was a good deal of ice lately formed, with smooth floes. They passed on near the foot of the bluffs, to see if there was any way of getting along the cliffs, making their way between the ice-wall and the foot of the steep slopes of the bluffs with great effort. The *débris* of stone, etc., from the cliffs above made the route almost impracticable for a sledge. Before reaching Black Horn Cliffs, they were obliged to find a route along the top of the ice-wall, and thus got a short distance along the bottom of these vertical cliffs. But now, from a fissure in the cliffs above, came a steep drift of very hard snow, slanting down to the water at its foot. To scale the cliffs by means of this drift was dangerous, as a slip would inevitably have taken one directly into the water.

By cutting steps in the snow they gained a considerable elevation, but, on looking round a point of rocks, the height beyond was so much greater and worse than they expected, that they could not proceed. All along shore was the crack of open water about a yard wide, with young ice beyond, through which a stone or fragment of ice might be thrown. Dense water-clouds appeared in many directions. They returned to camp, and, after enjoying some tea, Lockwood gave Jewell the tidal rod to make observations, while with Brainard he started out again, this time to the south and up a stream-bed, at whose mouth they were encamped, hoping to find a route back of the cliffs overland. They soon found themselves in a ravine with high, rocky sides, and encountered a steep snow-drift. Beyond was a small hole in the snow, which seemed to be a cavern or grotto formed of snow and ice, and probably running down to the bed of the stream—if that may be called a stream which has no water. Beyond this were exposed rocks under foot, and they saw ptarmigan-tracks, where the birds had used their wings in getting down a snow-drift. Finally, they came to a branch ravine from the southeast, the main stream leading off toward the south. They turned up the branch, and kept on for a while, when the high rocky sides seemed to come to a formation of ice like a glacier, a hundred feet high, at least, and very steep. The crest was perpendicular. The route thus far was difficult yet practicable, but it was clearly impossible for a dog-team to haul an *empty* sledge up this place, and yet it was the only place where there was anything else than an inclined plane of rocks. The glacier was covered with snow, but in many places the ice could be seen cropping out, the snow being only a thin covering. Some ice-grottoes were also seen. They clambered up the rocks to the left, and found themselves on a stony plateau. Off to the east was an elevated ridge or knoll, toward which they traveled about a mile and a half. On gaining it, the barometer showed an elevation of thirteen hundred feet. Toward the south was a chain of mountains running east and west, through the western extremity of which the main stream-bed they had ascended seemed to break, about six miles from the sea. The branch appeared to end at the glacier; but to the east of it the land sloped north and south, and formed a surface-drain which, running east, soon narrowed into a gorge, and, bending to the north, reached the sea just west of Rest Gorge, as well as they could make out. At the bend was a large formation of ice or snow.

They returned to camp at 3 P. M., and found every one there walking vigorously up and down to keep warm, or, rather, to keep from freezing, the thermometer marking -48°. Jewell left his beat every few minutes to note the height of the water on the tide-rod. There was now nothing else to do except to get into the sleeping-bags, and this in cold weather always involves a change of foot-gear. At six o'clock Brainard had prepared supper, and shortly after, the advance sledge-party was trying to sleep. Jewell kept on taking observations until after eleven, when he caught the high tide. It was a severe ordeal, but he preferred to do it, without assistance, as it was much better for the record.

Brainard complained of want of sleep, and Lockwood's rest was much the same as usual—an uneasy, oppressed feeling of being half asleep and half awake; every few hours getting broad awake, and wondering if it were time to rise, or how much colder his feet would have to get before freezing. Having decided to examine the main ravine running south, Lockwood started from camp before eight, with Brainard, Frederick, and Ellis. On reaching the branch, he and Ellis continued south, and the other two went up the branch. Continuing along between the high, rocky sides of the ravine, with abundance of hard snow under foot, but some bad snow-drifts, they found a very good sledge-route. After a while, they came to a huge formation of snow, filling the whole breadth of the ravine, and sloping up—in one place by a very easy ascent—to the west bank. Gaining this, they continued on and reached a ridge some twelve hundred feet high, which commanded a view of the sea, and of the valley to the south as far as the mountains. The valley seemed to grow wider and deeper as far as the mountains, through which it broke from a southwest direction. No break or defile of any kind offered an outlet to the east. Beyond the east bank was a wide plateau covered with stones, and about four miles from the sea. After taking a good survey of the country, they turned back toward the camp. Brainard and Frederick joined them some time afterward, and reported that they had cut one hundred and fifty-two steps in the side of the glacier to get up, and found that the branch extended a short distance beyond, but that a vertical ledge of ice some twelve feet high presented itself afterward, and that, on getting beyond this, they found themselves on a plateau covered with bare stones. Brainard thought the route utterly impracticable, and went no farther. He afterward said that they might be able to get round to Rest Gorge in two weeks, with the sledges and loads, by taking the sledges to pieces, and carrying them and the loads piecemeal over these obstructions. The young ice seemed to be getting thicker, and they began to think they might get around the cliffs after all. They had some tea and "pap," and began to calculate how many days it would take to reach Cape Bryant. During the afternoon, a way for the sledge was cut through a low place in the ice-wall, a short distance west of the camp, and two days' rations were also deposited in a *cache* on the hill. A slight wind blew during the day, and by eight o'clock all were in their sleeping-bags again, excepting Jewell, who kept up tidal observations until ten, securing a very satisfactory set, two high tides and the intervening low tide.

Thermometer during the night -43°. After breakfast, Brainard went down to the tide-gauge, and, coming back, reported that the rising tide had widened the crack a little, but that he had fixed it by chopping snow blocks and throwing them into the water. Being unwilling to risk everything on the young ice, thinking that it might break through, Lockwood put the five sacks of pemmican on the sledge, and leaving the tent, etc., and the supporting sledge-party packing up, he, Brainard, and Frederick started on. They reached the ice with no trouble, and, proceeding out from shore one or two hundred yards, turned to the east and went a short distance when, Frederick seeming to think the ice all right, Lockwood sent Brainard ahead with the axe, while with Frederick, having thrown off the load, he proceeded back for the rest of the stores, so as to take all on together. They had nearly reached the shore, when suddenly Lockwood saw two or three of the dogs in the water, and knew from Frederick's tones that something had happened. The ice was moving out from shore, and they saw no way of getting off. Lockwood called for Jewell, and then leaving Frederick and his team to find a way to shore if possible, started on the run to get within hailing distance of Brainard. He was speedily overtaken by Frederick and the dog-team, the dogs going at a fast gallop, and Frederick laying his whip about them in all directions. Lockwood proceeded to find some place to get ashore, but there was none, except at a little promontory of rubble-ice, in front of the camp, and about two hundred yards from the tide-gauge. Elsewhere up and down, as far as they could see, was a continuous belt of water, every moment getting wider. The ice had a motion toward the east, as well as out from the shore, and thus kept in position a small cake of ice by means of which Lockwood got on the promontory, and then directed the movements of the dog-sledge which now came along. On the way back they stopped and threw the pemmican on the sledge again, the ice being perfectly smooth and hard. They first saved the dogs, pulling them up one by one, and then, the little ice-cake seeming to keep its position, a bridge was made of the sledge, and all the pemmican saved. The ice continued to move out from the shore, until up and down as far as the eye could reach was a wide belt of open water. Before they left, it was in many places between one and two hundred yards wide, and the ice at the same time moving toward the east. They got ashore at eleven o'clock, and by 12.30 the sledge-tracks, which had been opposite the tidal rod, were opposite the camp, a distance of two hundred yards. While the sledges were being packed, a seal made his appearance and eyed the party curiously. The guns were not convenient, and he was not disturbed. Many water-clouds were seen to the north at this time, and the whole polar pack seemed to be on the move. They were all grateful for getting out of the trap so well. Referring to their living on the moving floe, Frederick made signs to suggest their eating the dog-pemmican; certainly this would have lasted a long time had they not frozen to death in the mean while, which they would have done very soon, as they were without sleeping-bags or alcohol.

There seemed nothing to do but turn about and go home, and yet Lockwood was extremely averse to the idea. The overland route looked well-nigh impossible, or something at least that could not be accomplished in time to allow them to reach the farthest of 1882. Lockwood's orders directed his return in case this contingency should arise, as well as in case of any "signs of the disintegration of the polar pack," or in case he became incapacitated for rapid travel. He walked up and down and thought of it for some time, both Brainard and Jewell having declared that there was nothing else to do but return. At 12.30, the teams being all ready, they turned toward the west. As they came near the slopes of Drift Point a very disagreeable south wind with drifting snow was met, which continuing to get worse, their cheeks and noses began to suffer, and therefore, at about two o'clock, they halted and pitched the tents, driving the pins first, and raising the tents afterward. By this time it was blowing almost a gale, and, the thermometer being very low, the tent was tied up, and they prepared to weather it out, Lockwood having a severe headache, which added to his tribulations.

The whole of April 5th was passed in the sleeping-bags, giving all hands an opportunity to meditate on the *delights* of an Arctic sledge-journey. The time was spent in sleep, or in trying to keep warm and sleep at the same time. During the day Lockwood counted up the exact number of rations remaining, and, still bent on his dream of the eighty-fourth degree, calculated that, if they could get around overland to Rest Gorge in five days, they could yet go to the farthest of 1882 and a few days beyond, provided the traveling was not worse than the previous year. He announced his intention accordingly. Brainard and Jewell were not hopeful, but willing to do their best in attempting it. One great obstacle was the lame and crippled condition of both Jewell and Ellis. The signs of disintegration in the polar pack, Lockwood proposed to disregard.

The wind continuing to blow, it was noon before they started off toward the east to reconnoitre; but, prior to this, Lockwood went up on the high ground back of the tents and saw a great deal of open water. Some time after starting, he stopped the sledges and went up on another elevation to reconnoitre, feeling that, if he went on and anything happened, his responsibility would be heavy, from his disobedience of orders. From this point could be seen a belt of open water running along shore, in both directions, for miles. In no place was it less than two hundred yards wide, and from that it increased to four and five hundred. Westward from the vicinity of Repulse Harbor, it extended in a lead, growing wider and wider, all the way across the straits, apparently to the vicinity of Lincoln Bay, where it seemed to swing round to the north. This lead was upward of five miles wide in the middle. Whether there were other leads south of it, between Newman Bay and Beechy, could not be determined. In the polar pack to the north were several small leads and a great many dark water-clouds. The ice was again noticed moving rapidly to the northeast. Beyond Cape Bryant, he supposed the ice to be intact, as in 1882, but around the cape, north of Britannia, they had then traveled on new ice, and, going out on the polar pack at Cape Dodge, just this side of the farthest, had traveled on it for several miles. The condition of this route now could not be known, of course, but what they had seen made the prospect very unfavorable. The signs of disintegration were unmistakable, and Lockwood therefore determined to turn back once again. Near this spot he remarked a very curious stratified floeberg. It was about forty feet high, and a dozen or more horizontal lines were very plain. The weather had now cleared up beautifully, and they were soon at Repulse Harbor. Here they left a short notice of their defeat in an English cairn, and, taking Beaumont's sextant, the English flag, etc., on the sledge, continued on their way to the mouth of Gap Valley, where they went into camp, and remained long enough to take a set of tidal observations.

The observations here were very satisfactory, and were kept up by Jewell for more than twelve hours. Brainard, with Ellis and the two teams and drivers, advanced the heaviest part of the loads *en route* nine miles to the shore of Newman Bay. Lockwood and Jewell remained in camp, and the former found it extremely monotonous, having nothing to do but to prepare supper. The only way to keep warm was by constantly moving about, and, as a cold wind was blowing, this in itself was not comfortable. The observations were very trying to Jewell, continued as they were long after the rest were in their bags.

On the 8th of April, they suffered more than usual with cold. The sleeping-bags, frozen stiff, were a long time in thawing out after they got into them. Dark water-clouds were seen along the northern horizon, although elsewhere the sky was bright and clear. One, particularly noticeable, to the northeast and near shore, looked like a huge cliff in a fog. They also noticed a movement in an ice-hillock some distance off the coast. It changed its angle to the east during their stay, and suggested open water across their route before reaching Cape Beechy. They left camp at ten, and found the traveling very good— rather improved by the late storm. Jewell and Ellis began to suffer again, and the latter was carried on the sledge several miles, the loads being very light. They soon reached the middle of the divide, and then the loads left on the shore of Newman Bay, making very fast time through the gorge, though the sledges had to be let down the snow-slopes and drifts by ropes. After stopping some time to take on everything, they proceeded slowly and reached the Boat Camp, and soon after Cape Sumner, where they stopped to make tidal observations, Lockwood and Brainard remarking what a particularly dreary and dismal place it was, and wondering if they should ever see it again. It brought to mind the trials and tribulations of the previous spring. Yet, in spite of those trials, the novelty of everything, and the imperfect equipment, that expedition was a success; and this one, notwithstanding their experience and the completeness of their arrangements, a failure. "Oft expectation fails where most it promises." Lockwood felt thankful that they had escaped from the ice-pack, and from passing the forty-eight hours of the recent storm upon it, living on the pemmican until finally frozen to death; but the sense of defeat was predominant. They passed a tedious, cold afternoon, but enjoyed a good dinner, having now an abundance of rations of all kinds. It warmed them up and put new life in all. Jewell saw, during his observations, a white owl flying overhead toward the east.

The morning of the 10th was bright, clear, and calm. They noticed a stratum of misty clouds, supposed to be water-clouds, hanging along the foot of the cliffs on the Grinnell Land shore, and extending from above Cape Beechy northward indefinitely. After passing through several bands of rubble-ice with great labor, and yet without having to double up, they found the tracks made on the outward journey, and followed them continuously. This saved a great deal of time in chopping and picking out a road. About noon they suddenly encountered a very cold south wind. It seemed to come out of Devil's Gap, Polaris Promontory, and as usual carried along a lot of fine drifted snow, continuing during the day. Their heavy loads made the dogs travel at a slow walk, otherwise, no doubt, both Jewell and Ellis must have been left behind or carried on the sledges. They went into camp on a hard snow-drift.

After an uncomfortable night, with the mercury at 45° below zero, they left camp and followed the old trail, as on the previous day, jolting along with little difficulty in the rubble-ice, the dogs doing admirably, bracing themselves to the effort at bad places, like so many men.

They reached Depot B at 2.50 P. M., and pitched the tents, this making the tenth time that Lockwood had crossed the straits above Fort Conger.

The traveling was tedious and slow, but they reached Depot A at noon, stopping only half an hour, and arrived at Fort Conger in the afternoon. Everything there was quiet as the grave. "General Grant" was the only one, man or beast, that knew of their approach and came out to meet them. Even when they passed the windows and reached the door, no one saw or heard them, and Lockwood walked in on Lieutenant Greely like a ghost, and simply said: "Well, I'm back again; open water at Black Horn Cliffs." Some of his further reflections were to this effect:

"Do I take up my pen to write the humiliating word *failed*? I do, and bitter is the dose, although it is now a week since first I tasted it. My return here, the inaction after two and a half weeks of activity, and the monotony, not to mention the disappointment of Lieutenant Greely, make it fresh as when first mixed. I tried yesterday and to-day to induce Lieutenant Greely to let me go out again, but he says this is our last year here, that I still have last year's work to fall back on, and, above all, that it is not *prudent*. I have a scheme by which I could travel four days beyond the farthest of '82, and get back here in forty-four days, leaving April 21st and returning June 3d—that is, provided an overland route around the Black Horn Cliffs can be found, and provided the conditions beyond are no worse than last year. My proposal was to take the two teams, the two Esquimaux and Brainard, five sacks of pemmican, one tent, two sleeping-bags, etc., and forty-four days' rations for the party. The five sacks would last the dogs twenty-three days, after which about eight dogs of the twenty would be killed one by one, and thus the remainder fed on the return. We should have to make long marches, it is true. Perhaps the refusal is for the best, and I still have the country southwest of the head of Archer Fiord to operate in; but I am reluctant to give up this scheme for passing 83° 24′." Everything at the station was very quiet, and much as when they left, except that a party had been sent for the boat at Thank-God Harbor.

XV.
ACROSS GRINNELL LAND.

While the disappointment which attended the late expedition was very great, it did not make Lieutenant Lockwood unhappy or morose. He was only convinced, perhaps, that when the ice and snow and storms, minions of the North Pole, undertake to play the game of April fool, they do it very effectually. The absence of so many of his companions from the station had a depressing effect upon his spirits, but as usual he prepared the report of his last journey, and duly submitted it to Lieutenant Greely, all the while suffering from the severe rheumatic pains which invariably followed his exposure to severe cold. Many of the men were complaining, and the weather outlook was not encouraging, and yet, after consulting with Lieutenant Greely, Lockwood fixed his mind upon an exploration up and beyond the Archer Fiord. His idea was to go west, at least as far as the English had gone along the northern shore of Grinnell Land, feeling that he could hardly fail of finding something of interest, and would perhaps make important discoveries. Indeed, he might be able to determine the coast-line on the west. As usual, he wanted the company of Sergeant Brainard and Esquimaux Frederick, and would be content with one dog-team and supplies for thirty days, with a proper supporting party for two days.

His spirits now became better than they had been, caused chiefly, as he confessed, by the glorious sun; and yet he could not refrain from thinking of home, and again resorting for comfort to his old family letters, which he had so frequently read before.

His late failure had been a disappointment to himself as well as to Lieutenant Greely and the men. Some of them seemed down in the mouth and gloomy, and, by way of cheering them, Lieutenant Greely informed them that he intended to leave Fort Conger on the 5th of August, or as soon thereafter as the ice would permit. The personal relations of Dr. Pavy and Lieutenant Kislingbury with Lieutenant Greely and himself were not what they should have been, and, instead of getting better, these relations seemed to grow worse. Could he not have gone abroad on these fatiguing journeys to escape such companionship, he would have felt utterly desperate. He certainly would cheerfully take any risks during the summer than longer endure the existing personal troubles. Lieutenant Kislingbury's only thought seemed to be that a sledge-party should be sent down to Littleton Island to have the ship leave her supplies at Cape Sabine, therein merely reflecting the latest opinion of the doctor.

The start for the western trip was made on the 25th of April, 1883, with two sledges, each drawn by ten dogs and carrying about one thousand pounds of rations for thirty days. They moved along the south side of the harbor over very soft and deep snow, through which the dogs labored, yet made their way with full loads. On getting near "Sun Land," however, the snow became abominable, and the traveling was as bad as they had ever experienced. After trying for some time to go ahead, but sticking incessantly, they turned short off to the left, and after a great deal of work reached the shore, Brainard *en route* falling down a crack, and Lockwood feeling convinced that his feet were frozen, as all sensation had left them.

Reaching Black Knob Point, where there was a tent, they found it blown down. After some delay in repitching it, they started overland toward Sun Bay, through soft and deep snow, and soon afterward reached Stony Cape, where they encamped, all the party being very much fatigued.

Resuming their march, they found the snow not particularly deep, but with a light crust, not quite hard enough to bear, which made the traveling fatiguing. They stopped to rest every hour, the weather being really too warm for comfort, so that Lockwood actually longed for the cold and hard work he had experienced in north Greenland. They reached Keppel's Head in three hours, and found that *Mr.* Keppel had a very stony face, and not a handsome head by any means, being a lofty promontory and precipitous mass of rocks, very grand and imposing. In two hours more they reached Hillock Depot, and stopped to get some corned beef left there by Lockwood in June of the preceding year, the English rations left there having all been eaten by foxes.

On reaching Depot Point, they transferred everything from the supporting sledge and sent it back to the station, afterward getting along with the whole load very well. The high, steep cliffs on their right threw their shadows almost across the fiord, and kept them out of the glare of the sun moving along the northern horizon. Fox-tracks constantly appeared. These tracks were found everywhere, and yet it was but seldom that the animals themselves were seen; and in thinking of their habits, Lockwood wondered if they laid up in store their surplus food against the days of want. A tame fox kept at the station would always take what was offered; but, when the ice-wall was pulled down, a large supply was found which Mr. Reuben had abandoned on regaining his liberty.

Greatly enjoying the pleasant weather, after finding some Esquimaux relics, and making a vain effort to surmount a glacier, they finally reached the head of Ella Bay, where, after some delay in finding freshwater ice, and snow hard and deep enough to pitch the tent, they went into camp. Lockwood and Frederick then took the team and empty sledge, and proceeded up a little water-course a few miles. Found less ice and more stones than they expected, but, having ascertained that they could advance up the valley with some extra labor, returned. Numerous fox, ptarmigan, hare, and musk-ox tracks were seen, but no game. Brainard became permanent cook, as the difficult business of making observations devolved entirely on Lockwood. The cliffs about here were grand, at least three thousand feet high.

Lockwood was disappointed in getting equal altitudes of the sun for longitude (time), the lofty cliffs shutting out the orb of light on each side of the meridian; and yet he had camped away out, a mile or two from the cliffs, in order to avoid this difficulty. This was one of the annoyances he had frequently experienced. After lying awake for hours, or taking his sleep by short cat-naps with one eye open, and running out in order to catch the sun at the right time, and all this after a tiresome march, it was very provoking to have "some miserable cliff" lift its ugly head right in his way. To get the local time *well*, it was necessary to take the sun's altitude some hours before noon, and then catch the precise instant of the same altitude in the afternoon, the sun being nearly on the meridian at a time midway between the times of the two observations. This middle time needed certain corrections, and then, the watch or chronometer being regulated to Greenwich or Washington time, the difference of time, or longitude, was known. The little streams occupying the valleys (or cañons, as they should be called) of this Arctic country are utterly insignificant compared with the depressions themselves. A great, ditch-like break in the country, from two to five miles wide and ten to thirty miles long, the sides of which are vertical walls rising thousands of feet, may be the bed of a little brook that in summer-time can be readily waded, and at other times of the year can hardly be seen under the universal mantle of snow. It was one of these that they followed in its windings. Here and there they would encounter very deep snow, and the sledge-runners would stick on the beds of stone, requiring all their efforts to get under way again. In about an hour they came to a long, level area, indicating Lake Katherine, which Lockwood had previously discovered and named when up near here in the launch, and then the view up the valley was unbroken as far as the glacier. Its terminal face could be clearly seen, looking like a little wall of ice three or four feet high, upon which one could readily step. Back of this the surface gently ascended until lost in the snow-covered mountain-side far beyond. The whole thing looked like a mass of barber's lather, flowing slowly down a deep ditch. For some hours, Lockwood and Brainard both thought there would be no trouble in getting sledge and dogs up the *little* face to the undulating and gradually ascending surface beyond. After proceeding some distance on the lake, Lockwood stopped the sledge, and with Brainard went off to the right, ascending a low ridge that ran parallel with the lake and between it and the high cliffs on the north side of the valley. They found the top to be four hundred feet high, and beyond was a wide ravine running down to the bay. There they saw the tracks of three musk-oxen that had evidently passed along on their way toward the fiord; also many tracks of foxes, ptarmigan, lemming, and hare. Probably, the chief reason for seeing so few animals, though so many tracks, was that the birds and animals (excepting the musk-ox) are all pure white in color for three fourths of the year. One might *look* at a hare or ptarmigan a few yards away and yet not *see* it. The lake called Katherine was found to be three or four miles long. At its farther end, the ground was quite bare of snow in places, and everywhere the snow was hard and thin, so that they went along very rapidly. Every half-hour, they thought, would bring them to the glacier, but the longer they traveled, the farther the glacier seemed to move away. When only a short walk from the glacier, as Lockwood thought, he stopped the sledge, and with Brainard went on ahead. The *face* seemed much higher than they had supposed it, but it was only after walking a mile that they realized what it was—a wall of ice, straight up and down, stretching a mile across the valley from side to side, and nearly two hundred feet high.

After surveying this wonderful object, they returned to the sledge and pitched the tent, seeing no way of proceeding farther; and there they remained a day or two to get a good look at the surroundings before deciding upon the proper course to pursue. A decided fall in the temperature was quite noticeable, due, doubtless, to the proximity of the glacier. They got to sleep after a while, and during the day took a good rest, getting up in the afternoon. The twain went again to reconnoitre, leaving Frederick to hunt, or amuse himself in any other way he chose. They went to the glacier-wall again, and followed along its foot to the south side of the valley. This wall was beautiful and imposing. From the top, one third of the way downward, the ice was of a charming green color, and looked like glass; below this came a white surface, in which small stones were numerous imbedded in the ice, with here and there streaks of a brownish color, like chocolate ice-cream mixed with vanilla. A close approach showed that it was earth. At the foot of the wall, probably concealing a "terminal moraine," was an undulating bank of snow, and over the upper edge of the wall hung wreaths of drifted snow that looked like the icing of cake. The ground for some distance out was strewed with blocks of ice and stone of all imaginable shapes and sizes. On reaching the corner of the glacier, a similar wall was seen extending up along its flank, abutting against an inclined plain of immense bowlders and masses of rock, the *débris* from the cliffs above. The angle thus formed was full of large blocks of ice, many recently detached from the wall of ice. Traveling along the flank proved so difficult that they took to the incline and scrambled for some time over immense masses of rock and snow, often across deep cracks and openings concealed by the snow covering them. After gaining an altitude of several hundred feet, they reached something like a terrace formation, from which they overlooked all the lower part of the glacier. It presented an undulating and gradually rising surface, extending up the valley fifteen or twenty miles, or more. Just opposite to them, a branch glacier came in from the north through a gap in the mighty cliffs. The slope of this branch in places was very precipitous, showing great rents and fissures. The surface of the glacier was free from snow, except, here and there, in what seemed little depressions in the ice. There was no way of climbing upon the glacier, much less of getting the sledge and dogs up. It would simply have been ascending a precipice of ice two hundred feet high. To get upon it had been their original intention, although Frederick went through a pantomime at the time, which they did not exactly understand, expressing how a sledge would go faster and faster, and finally shoot over the edge like a waterfall. Whether he ever had had such an experience in Greenland he did not say, but he would never have had it more than once. Seeing no way of getting on or along the glacier, except with the greatest labor, Lockwood proposed to Brainard that they should ascend the cliffs and get an outlook from the top. It did not seem very far to the crest, and accordingly they started, but a more severe climb they had never had, and hoped never to have again. It was a very steep incline of rocks and snow all the way up. When the barometer showed an elevation of twenty-five hundred feet, Lockwood found himself on a ledge of rocks from which he could get neither up nor down for some time. Beneath him was a steep surface of frozen snow, falling on which he would have gone down-hill like an avalanche. Brainard had inclined more to the left, and, by following the side of a steep gully full of ice, had got ahead of him and out of sight.

Finally, Lockwood reached what had long seemed the summit, and stopped to rest. Presently Brainard came in sight, and said the top was about a mile off. They then started together, walked over a gradually ascending surface like the top of a vast dome, covered with hard frozen snow and ice, and very smooth and slippery, giving them frequent falls, and at 4 A. M. reached the summit and viewed the country around for many miles. Being cold, they did not stay long —only long enough to take bearings by compass of several distant mountains to the south, snow and ice-clad peaks with many glaciers between. To the west the country was less broken, and seemingly was a lofty surface of snow and ice. They traced the glacier near their camp about twenty miles toward the west-south-west, when it, and the valley containing it, came to an end in a high mountain-ridge. This wonderful feature of nature possessed great interest for Lockwood. The face of the barometer gave an elevation of the mountain or cliff on which they stood of 5,050 feet above the sea-level. As their tent was only three hundred feet above tide-water, their climb had not been a small one. They descended the mountain readily, although they had to use hands as well as feet all the way down, in some places carrying with them a land-slide of earth and stones.

They were constantly deceived as to distances and heights. A headland on the fiord looked but a half-hour's travel away, yet it took two or three hours to reach it. So these cliffs, which looked from below like an easy climb, proved the highest and steepest in that benighted region. They got back to the tent after thirteen hours of as hard work as they had yet experienced, and completely tired out. They took meridian observation for latitude, and then enjoyed a hearty meal of ptarmigan killed by Frederick during their absence.

On the 2d of May, they left their beds and had breakfast at about midnight. Found it snowing and unpleasant. Saw little else to do than retrace their steps to Ella Bay, and thence proceed around to Beatrix Bay and try to get inland from that place; spent the day, however, in further reconnoitring, as Lockwood did not wish to leave before night. Brainard went over to the northeast corner of the glacier, but found no way of proceeding in that direction, and, after carefully studying the surroundings, Lockwood could see no means of getting on even with packs. Spent most of the day in taking observations, etc. Occasionally they heard a noise like thunder, caused by the falling in of sections of the great wall before them, more formidable than any to be seen in China. The ground at the foot of the wall was only the bed of a stream with blocks of ice, and here and there a big bowlder. Everything being packed up and ready, they started down the stream again, examining several deep breaks in the cliffs to see if there was any prospect of *flanking* the glacier by means of one of them, but without success. There was no way of getting up even a short distance, except by leaving dogs and sledge behind and taking to the knapsacks, which was not then to be thought of.

They got along without event and reached their old camp after midnight, pitching the tent farther toward the north side, in order to see the sun when ready to take observations. Shortly after getting in, Frederick laid his whip down for an instant, and the promising dog Barker gobbled up all except about six inches of the butt-end in much less time than it takes to mention the fact. The praises of Barker had been sung ever since his birth, and this was only one of many of the tricks by which he proved his proficiency. Frederick quickly made a new lash, however, and *gave it* to Barker on the next march.

On the 3d of May, as they pushed their way onward, they took a series of angles and paced distances to get at the height of the tremendous cliffs near at hand. The result gave an altitude of forty-one hundred feet, which was almost vertical, the *débris* extending a third of the way up, and not being quite so steep. They then followed the north shore to Record Point, and thence took a straight course for the head of Beatrix Bay. The cliffs were so grand that Lockwood never tired of gazing at them, wondering how they were first formed, and thinking what tremendous force of nature had scooped out the awful chasm that comprised the fiord. These walls, high as they were, were only one half or one third of the height of the great snow-covered elevations back of and beyond them.

The appreciation of the grand in this region was frequently marred by fatigue and hunger, and so it was on the present occasion, Lockwood being glad enough when, at half-past one, they reached the head of Beatrix Bay. In the valley which they now entered, they concluded to spend another day. This one, like nearly all the valleys in this region, was simply a cañon, a narrow, ditch-like formation, walled in by steep, high cliffs. It was occupied as usual by a very insignificant stream, the successor of some mighty mass of water or ice which had originally hollowed out the great gorge. This, and the head of Ella Bay, were the farthest reached by Lieutenant Archer, R. N., who explored the fiord named for him to find out whether it was simply a *fiord*, or a strait or channel, as the Polaris people had asserted it to be. His Mount Neville, thirty-eight hundred feet high, Lockwood looked for in vain as a regular head to the valley, and finally fixed it as one of the cliffs which, a little way back, rose slightly higher, to a dome. Archer was a day making the ascent. Lockwood and Brainard walked about four miles up the valley, and saw its termination nearly six miles beyond, when they retraced their course to camp, greatly disappointed in seeing no game, except two or three ptarmigans. The valley seemed practicable for the sledge, and so, after considering one or two narrow and rocky gorges which came in from the west, they determined to follow it to its head (north-northwest), and then seek farther a route in the direction desired, which was west or southwest. As they proceeded, the weather became bright and clear, and the mercury was only 2° below zero. They passed up the valley, leaving in *cache* for return two days' rations. The dogs were in excellent condition, and, in spite of stones, went along very well. There was some ice in the stream-bed, and of snow quite an abundance. Above the farthest reached the day before, a small lake was discovered—a level expanse of snow with ice beneath. The lower part of the valley had two distinct elevations, the stream-bed, a very easy grade, forming one, while along the stream extended broken terraces, termed shoulders, which from the cliffs projected out on either side, sometimes beyond the middle of the valley, which was from one to three miles wide. The breadth decreased as they ascended, and after several miles it was but a few hundred yards wide. At this point, they suddenly came to a place where the valley seemed to run out, the whole breadth being a mass of rocks. Good traveling was seen beyond, however, and, after working an hour doubling up (taking half-load at a time), they got over, and shortly afterward the real end of the valley was reached. They then turned short off to the north, and, going up a steep, rocky ravine, about midnight pitched the tent for further survey of the scene on the morrow.

From this camp a low-looking "hog-back" was seen to close in the head of the valley. They determined to ascend this and get a look at the country, it seeming certain that the *big* sledge could go no farther. After making some coffee as strong as it could be made, and drinking about a quart each, to bolster up their spirits, the twain again started out, leaving Frederick to crawl into his sleeping-bag or keep warm as best he might. They proceeded north up a rocky ravine about a mile, and then came to a level plain stretching northward, some half a dozen miles farther, to a line of cliffs running across which seemed to indicate another valley or lake. To the right were two or three high, dome-shaped elevations, and to the left was Mount Easy, so called, afterward, on account of the ease with which they ascended it, and in contradistinction to Mount Difficult, the last they had ascended. They soon came to a pretty little lake—Lake Carolyn—only a few miles long. This they crossed, and, in places where the snow had been blown off, they could see down through the beautiful transparent ice, seven feet in thickness, even to the stones on the bottom of the lake near the shore. This lake had an elevation of eleven hundred feet above the sea. In three hours from camp, they reached the top of the mountain, an elevation of 2,720 feet, and had a good view. To the south the country was very high, and several glacier-walls came into view, probably connections of the glacier above Ella Bay. The Henrietta Nesmith glacier, the Garfield range, and the United States Mountains, were plainly seen, and also the depression in which lay Lake Hazen. Snow and ice in every direction. The cliffs to the north of the camp were very conspicuous, but whether along a valley or lake they could not make out. They stayed on top two hours, and then descended the south side of the mountain through a deep ravine filled in places with snow-drifts, and lower down with stones and bowlders. However, they went down very rapidly, and got to camp in two hours. The cliffs to the north seeming to extend to the west, Lockwood decided to visit them and take that route. The only other feasible route was by way of the ravine they had descended from the mountain-top.

Shortly after midnight of the 7th, Frederick had the dogs and little sledge ready, and, with nothing upon it but the shot-gun, hatchet, and telescope, they all started. The dogs were irrepressible, and took the little sledge over the rocks in a way calculated to cripple all hands, for they had to run alongside and hold on to the upstanders to keep up. Occasionally a runner of the sledge would catch under a bowlder and bring the sledge to a sudden stand-still, the immense strain of the strong dogs threatening to break it. On reaching the lake, all three of the men managed to crowd upon the sledge, and the dogs went at a rapid trot over its smooth, level surface. Beyond Lake Carolyn was a ravine leading toward the river, and there the dogs took to a gallop, and in an hour they reached a rocky height overlooking a long, wide valley walled in on the north side by high, precipitous cliffs, and on the south by heights of even greater elevation, but not so steep. There seemed no way, however, to get down. The water-course from the lake here became a narrow gorge blocked with large bowlders, the spaces between which were full of soft snow. It was not inviting, but they tried it, and in an hour reached the river-bed, the descent being most laborious. Here they found themselves only four hundred feet above the sea-level, and, turning to the right, went down-stream in a northeastern direction, the barometer constantly showing that they were going *down*-stream. *En route* they passed over several small lakes formed by expansions of the stream. In many places the ice was very thick and beautifully transparent. Seven miles from Rocky Gorge, where they entered the river, they suddenly saw four musk-oxen. Frederick being very anxious for slaughter was allowed to go after them, while Brainard remained to watch the sledge and dogs, and Lockwood went off to the right to take some compass-bearings. After a while he heard a shot from Frederick, and saw one of the animals fall. The others did not seem at all frightened, but stood by their dead comrade until Frederick *drove* them away by throwing stones at them. The dogs became greatly excited, and, going to where the dead game lay—a second ox having been killed—they gorged themselves with the entrails until there was danger of ruining their own.

Having returned to the camp, Lockwood now projected a special trip westward of twelve days, and prepared his outfit as follows: Shelter-tent, sleeping-bags, axe, sextant, etc., telescope, shot-gun and ammunition, medicine, cook's bag, rubber blankets, small lamp, knapsacks, snow-shoes, rations for three at forty-five ounces each per day, and one sack of pemmican for dogs; total, 328¼ pounds. The *large* tent was left standing with the big sledge alongside and the American flag flying from the upstander. They got off at an early hour on the 8th with the dogs in excellent condition. Much work was required to get over the rocks, but after that they proceeded satisfactorily until near the valley. This was found to be quite wide for a region where everything of the kind was more like a cañon than a valley in the ordinary sense. Its width was two or three miles, or perhaps in some places four, and the general gradients of the stream-bed (Dodge River) were very slight, perhaps thirty feet to the mile. Narrow, deep cuts in the cliffs and high ground around indicated tributary streams.

Frederick having shot a hare, and gathered up the other food, they proceeded on their way, traveling now over thick, clear ice and hard snow, with now and then patches of stones. The valley seemed to come to an end some fifteen miles up-stream, a range of high hills running directly across it.

After various tribulations in exploring a side gorge, at midnight on the 10th of May the party resumed travel up the valley. The condition of the sledge-runners rendered it necessary to reduce the weight to the least amount possible. This doubtless pleased the dogs, for the driver had to restrain their ardor. Leaving the sledge to pursue its way along the base of the hills, Lockwood ascended a considerable elevation and obtained a good outlook over the country. He was very agreeably surprised to find at the farther end of a gap up stream an apparent prolongation of the valley in the same general direction. On either side of this prolongation was a range of low heights, while the intermediate surface looked very level—so level that he took it for a long lake. To the left, just outside the heights on that side of the valley, he could see at intervals a glacier-wall, the north boundary of a great *mer de glace*. About twenty miles distant, the valley seemed again to be shut in by a range of hills, but over the tops of them, and at a great elevation on the distant horizon, he saw what seemed to be a snow-bank. This he made his objective point. Passing onward through the gap, they came to a long and picturesque lake which was named Lake Nan after an interesting niece; and coming to a place near the end of the valley, a break in the low heights to the left revealed the glacier they had before seen. Its surface was very distinct. Extending to the south a few miles, it soon reached an elevation that formed the horizon in that direction. It seemed a vast undulating surface, and, as was afterward discovered, is the backbone of Grinnell Land. The wall of the glacier near which they camped presented a vertical face of solid ice 140 feet high. At intervals they heard the sound of falling ice—small fragments which became detached and dropped to the base. The altitude of this camp above the sea-level was found to be 1,240 feet, and of Lake Nan 920 feet; that of their last camp was 685 feet, and of the first camp in the valley, 420 feet.

Passing onward, they crossed several small lakes close along the wall, with brooks emptying into them from the north. In a few hours they were on the divide, the surface to the north having more slope than that on the other side. The summit gave an elevation by barometer of 2,610 feet, about 400 feet

147

higher than where they left the wall. They had an extensive view to the east, and could see Dodge River as far as they had explored it, also Mount Easy and the country adjacent. To the southeast, south, and southwest, was seen the glacier, which was named after Agassiz. It formed the horizon for half a dozen miles in these directions. All the ice-capped country and glaciers seen from the former camps were found to be connected with, and to form a part of this one glacier. Toward the north, the country had comparatively little snow. Presently they came in view of a mountain-peak toward the northwest, not many miles distant, which was recognized as Mount Arthur, the farthest point reached by Lieutenant Greely during the previous year. Away beyond it were seen very distinctly the United States and Garfield Mountains. Just to the west of Mount Arthur, they discovered a large lake, which Lockwood named Lake Fletcher. They were now on a surface rapidly sloping to the west. Some miles distant in this direction appeared a broken range of cliffs and mountains, and between their stand-point and these mountains was a wide valley, connected by a stream with Lake Fletcher, and a small lake, close to the Chinese Wall, which they called Lake Harry, the latter having an elevation of 1,320 feet. They crossed Lake Harry, and beyond it came to another called Lake Bessie, having an elevation of 1,630 feet, and covered with deep snow.

Reaching the cliffs to the west, they found the descent exceedingly precipitous and rugged. No other passage offered than that through a gorge which was filled with ice and hard snow, whose surface was almost perpendicular. As this was the only passage, they went into camp to devise ways and means. Next morning, Lockwood attached all the ropes he had, including dog-traces, to the sledge, and while he rode to guide caused the others to ease down the sledge. Unfortunately, the rope was too short, and those at the top let go. Gravity carried the sledge and rider down the foot of the slope, now somewhat reduced, with fearful rapidity, till they brought up against rocks covered with snow, fortunately without serious damage. The other men and dogs got down as best they could, the former digging footholds as they progressed.

Further descending the cañon, they came to another glacier stretching entirely across their way, and, as it seemed impossible to surmount it or the walls on either side, they came to a halt and enjoyed a night of rest. The next day they pushed on, though troubled with snow-blindness, and, overcoming the obstacle of the previous day, crossed a lake and encamped on its farther end. On the following day, after passing through a gorge, the outlet of the lake, between high cliffs, they were surprised to see a number of floebergs similar in every respect to the floebergs of the east Grinnell coast. At the same time they found the water to be *salt*, and saw the fresh tracks of a bear. These facts convinced Lockwood that they were near the western sea, probably at the head of a fiord. This soon became still more apparent. Here they also saw another glacier coming in some miles west of the last. They crossed a crack of open water, formed by the tide, and found themselves on well-recognized floe-ice, quite level but covered in places with deep snow. Ahead of them, twenty miles distant, on the opposite side of the fiord, was a bold headland, and toward this they now directed their course. This fiord, which Lockwood named after Lieutenant Greely, separated at its head into two bays. These he called, after Greely's daughters, Adola and Antoinette. The latter bay they were now crossing, while they bore away to the north. It had become very foggy, and was snowing and blowing hard. When some miles out they crossed other bear-tracks, and finally reached the cape for which they had been striving. Here the south shore of the fiord bent off toward the west-southwest being very wide and walled in on all sides by steep cliffs broken in a few places by branch fiords or bays. They encamped at the cape on the 13th, had supper, and soon turned in to sleep and fast as long as possible, or until the storm abated, as the party was now reduced to what they called a starvation allowance. There was nothing to do but to make observations when the sun appeared.

The mouth of the fiord at the north side was found to be about forty miles off, but the snow was deep and soft, and they could not attempt it without rations, all of which was extremely provoking. The sun became dimly visible through a snow-storm, looking like a grease-spot in the sky; but, notwithstanding, observations were attempted for latitude and longitude, and many compass-bearings were taken. At times everything was shut out of sight excepting the nearest cliff. Brainard feared they would have a very hard time in getting back, and Frederick evidently thought he was a long distance from Fort Conger, seeming rather "down in the mouth."

Soon after breakfast on the 15th, Lockwood and Brainard started to ascend the cliffs near by, the weather having partially cleared. They did so by means of a ravine opposite the camp, and had hardly reached the top before the snow began to fall again, and the wind to blow from the east; but, notwithstanding, they saw a large glacier to the south twenty or thirty miles away, and another to the northwest at about the same distance. The first was apparently an offshoot of the great "Chinese Wall" already mentioned. They saw also a lofty range of mountains far to the north, running generally parallel with the fiord. The cliffs to the west shut out the mouth of the fiord, and, before they could get far enough in that direction to see over them, the coming storm obscured almost everything. These cliffs were 2,140 feet high by the barometer, and almost vertical. The driving snow now became very uncomfortable, and, after going three miles westward, they concluded to return. *En route*, they found a number of fossils of what seemed to be trees, snakes, or fishes, Brainard being the first to notice them. They also saw a ptarmigan, an owl, and some snow-buntings, these being the only living objects observed. Reached the tent after six hours' absence, and found Frederick tramping around in the snow, not knowing what to do with himself. After supper, all three of the party with the sledge and dogs went an hour's journey toward the opposite shore of the fiord, ten miles away. The sky was partially clear, and they got a very good view down the fiord, the telescope bringing into view another cape (Cape Lockwood). Between that and the cape on the north side (Cape Brainard), they failed to see any land, though they examined long and carefully with the telescope. The fiord between those two capes was very wide. Several branch fiords, or what appeared to be such, were noticed. Cape Lockwood seemed to be on the farther side of one of these, or on an island. The country on both sides of the fiord was very elevated, that on the north side much broken, and that on the south, away from the fiord, apparently an ice-clad surface rising into immense, dome-like undulations against the horizon.

After a meager breakfast, they started on their return, finding the snow very deep and soft. The effect of short rations on the dogs was noticed. They saw two seals lying on the ice, which Frederick tried hard to shoot, but in vain. Lockwood was especially anxious to get a seal, for it looked as if they would have to kill one dog to save the remainder. After much trouble for want of food, they resumed their journey on the 17th, verifying at various points the observations that had been previously made in regard to the great ice-wall and the lake over which they had already passed.

On reaching the end of the lake, they began the ascent of the ravine. The snow at the head of the ravine was very soft and deep, and they had hard work to get through it. Arriving at the big snow-drift which they had descended with so much difficulty and danger, it became a question how to ascend, but they managed it by first cutting some steps and getting the dogs up, and then, attaching them by long lines to the sledge below, men and dogs together pulled the load up the almost vertical face. The party went into camp at the old place, and decided to kill one of the dogs, yet very reluctantly, Frederick opposing it. Brainard had suggested White Kooney, but Frederick named Button, a young dog. Button had eaten up his harness that morning, and this decided his fate. He was shot by Frederick, and soon the carcass was skinned and presented to his brethren. Old Howler at once seized a hind-quarter, but the others did nothing more than smell the meat. They walked around it in a reflective mood, debating whether to yield to their hunger or to their repugnance. When the party awoke next morning, nothing remained of poor Button but some of the larger bones.

On the 18th, Lockwood and Brainard ascended a neighboring mountain and got a look at the country. The ascent was easy and they gained the top in a short time; altitude, 2,008 feet. From this point they could see the "Chinese Wall" stretching off to the southwest forty miles, over hills and dales, as far as the glacier south of Fossil Mountain, although Lockwood could not recognize that particular glacier. The glaciers at the two ends of the lake, near Greely Fiord, were readily seen to be offshoots of the greater one, whose surface toward the south could be seen for several miles. In that direction, Lockwood took the bearings of several ice-capped mountains, one, as he thought, identical with a very high mountain seen to the south from Antoinette Bay. The "Chinese Wall" had the same general aspect everywhere—a vertical face of pure white or green ice upward of two hundred feet high, and extending across the country in a fashion he could liken to nothing else.

From here Lockwood made a short excursion by himself to Lake Harry, discovered a number of other small lakes, and obtained the altitude of several localities. He returned to camp only to find the dogs in a bad way for food, and a scarcity for himself and men. Resuming their course the next morning, after the dog Howler had performed the remarkable feat of stealing a piece of meat when it was cooking on the alcohol-stove, they passed many of the localities they had seen before, but in some cases hardly recognized them on account of the flying snow. Making two marches in twenty-four hours, they reached their first camp, and found the tent blown down, but the big sledge in its position, with the American flag flying over it as gayly as if in a pleasant and genial clime. The dogs were gratified with a good feast of pemmican, and the men themselves found it delightful, once more to have a full supply of food.

Their next move was for Archer Fiord, by way of Beatrix Bay and Record Point. They crossed another lake, where, as once before, they could see the bottom through ice that was seven feet in thickness, having revisited the north side of Musk-ox Valley, which was separated from the lake by a very low and narrow divide. Dodge River was seen bending off to the northeast toward Howgate Fiord. The surroundings were very picturesque, but barren and desolate in the extreme. They saw no signs of game, and even the poor, stunted vegetation of the region was wanting. Rocks and snow, with stretches of bare ground, composed the prospect.

The lake alluded to above was about twelve miles long—a considerable sheet of water—and, no doubt, in summer would be an interesting place to visit, as places go in the Arctic regions.

After camping they proceeded along to the east of Murray Island, the weather cloudy and calm. Depot Point was revisited, to look for the English rations, but nothing found.

Having killed a seal, they took the meat and blubber along, and camped about ten miles from Bulley's Lump, where they had a good feast of meat and liver. The latter was greatly relished, Brainard making it into many dishes.

On the 24th, they enjoyed their breakfast at midnight, Lockwood calling it a real *midnight mass*, as it was a black mass of seal-liver, English meat, corned beef, potatoes, and hard bread, all cooked together in one stew which was very good, notwithstanding its miscellaneous character.

The comments of Lockwood, in regard to the expedition, and how matters were at the station, were as follow:

"No such word as 'failed' to write this time, I am thankful to say, but the happy reflection is mine that I accomplished more than any one expected, and more than I myself dared hope—the discovery of the western sea, and hence the western coast-line of Grinnell Land. I have now the rather ponderous task of preparing a report, making a map, and writing out this journal from my notes. Tidal observations have been taken at Capes Baird, Distant, and Beechy, simultaneously, showing that the tides arrive at these places in the order named. This is very singular, as the previous expeditions into these parts established (?) the tides as coming from the north. This agrees, however, with the order of their arrival at Cape Sumner, Gap Valley, and Black Horn Cliffs, where I took observations in April. No more musk-ox meat left; it ran out on the 20th inst., and hunting-parties sent out April 25th saw nothing. I surmised as much, from the absence of game on my trip, though Brainard did not agree with me. Two seals have been shot, but only one secured.

"I find the social relations of our room not improved—rather worse than better. Dr. P., though he shook hands and asked me several questions as to my trip, relapsed into silence, which he seldom breaks. Lieutenant K. had but one question to ask. I often contrast ours with the pleasant relations of the English officers when here, and think how much happier we should be in following their example. As it is, I soon relapse into *ennui* and apathy. A sledge-journey, with all its trials, is preferable to this. I view those ahead of us with indifference, as it will rid me of this forced association. Another winter would render me a maniac, or put me under a cairn.

"The spirits of the men seem good. The sun has revived them. Merry groups may be seen at any time on the sunny sides of the house.

"How often do I think of home, which now seems to me like a series of pictures or objects long since seen! how often of my dear father, whom may a kind Providence spare for many, many years!

"Both Brainard and I lost a score of pounds weight on our late trip; but we are rapidly regaining our avoirdupois. My appetite is frightful, and nothing comes amiss. I want to eat every three or four hours. Fortunately, we have a supply of musk-ox beef on hand, having killed three recently aggregating four hundred pounds, to which are added many water and other fowl daily brought in. There was felt at one time some apprehension that our resource in this respect had disappeared, and fears were entertained of scurvy. The men seem to have fared so well that their appetites have become dainty. One would suppose that pork and beans were not staples at our army posts.

"Israel makes my *farthest* of the last trip, latitude 80° 47´, longitude 88° 29´. Hence my explorations extend over 2½° of latitude and 38° of longitude. Have plotted my western journey, and find that my farthest carries me far off the English map. I took latitude and longitude observations at every camp, and also frequent compass-bearings; to reconcile all these is a task.

"Rice has taken a photograph of my corner, where I do all my work and also sleep.

"Have been reading the authorities on glaciers, and regret I did not inform myself better before going out. But perhaps that Chinese Wall will make up for my short-comings.

"Those rheumatic pains I had a year ago have returned and trouble me much. I must be moving again soon.

"Several of the dogs, becoming mangy, have been shot. Poor old 'Howler,' whom we left on the ice-floe, hoping he would recover and follow us, was found dead near the same place. Oh! the hours of misery I have spent in sleeping-bags, kept awake by that howling brute—howling, perhaps, just because another dog looked at him! But, for all his howlings and stealings, the ex-king was a good worker and did his duty, and that should be all required of any one, man or dog. May he rest in peace in the happy hunting-grounds of the canine race! Frederick, I presume, will put on crape for him."

XVI.
PREPARING FOR HOME.

Hardly had Lieutenant Lockwood reoccupied his *corner* long enough to get thoroughly rested and warm, before we find him hard at work again and ready for any emergency. At the request of Lieutenant Greely, he undertook a task in which he himself feared that he manifested more zeal than discretion. Dr. Pavy, the natural history custodian of the expedition, having failed to render reports of the collections, or properly care for them, was relieved soon after Lockwood's return from the west, and the department was transferred to Lockwood. With very little aid from the doctor, he made lists and secured the specimens from further injury, the men having shown much industry and zeal in adding to the collection. In the mean time, Fredericks, who was a saddler by trade, rendered good service by making for Lockwood and the men seal-skin boots, which were of great use; and he also made himself useful by overhauling the sleeping-bags and making new ones for the contemplated boat-voyage to Littleton Island at a later day. Snyder had also made some wearing gear for use on board the relief-ship.

"What a change for us all," wrote Lockwood on the 3d of June, "if we ever return home! And how much to talk about, and how much to hear! Just two years ago, I left Baltimore on the Nova Scotia, to join the Proteus at St. John's. Open water is reported in the straits near Cape Baird. How eagerly we watch for any change that may effect our release!"

On the 22d of June, a party was sent up the Bellows for game and returned successful, having killed eight musk-oxen, one seal, and a few geese, all of which were duly brought in. Many waterfowl and ptarmigans were brought from other points; and then followed a grand dinner in honor of Dr. Pavy's birthday. To show the social relations of the officers, Lockwood says, "The only remark at dinner was a very sage one by myself, viz., that the sun was now on his way south, to which Lieutenant Greely assented.

"The men all busy and all cheerful. Lieutenant Greely remarked that it did not look as if the 'gloom which their coming fate cast over the spirits of the men' was quite as deep as Lieutenant Kislingbury thought it to be. Another day gone," wrote Lockwood—"another day nearer the end of our stay here! A miserable, gloomy day it is too. Snow, or snow mixed with rain, all day, and last night it blew a gale from the right direction to clear away the ice—north-east. I think myself now in excellent condition for a hermit's life, having had two years' experience of a life not very dissimilar."

On the 3d of June, Lockwood made the ascent of an immense "hog-back" north of the station. Hog-back was the term used by the English to designate the oval-shaped elevations so common in this region, being neither mountain nor table-land, but immense undulations which, with more or less slope, rise three, four, or even five thousand feet above the sea-level. He was the first to ascend this one, and did so to view the country northwest of it, which he desired to explore. It was the highest of a series of ridges, half a mile or so apart, each just high enough to suggest the idea of its being the genuine top, but showing another beyond still higher. He pressed on, frequently resting, and finally *did* reach the top, and saw, beyond, the United States Mountains in the distance. The view from this elevation, more than half a mile above the sea-level, was superb. The straits seemed one solid mass of ice. The Greenland shore and Archer's Fiord were in full view. The whole land was made up of mountains.

The 4th of July was celebrated by a game of baseball, in which Lieutenant Greely took part; also the Esquimaux, but they confined themselves to running after the ball. A good dinner followed, to which Lieutenant Greely contributed four bottles of Sauterne; but the doctor declined the wine, and made a hasty meal. They also had a rifle-match. Several of the men donned white shirts and other "store-clothes," metamorphosing themselves completely, flannel shirts, with trousers in boots, being the usual costume.

On the same day Lieutenant Greely issued an order directing Dr. Pavy to turn over to Lieutenant Lockwood all the medical stores, journals, and collections, the former having declined to renew his engagement, which had expired. On the 11th of July, Lockwood started with Brainard on an exploration toward the northwest with a view of reaching, if possible, the United States range of mountains. They carried an outfit weighing one hundred pounds, or twenty-five pounds for each man at the start, as Henry and Biederbick were to help them with the impedimenta for one day and then return. They went without sledge or tent, and carried only blanket, sleeping-bags, a small lamp, and a few pounds of food, with instruments, snow-shoes, etc. They soon reached the top of the hog-back beyond "Sugar-Loaf," and afterward the true hog-back Lockwood had visited before, finding it 2,700 feet high. Thence they kept a north-northwest course toward a prominent glacier in the United States Range, moving about parallel to North Valley Creek, which empties into St. Patrick's Bay. After traveling fourteen miles they camped—that is, selected as smooth and sheltered a spot as could be found, made some tea, spread out the sleeping-bags, and crawled in.

Henry and Biederbick left the next morning evidently well satisfied to forego the pleasures of this trip. Their departure rendered it necessary to reduce the load somewhat, which was done by leaving behind the snow-shoes and rubber spread, trusting to luck to find a bare spot for their sleeping-bag. After tramping through much wet snow alternating with mud and stones, and getting their feet soaking wet, they came to two deep gorges close together, each occupied by a considerable stream of water. They crossed these and ascended a dome beyond, three thousand feet high, and thence came to a still larger stream whose gorge was one thousand feet deep. Here they stopped for the night after a tramp of twelve miles. The next morning the sky was overcast, with barometric indications of a storm; but they continued their way with reduced loads, having only one day's food left. Following the stream northwest a few miles, they crossed it and ascended a high elevation, from which the United States range could be very distinctly viewed, and then came to the conclusion that they had gone far enough.

With the telescope they could see distinctly, about twenty miles away, the walls of the great glacier, and its face ten miles wide. In fact, the whole range was full of glaciers. The country intervening between them and the glaciers seemed comparatively level. At noon they started back, and did not stop until the camping-place of the night before was reached. Thence, after a drink of tea and something to eat, abandoning their sleeping-bags, they made for their first camp, where had been left the rubber spread and one extra bag. The traveling was execrable, but they reached Fort Conger on the 14th, hungry, tired, and decidedly used up.

On the 24th, preparations began for the proposed boat-journey toward the south on which they would start when the ice would permit. Lockwood, in obedience to a general order, prepared to take no clothing except what he wore, and the few pounds of his baggage would consist of his journal and other papers. He felt depressed and low-spirited, and totally indifferent as to the risks they were to encounter.

The straits were reported clear of ice below Cape Lieber on the 26th, but the bay near by was still full, though with many leads. Every preparation was made to leave on the 1st of August, if possible, or as soon after as the ice would allow. The men fiddled and sang, and seemed in joyous spirits; and the hilarity was kept up by the dogs Ritenbank and Ask-him having a terrible fight, resulting in victory to the latter. The probable consequence was that Ask-him would now be king. Ritenbank went about with his head down and tail between his legs, a dethroned and friendless monarch. The usurper's reign, however, was likely to be a short one, as, on the party's leaving, the dogs would either be shot or left to starve to death.

The 5th of August arrived, and the ship was the only thing talked about. Some of the men reported smoke down the straits, but it was soon found to be only water-clouds or fog. In the midst of these excitements, Lockwood gave expression to the following feelings: "As the time for moving approaches, I feel a singular apathy. If we had plenty of fresh meat and more good books, I could stand another winter here."

Soon after, heavy winds from the south making great changes in the condition of the ice, active preparations were made for leaving.

Lockwood writes: "I don't feel as though I was going away, much less toward the south. Have felt more stirred up on beginning a sledge-journey."

TABULATED STATEMENT OF THE DISTANCE TRAVELED TO LOCKWOOD ISLAND.

	DISTANCE TRAVELED.				TIME.		
	Adv	Tr	Add	Tot	Adv	Tr	MPH
	MILES—GEOGRAPHICAL.				HOURS. GEO. M.		
OUT.							
Fort Conger to Boat Camp	48	67	157	224	21½	28¼	2·23
Boat Camp to sea-coast	36	86	25	111	18¾	44⅓	1·92
Sea-coast to Cape Bryant	37½	103½	12	113	21½	47¹/₁₂	1·74
Cape Bryant to Cape Britannia	60	118	..	118	32	55⁵/₁₂	1·87
Cape Britannia to farthest	95	95	..	95	39⅔	48⅙	2·39
Total (out)	267½	469½	194	701	133½	223¾	2·07
BACK.							
Farthest to Cape Britannia	95	95	..	95	37⅓	41¾	2·52
Cape Britannia to Cape Bryant	60	60	..	60	25¾	28	2·33
Cape Bryant to Boat Camp	61½	61½	..	61½	27¼	36½	2·25
Boat Camp to Fort Conger	48	48	..	48	22½	28⅓	2·13
Total (back)	264½	264½	..	264½	112⅚	134 2/12	2·34
Aggregate (out and back)	541	734	194	965½	245 11/12	357⅚	2·20
Aggregate (out and back) in statute miles	623	..	..	1069			

Key to Headings:
Adv: Advanced.
Add: Additional miles traveled.
Tr: Traveled.

Tot: Total.
MPH: Number of miles per hour.

The word "advanced," both here and in the journal, refers to the simple distance from camp to camp, and the actual time occupied in making that distance—all stops *deducted*.

The word "traveled" includes total number of miles traveled—the number of miles advanced added to those traveled in going back and forth in "doubling up." The time corresponding refers to the whole time from leaving one camp to arriving at the next, all stops included.

The "additional miles" refer to incidental journeys not numbered as marches.

The rate per hour is computed from the distance and time *advanced*.

The whole statement is confined to the dog-sledge.

XVII.
HOMEWARD BOUND.

The time having arrived, the final orders were given for the Arctic exiles to make ready for the first stage of travel leading to their far-distant home. They were now to leave the station at Fort Conger, and, as best they could, find their way to Littleton Island, where they hoped to meet a vessel that would take them back to Newfoundland. They were to depart in boats, viz., the steam-launch Lady Greely, a whale-boat, an English boat of which they had come into possession, and a still smaller affair, that might prove serviceable for special purposes.

The journal kept by Lieutenant Lockwood after his departure from Fort Conger was written in short-hand, as always while in the field, and is a very complete record. In the following pages, only a brief summary of purely personal incidents will be attempted, without presuming to give the phraseology of the youthful explorer.

On the 9th of August, the little fleet pushed off from shore, laden with the twenty-five adventurers and a comfortable supply of provisions. They reached Bellot Island without much trouble, but afterward encountered a good deal of ice, and, while working very hard to get through, Rice accidentally fell overboard, which was for him a poor beginning. The ice continued to be troublesome until the close of the next day, when the boats were so severely nipped that they had to be drawn up on the floe. Afterward, open water appearing all the way across the fiord, the launch and the other boats made a successful crossing nearly opposite Sun Bay. They reached the depot near Cape Baird, at about 2 P. M., up to which hour, from the time of leaving Fort Conger, they had not been able to secure any sleep, nor anything to drink but cold water. Reaching Cape Lieber on the 11th in a snow-storm, they landed on a bluff about a mile from the cape, where they waited for the ice to move, so that they might continue on their route toward the south along the western shore of the strait. The only animals seen in that vicinity were two narwhals, fighting near the shore. The fog now became so very dense that no headway could be made, and this gave them an opportunity to obtain some needed rest. Their next advance was in the midst of a severe storm of wind and snow, in spite of which they reached Carl Ritter Bay on the morning of the 12th. The next morning, while they had open water near the shore, they discovered ice-barriers extending to the south as far as they could see. At this point a young seal was killed, which was greatly enjoyed by all of the party; but this luxury, in the case of Lockwood, was counterbalanced by the discomfort of sleeping on shore without any protection excepting that of his bag. He also spent several nights on a floe-berg, where, by laying his sleeping-bag on a sheepskin, he slept more comfortably. From the 13th until the 20th, when the party reached Rawlings's Bay, it was a continual conflict with floating ice, snow-storms, and fog, the monotony of the struggle having been broken by an accident to the launch, and also one to Lieutenant Greely, who had a fall into the water, from which he was rescued without harm. At all the places where they encamped, they had great difficulty in securing a safe harbor for the launch. Having passed across Richardson Bay in safety and reached Cape Collinson, they found about one hundred and twenty, out of two hundred and forty, English rations which had been deposited there, the missing portion having been eaten by the foxes. On the 22d they reached Scoresby Bay, where observations of the strait showed it to be full of floating ice; and in this vicinity they were brought to a halt by the ice-pack near the shore at Cape John Barrow. Here the boats were pulled up on the floe, and, as the thick sludge-ice was all around, no open water in sight, and the supply of coal getting very low, the prospect was gloomy in the extreme. When able to continue on their course, the travelers were still greatly troubled by heavy fogs, and while passing over a space of open water, abounding in floe-bergs which could not be seen, they were in constant danger of being lost. Notwithstanding all these obstacles, they pushed their way onward, and in due time reached Cape Louis Napoleon, Cape Hawks, and Princess Marie Bay, when they were again stopped by the floating ice, and detained by the newly formed ice.

In his desire to comply with the order as to weight of baggage, Lockwood had left his seal-skin coat at Fort Conger, but this step he afterward regretted, as the weather continued stormy, and he was greatly exposed to the cold. To this was added the misfortune of having a badly fitting seal-skin boot which gave him great pain, so that he had to resort to a pair of moccasins. When the boats were caught in floes and detained for days, the only exercise available was that of walking over the level floes. Some of the men were wont to march around, under the light of the moon, singing aloud their wild and uncouth songs. When tired of walking, Lockwood would creep into a cozy corner of the launch, and pore over a pocket copy of Shakespeare which he had fortunately brought along; and then, after getting into his sleeping-bag, his thoughts would wander far away and find expression in such words as these: "What are they doing at home? How often I think of the dear ones there! The dangers and uncertainties ahead of us are only aggravated by the thoughts of the concern felt by them on my account. Most of us have given up the idea of getting home this fall."

On the 3d of September, while in the floe below Cape Hawks, Lieutenant

Greely held a consultation with Lockwood, Kislingbury, Pavy, and Brainard, expressing the opinion that their situation was critical, and that they were really working for their lives. One of the suggestions was that the launch should be abandoned, and further progress made in the smaller boats along the western shore of the strait; but to this, Greely and the majority objected, still hoping that they might yet be able to reach Littleton Island through a lead or over the young ice. On the 6th the hunter Jans killed his fourth seal, and was rewarded by a drink of rum. After five more days of travel, and while approaching Cocked-Hat Island, there was a great excitement caused by the report that one of the men had heard the barking of dogs, whereupon guns were fired and a flag displayed; but all the commotion ended in nothing. The tides were contrary, the small boat was abandoned, and the outlook was very gloomy. The faithful Esquimaux, Frederick, who had latterly been somewhat unlucky as a hunter, now came to the front by killing a seal that weighed six hundred pounds, receiving the usual drink of rum. On this occasion Lockwood mentioned that he swallowed a cupful of the seal's blood, and found it somewhat tasteless. On the 5th of September, the party after great labor came abreast of Victoria Head and Cape Albert, and while drifting along on the floe the American flag was hoisted over the launch, and the fire under the engine was put out to save coal, Lockwood enjoying a little needed sleep. On the 7th they came in sight of the coast extending from Alexander Harbor to Cape Sabine, and the impossibility of proceeding in the launch becoming apparent, it was decided to resort to sledge-travel, two of the sledges to carry a boat each, and both of them to be drawn by the men. When they were fully prepared for moving, it was found that one of them weighed 1,700 pounds and the other 2,100 pounds. Owing to the various difficulties which soon beset the travelers, they were obliged to abandon one of the boats, whereby it became necessary to retrace several sections of the journey for the purpose of bringing on the extra supplies, thus adding greatly to the fatigue of the men. Lockwood now expressed his doubts as to whether he would live to write out his notes, and also his fears that the floe upon which the party then were, might take them down into Baffin's Bay. Not only were they at the mercy of the floe, but the currents were contrary, sludge-ice abundant, and their supply of food reduced to seal-blubber, bread, and tea. At one time, strange to say, their position in the straits was directly north of Littleton Island, and nearer the Greenland coast than that of Grinnell Land. It now seemed to Lockwood that there was nothing ahead of them but starvation and death, and yet the men kept up their spirits in a manner that greatly surprised him. One of the floes upon which they had drifted for many days, when found to be cracking in one or two places, caused the party to move upon another nearer the shore, and in a short time the floe previously occupied was entirely broken up. On the 29th of September, the floe on which they were floating, finally touched another toward the west, and that another connected with the shore, by which means they were enabled to reach the land, very thankful to be in a place of security once more. The locality was really a rock forming a promontory between two glaciers, and thought to be about thirteen miles directly south of Cape Sabine. To that place a reconnoitring party was at once sent, but the cape could not be reached on account of open water near it, and the party was compelled to return. In the mean time, arrangements were made for building out of stones and ice the necessary huts for protection during the coming winter, should it be their fate to remain there. While this work was progressing, it was decided that the daily rations would have to be reduced. Lockwood expressed the opinion that they had only three chances for their lives: first, the chance of finding an American *cache* at Cape Sabine; secondly, a chance of crossing the straits, here thirty-five miles wide, when their provisions were gone; thirdly, the chance of being able to kill enough game for their support during the winter. A second effort was made by Rice and a party to reach Cape Sabine, which was successful. They not only brought news about the wreck of the Proteus, but also a copy of the Army Register for 1883, in which appeared Lockwood's name as a first lieutenant. Rice also succeeded in discovering the English *cache* with two hundred and forty rations, the *cache* left by the Neptune in 1882, and the stores brought from the wreck of the Proteus in 1883, all of which information was hailed with delight by the party. Among the stores left by the Proteus, a newspaper slip was picked up, from which was gathered the news that President Garfield had died; that the Jeannette had been lost; and that serious apprehensions were felt in the United States about the fate of the Greely Expedition. This latter intelligence gave Lockwood great pain, seeming almost prophetic, except in the remark "lying down under the great stars to die!" and induced him to make this record: "This article gives me great pain, because of the alarm and sorrow which must be felt by my dear father and mother and sisters on my behalf. Should my ambitious hopes be disappointed, and these lines only, meet the eyes of those so dear, may they not in thought add to my many faults and failings that of ingratitude or want of affection in not recording more frequently my thoughts regarding them!"

One of the results of the trip made by Rice to Cape Sabine was the selection of a spot, between the cape and Cocked-Hat Island, for a home during the approaching winter. Here, officers and men alike laboring, a new hut was built, which was forthwith occupied by the party, all the supplies being at once brought from the camp south of Cape Sabine. The place where they now found themselves established, Lieutenant Greely called Camp Clay, in honor of one of the party—a grandson of Henry Clay—who had been attached to the expedition until it reached Lady Franklin Bay, whence he returned home on account of his health. As soon as the new hut was occupied, the announcement was made that six of the party were on the sick list; but shortly afterward, and notwithstanding the deplorable condition of affairs, Lockwood recorded the following in his journal: "We are all now in comparatively high spirits, and look forward to getting back to the United States with a great deal of certainty. We shall have to live on half-rations or less until April, and there will be shortness of fuel. Many hardships are obvious, but we all feel sound again."

On the 23d of October, twelve of the party went from Camp Clay upon a visit to Cape Sabine, and, while some of them opened the English *cache* at the south side of Payer Harbor, Lockwood built a cairn there and deposited under it, among other things, the records of the expedition, with a note in lead-pencil to the following effect:

> "*October 23, 1883.*—This cairn contains the original records of the Lady Franklin Bay Expedition, the private journal of Lieutenant Lockwood, and a set of photographic negatives. The party is permanently encamped at a point midway between Cape Sabine and Cocked-Hat Island. All well.
>
> "J. B. LOCKWOOD,
> "*First Lieutenant Twenty-third Infantry.*"

On their way back to Camp Clay, Dr. Pavy met with an accident to one of his feet, and, while most of the party went on, Lockwood and Ellison remained behind to look after him. When night came on, they lost their way, stumbling and floundering over the rubble-ice until overcome by fatigue and hunger; but were revived by a limited mutton stew on their arrival at the camp. One of the results to Lockwood of his Samaritan conduct was an accident to one of his knees, which gave him trouble for several days, and prevented his being as useful as he desired in contributing to the comfort of the party. It was about this time that Lieutenant Greely declared his intention of reducing the rations, all assenting, so that they might last until the 1st of March; and this fact, added to the discovery that some of their meat was far more bony than it should have been, caused some consternation. Cold, dampness, darkness, and hunger continued to be their hourly and daily portion, the allowance of food being only about one fourth of what they actually needed.

XVIII.
THE FINAL CATASTROPHE.

While the following pages will contain necessarily brief notices of the life of the party during an entire winter, they must conclude with the record of the great calamity which befell the band of heroes. Shortly after they found themselves settled for a campaign of idleness, as they expected it to be, Lockwood was again confined to his sleeping-bag on account of an injury to his feet which had not been properly protected; his discomforts being aggravated by the reflection that both provisions and fuel were beginning to reach a low-tide level. The constant hunger which was experienced by all hands went far to make their circumstances dismal and depressing; while the only entertainment that could be provided was the reading aloud, by one of the men, of a story and some newspaper scraps which Rice had picked up at Cape Sabine. A little excitement was afforded by a lottery for the distribution of some clothing and two mattresses which had been brought ashore from the Proteus, one of the latter falling to the lot of Lockwood. And now came a proposition for a sledge expedition, not to discover islands, glaciers, fiords, and prominent capes, but to go after the abandoned whale-boat which had floated down with the floe. This must be broken up and used for fuel. Then followed another expedition, occupying not less than eight days, to Cape Isabella, to obtain one hundred pounds of preserved meat left there by the English. Feeling the want of exercise, Lockwood occasionally took a long walk, and on one occasion was so hungry when he returned, that he could not wait for the regular evening meal, but fastened upon a lot of moldy potatoes which had been abandoned, and with these filled his stomach, almost expecting that the feast would cause his death. Some of the men went still further, for, when a blue or a white fox was killed, even the entrails of the animal were devoured. Food was the constant subject of conversation with all of the party—what they would be able to get, what they had enjoyed in former years at their distant homes, and what they expected to enjoy after their return from the North. Not only were their supplies getting lower day by day, but the only warm thing they could now afford was a cup of tea, excepting on Sunday, when they had a little rum with a bit of lemon.

On the 25th of November, the sun disappeared from view, not to be seen again until the following February, and now the gloom of the time and place was greatly increased. On that day Lockwood recorded in his journal the following: "I have intended writing a letter home recounting my experiences since leaving Fort Conger, but so far the discomforts of this life have prevented me. It is difficult to get the blubber-lamp for more than a few minutes during the day, and sometimes it can not be had at all. The lamp is blown out every evening when we are ready to retire, which is generally about eight o'clock."

Nor were their troubles in any way alleviated by the discovery that one of the men had been seen, or was suspected of, visiting the store-room to fill himself with food—especially despicable thieving. The expedition to Cape Isabella resulted in finding the food which, however, was abandoned in returning, as one of the men, Ellison, became very sick, and had his hands, feet, and nose frozen. He was brought home by a relief party in a helpless condition, Lockwood and the other men of the party having completely worn themselves out by exposure to the cold and hard work. As it was feared that the men would become insane if they did not stop talking about food, Lieutenant Greely began to deliver some lectures on the geography of the United States and their natural productions; and this was followed by miscellaneous discussions in regard to places for business. Whistler, for example, praised the city of Independence, in Kansas, as a splendid place; Long said he was going to set up a restaurant at Ann Arbor in Michigan; Fredericks would follow suit at Minneapolis in Minnesota; while Jewell counted upon a grocery-store in Kansas.

After commenting upon the terrible weather, Lockwood gave expression to the following: "These short rations make me feel the cold dreadfully. It is a constant effort to keep one's hands and feet comfortable, or even comparatively so. I find my spirits first up and then down. Sometimes, when I think of the months before us of this life of misery and suffering, I do not see how we can possibly pull through. At other times I feel much more hopeful; but this is a life of inexpressible misery."

For several days before the arrival of Thanksgiving-day, a great feast was anticipated and on that day enjoyed, including a favorite dish called by them "*son-of-a-gun*," composed of bread, raisins, milk, and a little blubber; nor did the exiles omit the reading of a few chapters from the Bible. In the evening Lockwood entertained the party with his experiences as a farmer at Annapolis, all being interested, and he wound up by inviting the whole of the company to assemble there and enjoy a dinner with him on the next Thanksgiving-day, the said dinner to be composed in part of a roast turkey stuffed with oysters and eaten with cranberries. In return for this compliment, each one of the audience invited Lockwood to partake with him of a feast after their return home, and expatiated with great gusto on the dishes that he proposed to have served. The promise made by Lynn was a roasted turkey; Ralston, hot hoe-cake; Ellis, spare-rib; Long, pork-chops; Biederbick, old regiment dish called buffers; Connell, Irish stew; Bender, a roasted pig; Snyder, tenderloin-steak; Brainard, peaches and cream; Fredericks, black cake and preserves; Saler, veal cutlets; Whistler, flapjacks and molasses; Jewell, roasted oysters on toast; Rice, clam-chowder; Israel, hashed liver; Gardiner, Virginia pone; Ellison, Vienna sausage; Pavy, *pâté-de-fois-gras*; Henry, Hamburg steak; Kislingbury, hashed turkey, chicken, and veal; Greely, Parker House rolls, coffee, cheese, omelette, rice, and chicken curry. It was after this jolly discussion of imaginary good things that the party sat down to a stew of seal-blubber and nothing more. The next day Lockwood partook of his first dish of seal-skin which he found as hard to digest as it was difficult to swallow.

On one occasion, when nearly all were asleep, a scratching noise was heard upon the roof, and it was ascertained that a blue fox was trying to make an entrance. The same night the ears of the sleepers were saluted by a loud roar, caused by the ice moving down the straits, a sound most terrible to human nerves. At one time, after Lockwood had expressed his gratitude for enjoying warm feet for a whole night, he resumed the subject of food, and then penned the following: "My mind dwells constantly on the dishes of my childhood at home. O my dear home, and the dear ones there! Can it be possible I shall some day see them again, and that these days of misery will pass away? My dear father, is he still alive? My dear mother and sisters, Harry, and my nieces and brothers-in-law, how often do I think of them! Only three days more to the top of the hill!" (alluding to the longest night, or winter solstice).

"As to my bread, I always eat it regretfully. If I eat it before tea, I regret that I did not keep it; and if I wait until tea comes and then eat it, I drink my tea rather hastily and do not get the satisfaction out of the cold meat and bread I otherwise would. What a miserable life, where a few crumbs of bread weigh so heavily on one's mind! It seems to be so with all the rest. All sorts of expedients are tried to cheat one's stomach, but with about the same result. By way of securing the idea of a warm piece of meat, I sometimes pour upon it a bit of my hot tea, but the effort proves futile."

On the 21st of December, the day which Lockwood had long been anticipating with pleasure, he expressed his gratification in these words: "The top of the hill! the most glorious day of this dreary journey through the valley of cold and hunger has at last come, and is now nearly gone. Thank God, the glorious sun commences to return, and every day gets lighter and brings him nearer! It is an augury that we shall yet pull through all right." In view of his ultimate fate, how unutterably touching are these hopeful words!

Before the close of that day, however, he made another record in his journal, which forcibly illustrates their deplorable condition, as follows:

"Had a good fox-stew this evening. By a great effort I was able to save one ounce of my bread and about two ounces of butter, for Christmas. I shall make a vigorous effort to abstain from eating it before then. Put it in charge of Biederbick as an additional safeguard."

Among the entertainments enjoyed by the party were lectures by Lieutenant Greely on the several States of the Union. After one of them, on Louisiana, had been delivered, Lockwood added to it an account of his trip from Baltimore to Texas, and that from New Orleans to Cincinnati, all of which narrative was well received.

For several days before Christmas, all were eagerly looking forward to the grand forthcoming dinner and talking about it, a number of them, like Lockwood, saving up a part of their scanty daily allowance for the occasion. Lockwood mentioned that when he proposed to exchange the promise of a fine Christmas-dinner on their return home for a piece of dog-biscuit delivered at once, he found no one ready to accept his *liberal* offer. The Christmas-dinner was similar to that on Thanksgiving-day; various songs were sung, and, at the close of the feast, hearty cheers were given for Lieutenant Greely, Corporal Ellison, Rice the photographer, and the two cooks.

On Christmas-night all the party enjoyed a refreshing sleep, and the next day there was much talk about the distant homes and friends. Lockwood was greatly pleased to learn that his comrades had formed a high opinion of his father from what Greely and he had occasionally told them; and, while describing the family reunions in Washington, he was affected to tears for the first time during his Northern campaign, excepting when Rice had come from Esquimaux Point with the Garlington records, when his tears were the result of gratitude.

In a region where eating had become pre-eminently the chief end of man, it is not strange that the business of marketing should have become popular. How it was managed may be gathered from the following paragraph: "To-day has been a market-day, everybody trading rations—bread for butter, meat for bread, bread for soup, etc. A great deal of talking done, but not many solid trades made. I traded about half of my to-morrow's *son-of-a-gun* for about eight ounces of bread; then I gave Brainard one ounce and a half of butter for two dog-biscuits, but my trading did not prove profitable."

As for New-Year's-day, it came and departed without any special demonstrations: the *son-of-a-gun* was enjoyed by all parties; many of the ice-bound hearts were warmed by memories of home; and Greely and Lockwood had a long talk about the condition of affairs, and the prospects for the future.

The business of trading among the explorers being discouraged, did not long continue, but was succeeded by some other importations from civilization, viz., the taking of property of other people without leave or license. A report was made to Lieutenant Greely that some one had taken a quarter of a pound of bacon, left in the stearine by the cook; also that a barrel of bread had been broken open and two pounds taken away. This proved that the bears and the foxes were not the only thieves to be found in the Arctic regions. The man suspected of the deed was closely watched and had a narrow escape from being properly punished.

On the 10th of January, the case of poor Corporal Ellison was again brought up for discussion and prompt action. It had been hoped that his frosted feet would be restored to their normal condition, but this was not to be, for they were both amputated by Nature, and two of his fingers besides. Strange to say, this was accomplished without his being aware of what was taking place, so little vitality remained in these parts. When we recall the sufferings of this man, in connection with his surroundings and his distance from the comforts of home, we must conclude that the stories of fiction can not eclipse the wonders of actual life and experience. What a combination there of cold and hunger, bodily pain and mental anguish, darkness and perpetual storms!

As we pass over the daily records made by Lockwood in his journal at this particular time, we find food and the dangers of starvation to be the absorbing themes. It seems strange that, in a land of ice and snow, there should have been any apprehensions about a sufficient supply of drinking-water; but this was the case, and the fact came home to the exiles when they found that their supply of tea had to be reduced to half a cup per man. Good water was not only scarce, but could not be obtained from the neighboring lake, their sole dependence, without great toil in chopping away the ice. They had the ice, of course, but there was not sufficient fuel to reduce it to a liquid.

As they could keep warm only by remaining in their sleeping-bags, the manner of visiting each other was simply to exchange sleeping-bags; and thus, when Lockwood wanted to have a talk with Greely, one of the companions of the latter would exchange bags with the visitor.

On the 18th of January, another cloud was thrown upon the party by the death of Cross. He died of a kind of heart-disease, induced, it was supposed, by intemperance in drinking. For several hours before his death he uttered low moans which seemed a kind of echo from the grinding of the far-off ice-fields. His remains were enveloped in coffee-sacks and an American flag, and deposited in a stony grave near the neighboring lake, the only funeral remarks having been made by Lieutenant Lockwood.

On the 21st, Lockwood had a talk with Greely about his own health; said he was very weak, and had been so for two weeks, but had not mentioned it for fear of depressing the men; he could not account for it, and concluded by saying that if he should not be well or better when the time came to make the contemplated passage of the straits, he desired to be left behind with his share of the rations, and then be sent for from Littleton Island. To this Greely replied that he would never harbor such an idea for a single moment; that he would never abandon a living soul.

On the 2d of February, Rice and Jans started to test the passage of the straits, hoping to reach Littleton Island, where they expected to find some provisions or a relief-ship. But, alas! they were stopped by open water, and not successful, though they traveled about fifty miles up and down the floes, and were absent four days. Owing to the bad weather, they did not even get a glimpse of the coast of Greenland. All were greatly disappointed, and some felt that death from starvation was staring them in the face; and yet they found some relief in the increased light preceding the reappearance of the sun. Lockwood, who now became despondent and apathetic, endeavored to peer into the future, and wondered whether his bones were really to be left in the Arctic regions. He mourned over the fact that he had not been as good a son and as kind a brother as he might have been, and hoped that the dear ones at home would remember him as he wished to be, and not as he had been. As to the end, he hoped it would come soon, whatever it might be; and he declared himself possessed by a feeling of indifference to hunger, cold, and gloom, "all of them enemies of existence." After mourning over the approaching fate of Ellison, he recorded these touching words: "How often I think of the dear ones at home, the Sunday evening reunions, and all the bright and happy pictures that present themselves! My dear, good old father! may he look with charity on my many short-comings! My dear mother and sisters and Harry, brothers-in-law, and nieces! I trust that they are well and happy, and, if I do not pull through this, will learn to look on my memory kindly!" An allusion that he now made to his companions in suffering was to this effect: "The party presents a bold front, and is not wanting in spirit. If our fate is the worst, I do not think we shall disgrace the name of Americans and of soldiers." The attempt of Rice to cross the straits to Littleton Island was heroic in the extreme, and his pluck was further exemplified by a proposition that he submitted to Greely to make a second effort to cross the straits, and that, too, unattended by any companion; but the idea was not sanctioned.

On the 22d of February, strange to say, a raven made its appearance in the vicinity of the Arctic camp, but was not killed, although it might have been enjoyed at the forthcoming dinner. It must have been a great relief to some of the party that it disappeared without uttering its dreadful cry, "*Nevermore!*" as translated by the poet, Poe.

On the 27th, not knowing what might happen to him, Lockwood wrote the following in his journal: "The chronometer in my pocket is the one used on the trip to 83° 24´ and on all my trips in this region. My intention is to buy it, but, in case I do not get back, I would have it purchased and kept in the family."

When the sun first made its appearance above the horizon, as it carried his mind away to his far-distant home, he gave expression to this emotion: "O God! how many years of my life would I give to be there!"

Every day, observations were made from neighboring elevations to ascertain the condition of the straits separating them from the Greenland coast which was distinctly visible in clear weather, hoping without hope to see it frozen over from shore to shore; but the lateness of the season precluded all reasonable expectation of such a result, and the daily reports of open water were depressing in the extreme. On the 13th of March, the announcement was made that the supplies of coffee, chocolate, and canned vegetables were all exhausted, and that henceforth they would have to depend almost entirely on pemmican, bacon, bread, and tea, all of which, though given in one-third rations only, would not last for more than a month, thus leaving them without supplies to cross the straits in the event of a satisfactory freeze. In view of all these circumstances, it is impossible to imagine how they could quietly continue their preparations for a journey to the supposed goal at Littleton Island. Surely the hope which inspired the sufferers was eternal and supreme in its strength and pathos. "The straits," said Lockwood, "are open, and I see no prospect of their freezing so that we can get across. Of course, I hope to the contrary; for this means death, if we can find no game here." On a subsequent day he writes as follows: "We look to the end with equanimity, and the spirits of the party, in spite of the prospect of a miserable death, are certainly wonderful. I am glad as each day comes to an end. It brings us nearer the end of this life, whatever that end is to be."

On the 23d of March, the last of the regular fuel was exhausted, and the food was so nearly gone that the men actually began to collect their seal-skin clothing and foot-gear for any emergency that might happen. Game was not only scarce, but the men were getting almost too weak to endure a hunt. To avoid long tramps, which were sure to be unsuccessful, they turned their attention to shrimp-fishing, but, as one man could only get three pounds in one day, the prospect in this direction was not hopeful.

During the month of March and the early part of April, there was nothing done by the able-bodied members of the party but to try to secure some game, the only incidents occurring to interrupt the monotony being the deaths of the Esquimaux Frederick Christiansen, and Sergeant Lynn. The former had been complaining for a week or more, but nobody thought him in danger, and he died unexpectedly. Lockwood's tribute to him was to this effect: "He was a good man, and I felt a great affection for him. He constantly worked hard in my service, and never spared himself on our sledge-trips. His death makes me feel very sorrowful." He was buried by the side of Cross, near the lake. The death of Lynn was also unexpected. He fully appreciated his condition, and gave some directions regarding his last wishes. He was much liked, and highly spoken of by all. After the burial service had been read at the house by Lieutenant Greely, his remains were also placed by the lake-side with those of Cross and the Esquimaux.

The drama was about to close, the curtain already falling upon the band of heroes:

"And their hearts, though stout and brave,

Still, like muffled drums were beating

Funeral marches to the grave."

The phantom of Starvation, which had long been following them over the ice and snow, and dallying with their hopes and fears as they lay in their comfortless camps, had now become a terrible reality, determined to assert all his powers. Three of his victims were already under the snow, and were soon followed by several others, including the one who had directed them in many of their duties and befriended them in trouble, and whose honored name, attached to a noted island and a famed headland in the Arctic world, will be forever remembered with pride and affection by his countrymen.

The concluding paragraph in Lieutenant Lockwood's journal was written on the 7th of April, 1884, and alludes to the sickness and death of his two comrades. In the last allusion that he makes to himself, he speaks of his excessive weakness, and of the fact that he could not rise from his sleeping-bag without great difficulty. His death occurred two days afterward.

Having been permitted to examine an elaborate and interesting journal kept by Sergeant Brainard, a few notices relating to the closing days and the death of Lieutenant Lockwood are reproduced, as follows:

January 12, 1884.—Lieutenant Lockwood is very weak. He has been saving the greater portion of his bread and meat for several days, and talks to himself about food. He frequently looks intently at the lamp, and requests that it be kept burning all night.

January 20th.—Lieutenant Lockwood is growing weaker and weaker. He said to me a few days ago, "Brainard, I have lost my grip," meaning that he had lost his last hope of life.

January 24th.—Lieutenant Lockwood seems to be in better spirits to-day.

January 28th.—The doctor said to-day that if Lieutenant Lockwood did not brace up, he would never recover.

January 30th.—Lieutenant Lockwood is growing steadily weaker, and talks but seldom now. I wish he would try to be more cheerful.

February 15th.—Lieutenant Lockwood is better, but does not improve so rapidly as I would wish.

April 4th.—The rations of Lieutenant Lockwood and Linn have been increased to one fourth of a dovekie each per day.

April 5th.—I am afraid that Lieutenant Lockwood and Linn will soon follow the faithful Esquimaux, who has just died. They can not, or they will not, eat shrimps any more. Although they are both given an extra allowance of dovekie, it is not sufficient to restore them.

April 7th.—Lieutenant Lockwood and Jewell will soon follow Linn. They are very weak and failing rapidly.

April 8th.—Lieutenant Lockwood fell in a faint in the alley-way, and much difficulty was experienced in resuscitating him.

April 9th.—Lieutenant Lockwood became unconscious at an early hour this morning, and at 4.20 P. M. he breathed his last. His end was painless and without a struggle. This will be a sad and unexpected blow to his family, who evidently idolized him. To me it is also a sorrowful event. He had been my companion during long and eventful excursions, and my feelings toward him were akin to those of a brother. Biederbick, who was with him at the last moment, and I straightened his limbs and prepared his remains for burial. It is the saddest duty I have ever been called on to perform, and I hope I may never experience the like again. A few days prior to his death he had spoken of writing to his family, but, owing to weakness, had deferred the matter until too late.

April 10th.—The last sad rites were performed over the remains of our late comrade, and he was interred with the others on Cemetery Ridge, Lieutenant Greely reading the Episcopal service.

To the above may be added the following remark made by Brainard in regard to his friend Lockwood: "The lieutenant was buried in an officer's blouse. It affected me deeply to pass his grave, as I thought of the leader of our little party which had carried the Stars and Stripes beyond the English Jack; but this feeling soon wore away, and, as I had so many other horrible things to occupy my mind, I became somewhat indifferent."

But wholly indifferent he could not be, even when he saw two men in one sleeping-bag, one of them a corpse, and the other too weak to assist in pulling the body out for burial.

Another and most touching reference made by Brainard to the burial-place of his friend Lockwood occurs in his journal under date of May 31, 1884, and is as follows: "In my daily journeys across Cemetery Ridge, it was but natural at first that my reflections should be sad and gloomy. Here lie my departed comrades, and to their left is the vacant space where, in a few days, my own remains will be deposited if sufficient strength remain to those who may survive me. The brass buttons on Lieutenant Lockwood's blouse, worn bright by the flying gravel, protruded through the scanty covering of earth which our depleted strength barely enabled us to place over him. At first these dazzling buttons would awaken thoughts of those bright days spent at Fort Conger, of the half-forgotten scene of his death, and of the universal sorrow that was felt at his departure. But later my own wretched circumstances served to counteract these feelings, and I would pass and repass this place without emotion, and almost with indifference."

The supply of food had been almost entirely exhausted during the first few days of April, and it was impossible to obtain any game or rations from distant caches. An effort made by Rice to secure certain provisions that had been abandoned on a former expedition in order to save the life of Ellison when frozen, resulted in his own death, breathing his last in the arms of Fredericks, his only companion, who buried him in a lonely, ice-made grave. Nor were the horrors of the situation lessened by the discovery that the man Henry had been guilty of stealing their food, for which, after ample warning, under orders from Lieutenant Greely, he was summarily shot, according to the law of self-preservation. His remains were not deposited in the cemetery, but by themselves in a place near by.

The total number of deaths out of the twenty-five composing the complete party of explorers was nineteen, and, while twelve of them were buried at Camp Clay, the remainder, like the lamented Rice, were buried elsewhere or where they died. Jans was lost in his kyack. During a discussion that occurred, about the final disposition of the dead, Lieutenant Greely expressed the wish that the remains of his men might be left undisturbed. They had died, he said, beneath Arctic skies. Arctic desolation witnessed their sufferings, heard their cries of anguish. They are buried in Arctic soil. Let them lie where they fell. Lockwood told me that he wanted to rest forever on the field of his work. Why disturb them? Why not respect their wishes?

Before closing this chapter it seems proper that an allusion should be made to alleged cannibalism at Camp Clay. The writer of this was informed by Sergeant Brainard that such might have been the case, but that not a single one of the survivors had ever known or witnessed anything of the kind. So far as Lieutenant Lockwood was concerned, it was positively established, by unimpeachable testimony, that his remains were not mutilated in the least degree. When carefully carried, with all the others, on board the ship that was to bring them to the United States, his remains were perfect in every respect, and of this his father has the assurance of those who saw them.

In view of the fact that Sergeant David L. Brainard accompanied Lieutenant Lockwood in all his explorations, it seems only proper that a notice of his life should appear in this volume. He was born in Norway, Herkimer County, New York, December 21, 1856, his parents having come from Massachusetts. His father was of French extraction and his mother of English stock. He attended a district school until his eleventh year, when he removed with his family to Freetown, Cortland County, New York, where he attended the State Normal School. On the 18th of September, 1876, he enlisted at New York city in the regular army, being assigned to Company L, Second Cavalry, then stationed at Fort Ellis, in Montana Territory. He joined his troops late that year after an arduous journey of five hundred miles on horseback from Corinne, Utah. In the following spring he participated in the Indian campaigns under General Miles, along the Yellowstone River and its tributaries, and was wounded in the face while in action with the Sioux, at Muddy Creek, Montana, May 7, 1877. In August of the same year, he was selected as one of four men to act as escort to General Sherman and party in their tour through the National Park. In October following, he was made a corporal, and in July, 1879, was promoted to be a sergeant. He was frequently in charge of parties in the field on detached service, and was intrusted with important missions by his commanding officers. Lieutenant Doane, Second Cavalry, recommended him for detail on the Howgate Polar Expedition in May, 1880, Brainard visiting Washington for that purpose. The enterprise having been abandoned, he was ordered back to his regiment at Fort Assiniboin, on Milk River. Early in the spring of 1881, Lieutenant Greely requested his detail on the Lady Franklin Bay Expedition, and, on his arrival in Washington, appointed him first sergeant of the expedition, which position he held during the three years of Arctic service. On the 1st of August, 1884, he was transferred, with the rank of sergeant, to the United States Signal Corps, having always acquitted himself with ability and honor as a man, a soldier, and an explorer.

XIX.
THE WOEFUL RETURN.

Without stopping to discuss the action of Congress or the Government officials in regard to sending relief to the Greely Expedition, the writer desires to mention that the names of Senator Joseph R. Hawley and Representative E. John Ellis, because of their manly action in Congress in behalf of the suffering explorers, are far more deserving of places on the charts of the North than those of many others which have thus been honored. In 1882 a vessel called the Neptune, Captain William Sopp, was chartered at St. John's, Newfoundland, and with a full supply of provisions was dispatched for Lady Franklin Bay, but failing in her mission returned to Newfoundland *without leaving* any of her supplies in the North, but bringing them all back to St. John's! In 1883 the steamer Proteus, Captain Richard Pike, was rechartered at St. John's, and with a full supply of provisions sailed for Discovery Harbor, but was crushed in the ice near Cape Sabine, her crew succeeding in landing in a safe place a small part of her cargo, some of which was subsequently utilized by the Greely party.

In 1884 a third rescuing expedition was organized and dispatched for the relief of the Greely exploring party. That expedition was composed of a squadron of three ships, the Thetis, the Bear, and the Alert, under the command of Commander Winfield S. Schley, of the United States Navy. They left St. John's on the 12th of May, and, after the usual tribulations along the western coast of Greenland, reached the vicinity of Cape Sabine, and discovered the Greely party at Camp Clay, on Sunday, the 22d of June, seventy-three days after the death of Lieutenant Lockwood. The discovery was then made that, out of the twenty-five men connected with the Greely Expedition only seven were alive, viz., Lieutenant Greely, Brainard, Biederbick, Fredericks, Long, Connell, and Ellison. As soon as the survivors could be relieved and transferred to the ships, the remains of the dead were exhumed with care and taken to the ships for transportation to the United States, excepting the remains of Esquimaux Frederick, which were left at Disco.

As the pictures presented by the survivors lying in their camp, dazed with suffering and surprise and a joy they could not manifest, and the incidents they subsequently narrated of intense suffering, can only prove heart-rending to the reader, they will not now be dwelt upon. The departure of the ships, with their strange list of dead and living passengers, seemed to enhance the gloom which filled the sky and rested upon the sea. Their condition was so deplorable, that a delay of a very few days would have left none to tell the tale of woe and suffering. At least two could not have lived twenty-four hours. That this time was gained, under the stimulus of the twenty-five thousand dollars reward, appears from an article written by an officer of the Relief Expedition and published in the "Century" of May, 1885, as follows:

"The reward of twenty-five thousand dollars that Congress had offered for the first information of Greely had incited the whalers to take risks that they otherwise would have shunned. They had expressed a determination to strive for it, and were ever on the alert for a chance to creep northward. The Relief Squadron was determined, on its part, that the whalers should not secure the first information, and were equally zealous in pushing northward. It was this rivalry (a friendly one, for our relations with the whaling-captains were of the pleasantest nature) that hurried us across Melville Bay and brought us together within sight of Cape York. It had been thought possible that Greely or an advance party might be there."

Mr. Ellis proposed in the last session of Congress that, as the reward had not been spent, yet had contributed to the rescue, it should be appropriated to building, at Washington, a monument to the dead.

The temporary halt at Disco Harbor was saddened by the death of Ellison, after prolonged sufferings, as if his noble spirit was determined to join its departed comrades in their passage to the skies from that Northern Land of Desolation.

In the official record of the Relief Expedition, Commander Schley makes an allusion to the important part taken by Lieutenant Lockwood in the Greely Expedition which should be repeated in this place. After submitting certain papers which had been found in a cairn at Breevort Island, he says: "It was a wonderful story. It told how the expedition, during its two years at Lady Franklin Bay, had marked out the interior of Grinnell Land, and how Lockwood had followed the northern shore of Greenland, and had reclaimed for America the honor of 'the farthest north.'"

On Thursday, the 17th of July, the Relief Expedition arrived at St. John's, Newfoundland, where they were kindly welcomed, and the tidings of their arrival promptly telegraphed to the anxious multitudes in the United States. Complete arrangements were made for the continuous voyage of the living and the dead to their several homes.

In a dispatch which the Secretary of the Navy sent to Commander Schley, on the day of his return, he said, "Preserve tenderly the remains of the heroic dead," and that order was duly obeyed. They were placed in metallic caskets, and the squadron sailed from St. John's on the 26th of July, arriving at

Portsmouth, New Hampshire, on the 2d of August. As the first duty after a battle is to bury the dead, it is to be regretted that this was not done before the display was made at Portsmouth. It was not thus that England received her victorious fleet from Trafalgar, bearing home the remains of the dead hero Nelson. The mutilated remains of the dead should first have been delivered over to the bleeding hearts that awaited them. While so many unurned corpses remained in the ships, the celebration was but a ghastly jubilee. Requiems should have been chanted before pæans were sung. The only casket removed from the ships at Portsmouth was that containing the remains of Sergeant Jewell, who was a native of New Hampshire. The squadron now sailed for New York, and on its arrival, the 8th of August, was received with great enthusiasm. Here the remains of the dead were delivered to the custody of the army commander at Governor's Island, by whom the final dispositions were made. The remains of Lieutenant Lockwood were forwarded to Annapolis and placed under a military guard, in the church of St. Anne, where the young hero had been baptized, confirmed, and received his first communion. The funeral was of a military character, and the attendance was very large, comprehending all the naval, military, and civil organizations of the city. Recalling the words of the poet Whittier, many of the mourners present must have felt their special force, when he says:

"I know not what the future hath

  Of marvel or surprise,

Assured alone that life and death

  His mercy underlies."

The remains of the hero lie in the beautiful cemetery of the Naval Academy, overlooking the place of his birth and the scenes of his childhood. An appropriate tomb was erected over them, bearing this inscription:

JAMES BOOTH LOCKWOOD,
LIEUTENANT UNITED STATES ARMY,
BORN AT ANNAPOLIS, MARYLAND,
October 9, 1852,
DIED AT CAPE SABINE,
April 9, 1884.

"The sufferings of this present time are not worthy to be compared with the glory that shall be revealed in us."

On the day that the rector of St. Anne's church, Rev. William S. Southgate, gave notice of the time of the burial, he made the following remarks:

"One of the truths of the Bible, taught us by the Church, the most difficult to receive and to hold practically, is that expressed in the words of the Collect for the last week: 'O God, whose never-failing providence ordereth all things both in heaven and on earth.'

"The difficulty arises from the fact that in so many cases we can not discover either the justice or the mercy or even the expediency of that ordering.

"And yet at times we get a glimpse of light that reveals much of the fitness and beauty of this divine ordering of events. Here is an example before us. There is a peculiar appropriateness in the ordering of events that brings James Booth Lockwood here to be buried. Born in this parish, baptized here, confirmed in St. Anne by Bishop Whittingham, April 19, 1868, he received his first communion at this altar on Christmas-day of the same year. The rector of the parish, who presented him for confirmation and administered to him the holy communion, has just been called suddenly to his rest. In the midst of untiring labors the call found them both at the post of duty, and both were taken away while in the performance of that duty. But there was something peculiarly sad in the circumstances and mode of young Lockwood's death—circumstances due partly to the nature of the work in which he was engaged, partly to the fault of others. But what matters it how or when he died, if found at Death's call doing the duty assigned to him?

"One of the earliest of the adventurers along this coast, then as little known to the world as the Arctic regions are now to us, when his little ship was overwhelmed by the stormy sea, comforted the frightened and trembling helmsman with the assuring words, 'My child, heaven is as near to us by sea as by land.' And so what matters it where we die and how we die, so long as we are reconciled to God, and are faithfully fulfilling our calling? May God give us grace so to live that we may never be afraid to die in any place or in any manner!"

That the story and the fate of James B. Lockwood excited a profound sentiment of sorrow and admiration throughout the entire country was manifested in many ways, and a notice of some of them will form an appropriate conclusion to this *in-memoriam* volume. Among the first tributes of honor and affection was the following official order published by the colonel of his regiment, announcing his death to the military associates of the young soldier:

[ORDER, NO. 46.]
HEADQUARTERS TWENTY-THIRD INFANTRY,
FORT WAYNE, MICH., *July 25, 1884.*

Another name is added to the list of our honored dead. The official announcement is received from the War Department of the death of First-Lieutenant James B. Lockwood, at Camp Clay, near Cape Sabine, Smith's Sound, Arctic regions, April 9, 1884. He was assigned to this regiment as second lieutenant, October 1, 1873, and promoted first lieutenant March 15, 1883. He served with distinction throughout Arizona, Nebraska, Kansas, the Indian Territory, and Colorado, always performing with zeal and thoroughness the various and complex duties that usually fall to the lot of the young officer. In 1881 he turned from the arduous duties and savage warfare of frontier life to face still greater hardship and danger, and finally to lay down his life in those frozen and inhospitable regions which have proved the sepulchre of so many heroes before him.

Lieutenant Lockwood was a young officer of great promise in his profession; of a noble and exalted character, his fine mind tended constantly to the investigation of scientific truths. When the privations, the suffering, and the achievements of the "Lady Franklin Bay Expedition" are fully related, higher authority will doubtless pay a more fitting tribute to the worth, the fortitude, and the matchless courage of an officer who, in Arctic exploration, has carried the American flag to a point in advance of that of any other nation.

His reward is an imperishable fame, which he sought with even greater resolution than leads the soldier to the cannon's mouth. The pleasant smile and manly form of our comrade are lost to us forever, but his name and memory will be always green in our hearts.

Officers of the regiment will wear the usual badge of mourning for thirty days.

By order of Colonel BLACK:

T. G. M. SMITH,
First Lieutenant and Adjutant Twenty-third Infantry.

When the news of Lockwood's fate was known at Fort Leavenworth, Kansas, arrangements were at once made, by those who had known and loved him there, to erect a tablet to his memory in the handsome post chapel at that place. When completed it was placed in a conspicuous position, and bore the following inscription:

IN MEMORIAM
JAMES B. LOCKWOOD,
FIRST LIEUTENANT TWENTY-THIRD INFANTRY,
A MEMBER OF THE
GREELY POLAR EXPEDITION,
DIED AT CAPE SABINE, GRINNELL LAND,
April 9, 1884.

This tablet was erected chiefly at the expense of Lockwood's old regiment. To one of the officers General Lockwood presented a sword that had belonged to his son, and, in his acknowledgment, that officer made this remark: "As a friend of your son, I shall take pride and comfort from having in my possession the sword of a friend, who lived so nobly and died so honorably. Should you desire it to come back to your family when I have joined your son, I hope you will tell me so, and I will provide accordingly." Among those who earnestly co-operated with this gentleman in erecting the tablet was one who wrote to his fellow-officer as follows: "No two people, outside of Lockwood's own blood relations, loved him more than you and I. And yet I do not know that I am right in calling his end untimely. He died, as he had ever lived, in the discharge of his duty, and I imagine, when the records of the expedition become more known, it will be seen that his duty was well done to the end. He was a man, and has died like one. God grant that when our time comes it may find us, too, in the discharge of our duty!"

During Lieutenant Greely's sojourn in Portsmouth, when on his way home, and while yet too feeble to use the pen, he dictated the following letter to General Lockwood:

PORTSMOUTH, N. H., *August 9, 1884.*

MY DEAR GENERAL LOCKWOOD: Had I not seen Commander Sigsbee, and given to him such information as he wished, and as I knew would be most important to you in regard to your son, I should have attempted an earlier letter to you. I am still unable to write to you by my own hand. As I told Commander Sigsbee, James died from water around the heart, induced by insufficient nutrition. His last days were quiet and painless. He did his whole duty as a soldier and an officer. His loyalty to truth, fidelity, and zeal could always be relied upon by me. His unvarying kindness, his gentleness, his deep interest in and toward the men of the expedition indicated a nature thoroughly imbued with the essential and fundamental principles of Christianity, and won for him their good-will, confidence, and affection. I feel that you and Mrs. Lockwood may well be proud of such a son. His daily conversation during the past winter told us how much he loved his parents, and how deep and close were the bonds of affection which united him to his sisters and brother. He seemed to feel that he had not done full justice to the many and great advantages that you had given him, and hoped to make amends in the future. His innate modesty in this, as in other matters, I think did scant justice to his true merits. I write by Mrs. Greely's hand—she joins me in sympathy and condolence. I feel that this letter insufficiently informs you regarding James. From day to day he intended to write you, but delayed too long. His diary, in short-hand, was kept up, I believe, to the day preceding his death.

Sincerely yours,

A. W. GREELY.

Another letter from Portsmouth, written by Sergeant D. L. Brainard in answer to some inquiries made by General Lockwood, was as follows:

PORTSMOUTH, N. H., *September 4, 1884.*

General H. H. LOCKWOOD.

DEAR SIR: Your letter of the 22d ult., requesting information of the missing effects of your dear son, which had been committed to my care, is just received... . The effects in question, excepting the ring and coins, I turned over to Major Greely before leaving this city in August. The two latter articles I afterward found and gave to Mrs. Peck, who, with her husband, called on me at the Parker House, in Boston. The setting of the ring, I am sorry to say, was not found after his death, although diligent search was made. He had spoken of it but a few days before his death, and expressed great concern for its safety. It was supposed to be suspended from his neck in a small parcel, but search revealed nothing. The compass was among the effects I transferred to Lieutenant Greely, as were also two pencils, his pipe, spoon, knife, etc. With reference to the inner life of your son, do not feel any concern. Although not an open professor of any particular creed, he followed closely the golden rule during my acquaintance with him. When I reach Washington I shall be glad to call on you. In the mean time I shall willingly answer any question with regard to his life in the frigid zone that you may desire to ask. Place no reliance on any of the adverse newspaper reports that are occasionally seen reflecting on his conduct; they are not worthy of a moment's thought. Hoping that the articles have reached you in safety ere this, I am, very sincerely yours,

D. L. BRAINARD.

Another and a very handsome letter sent to General Lockwood by an officer of the army, who had long known the son, was as follows:

"SAN ANTONIO, FLA., *July 25, 1884.*

"MY DEAR GENERAL: The newspapers tardily convey to me the news of your son's heroic death. I can not express to you how much both my wife and myself were affected by this intelligence. I knew your son from his entry into the Twenty-third Infantry in 1873 until I was promoted to the Twenty-second in 1879, and formed so high an estimate of his sterling soldierly character that it is inexpressibly sad to think of his career being cut short at so early an age. But, though early, he has nevertheless left his mark on the scientific record of the country—a record which can never perish while the frozen North continues to hold the secrets he has more nearly penetrated than any other explorer of those regions. This must be, my dear general, some consolation to you, though I well know that it can not wholly atone for the loss of your noble son. But, as time passes, this reflection may soften your paternal grief.

"A life-work need not extend to the allotted threescore years and ten. In the providence of God it often compasses a much smaller period of time; when it is accomplished, God calls the worker home.

"Who shall measure the work your son accomplished in the examples he gave of fidelity to duty, of heroic fortitude? How many fainting souls in the future, reading of his devotion, will be strengthened to go forward in the paths marked out for them! That your grief may be in time assuaged by these reflections is the prayer devoutly offered by your sincere friend."

Many private letters of condolence and sympathy were written to the parents of the deceased, by personal friends and others, some of which serve to illustrate the character of the departed. One of these friends wrote as follows:

"The tender regard and sincere love I had for James prompts me to write to you and express my heart-felt sorrow in losing him. We were dear friends for years, and a more upright and honorable man never lived, and our regiment has lost a member who can never be replaced, and the memory of him who died far away from us can never be forgotten."

In another letter a friend wrote as follows:

"Dr. B——, U. S. A., one of James's most intimate and best friends, desires me to say that, of all the men he knew, James was to him far dearer than any other. As for myself, I shall always hold James dear to my heart, and hope some day, when all things pass away, to meet him in that happy land where our loved ones are gone."

In another letter occurs the following:

"Lockwood was among the best young officers of the regiment. Very attentive to duty, and correct in habits, his promise of usefulness was unusually great. I hope that the knowledge of duty well performed, and under the most trying circumstances, may in some degree ameliorate your great grief."

Another friend writes:

"I but echo the feelings of all in the Twenty-third Infantry who knew your son, in saying that your great loss is partly theirs. His kindly and generous impulses, his sterling integrity, and his thoroughness as an officer and a gentleman, secured and retained for him the substantial good-will and friendship of all. And while we may grieve at the mournful end of his career, yet this feeling is somewhat neutralized in the melancholy satisfaction of knowing that he died on the field of honor."

In another letter from one who had been in the army and on the staff of General Lockwood at Accomac, Va., occurs the following most admirable and appropriate passage: "I do believe, dear general, that all is well with your son. Standing where no human footstep had ever trod before, seeing what no eye had ever before beheld, alone amid the awful silence of that frozen deep—alone with God—there must have been communings with the Holy One of more import to James than all else besides. And at the last day you will again see your son in glory, wearing the crown of those made perfect through suffering."

Besides the many letters written by personal friends, there were others from perfect strangers, who had either served under General Lockwood in the army, or been especially interested in the fate of the youthful hero.

Among the strangers who wrote letters of condolence was the Rev. William E. Griffis, D. D., of Schenectady, N. Y., who had preached a sermon on the conquests of peace, and in which he made the following allusion to Lieutenant Lockwood: "The laurels that repose on the memory of Lieutenant Lockwood are better than battle-honors or wreaths after bloody victories." It was his opinion that the Arctic secret would yet be won; and that Lockwood and his brother heroes were doing the will of God as explorers in the far North.

On the 20th of July, 1884, the Rev. Dr. John S. Lindsay, of St. John's Church, in Georgetown, delivered a sermon in which he alluded to the return of the Greely Expedition, and especially to Lieutenant Lockwood, who had been one of his parishioners. He said: "Just a few days ago we were plunged into sorrow by the news that among the living of the latest Arctic expedition who had been rescued was *not* our young townsman, the son of one of the most honored members of this congregation; the dispatch that brought the glad intelligence that six were saved was soon followed by the sad announcement that he, vigorous as he was, had sunk under the rigors of the climate, worn out by work and want. Has he left no lesson for you and me, for all his fellow-men? Think of his ceaseless endeavor, of the courage and devotion with which he bore the brunt of the exploration, and wore away his own strength in seeking food for his comrades and himself! See him, with a single companion, penetrating nearer to the north pole than any other man had ever gone, however daring! When he had done his whole duty, more than had ever been done before, he lies down to rest—to die.

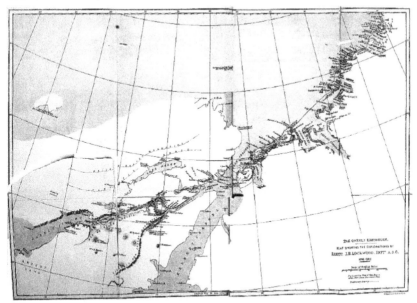

THE GREELY EXPEDITION.
MAP SHOWING THE EXPLORATIONS BY
LIEUT. J.B. LOCKWOOD, INF'T . A. S. O.
1882-1883
High-resolution Map

"Most fittingly did his brother explorers give his name to this spot, the farthest land north trod by human foot. Lockwood Island shall stand, as long as the earth endures, amid the awful wastes and silence of these mysterious regions, as the monument of this brave young soldier. A child of the Church, the subject of ceaseless prayer—of yours, of mine, of his family—we trust that his spirit, chastened and exalted by the hardships he endured, winged its flight from the inhospitable land that refused sustenance to his body, and now rests and waits in the paradise of God. We mingle our tears with his father's and his mother's, and with those of all who loved him; but out of the deep we rejoice in the record he has left behind of devotion to duty even unto death. Surely no life is short in which so much is done, or in vain that gives such instruction and such inspiration to other lives. In conclusion, let us not cast away our faith in God, because of the mysteries and trials and sufferings of life."

Lightning Source UK Ltd.
Milton Keynes UK
UKHW010635240820
368739UK00001B/227